Overtake

VANSTONE RACING
BOOK 1

S.J. SYLVIS

SJ SYLVIS BOOKS LLC

Published: SJ Sylvis Books LLC
sjsylvisbooks@gmail.com
Cover Design: Ashes and Vellichor
Art by: Illustrious Jane
Editing: Jenn Lockwood Editing
Proofing: Emma Cook | Booktastic Blonde, Sarah Plocher |All Encompassing Books

S. J. SYLVIS

OVERTAKE

Vanstone Racing Series

ELECTRIFYING.

That's what it's like to be in this seat.

Zero to sixty in 2.6 seconds with nothing but my pulse strumming wildly underneath my skin.

I check out mentally, and for a moment, it's just me, the track, and my car.

Unfortunately, it all comes rushing back in when I get a glimpse of blue in the corner of my eye. One of Vanstone's drivers has been harassing me from the beginning of the race, both of us neck and neck, and with each chicane, he tries to overtake me.

My father's voice probes the inside of my ear, and I swallow a growl. The concentration I hold is impenetrable, even with his seething tone floating around my helmet.

"You need to be more aggressive," he says, his words thick with irritation.

"I'm ahead," I argue.

There's a corner coming into view, the same corner I've been cutting as short as possible.

"He's struggling with the corners. Maintain your position," he reiterates.

My heartbeat quickens with every demand, and just like every race since I was a child, I silently ask myself *why*.

Why do I try so hard to prove that I'm the best to a man who continuously reminds me that I'm the opposite? Why do I work my ass off, day in and day out? Why am I here? In *his* car?

But then, suddenly, the tires beneath me vibrate, the carbon fiber and metals of the car that surround me shake my bones. The taste of victory, so fucking sweet, sits on my tongue as the podium dangles right in front of me.

It's the *only* thing in the world that has given me a high.

It's the only thing in the world that I've ever been praised for, even if short-lived.

"Rome!" my father barks my name, as if I've gone somewhere. "Don't brake until I tell you to."

I grit my teeth. "I've been braking fine the entire race."

"Don't fucking argue with me on this. Do you want to win? Or do you want to be a failure?"

If it wouldn't fuck up my focus, I'd roll my eyes. What an *insolent* fucking question.

The corner is in front of me, and I wait like the prodigal son that I am, keeping my foot off the brake until his demand strikes through. Except, he doesn't, and panic claws up my throat.

My foot hovers until, finally, his barking demand cuts through. "Now!"

I brake, a snarl already on the edge of my lips from causing me to lose position with the late braking, but to my shock, I'm still ahead.

"I can't believe that fucking worked," I mutter, shifting my focus to keep my position.

"I told you to trust me, son."

I recognize that tone. Pride, but something else too. Conceited yet patronizing—both things my father has been labeled as throughout the years of taking Pierce Racing to the top.

Two more times around the track, and my braking is somehow even tighter.

I'm driving aggressively, braking quicker than I ever have, taking corners sharply without colliding with the wall or, worse, another driver.

My father's calm assurances keep me level-headed, but something red is flashing on my steering wheel that is no longer every few miles but instead a constant.

"Is my brake temp high?"

My father doesn't answer right away. There's whispering in my helmet, and I've been in the racing world for long enough to know he's checking with the rest of the crew.

The same corner comes into view, and my hands tighten on the steering wheel.

"Yes or no?" I snap.

"The brakes are hot but stable. Brake the same you have been–"

There's a shuffling in my ear along with another voice that isn't my father's. "Your brake temps are critical. Back off, back off!"

Vince?

He cuts through again. "Listen to me, Rome!"

I shake away the confusion and feel for my brake, but nothing happens.

Panic sets in, the brake seemingly gone.

"Fuck–I can't!" I press down again. "Dad! I have no brakes–"

Fear spikes, and I brace myself for impact.

I collide against the sidewall with a substantial amount of force, my father's and Vince Halston's arguing echoing in my ear.

"Ah!" My brain ricochets off the inside of my skull, pain deepening in my temples as I spin around too many times to count.

White flashes in my vision, and my eyes close.

I come to a stop, and my body grows stiff. Confusion swarms in like a thousand wasps from a nest.

My dad and Vince.

They're arguing as I chase Tessa around with Graham and Beck.

"Guys, stop chasing Tess." Van, the oldest of the Halston siblings, always reprimands us. He's got his glasses perched on the tip of his nose and a notebook in his hand.

"She stole my gum!" Graham argues.

"Did not!" Tessa whines as she slides in between two giant racing trailers.

"Did to!" Graham argues from behind me.

I'm faster than the rest of them, and I can catch Tessa easily.

I glance over my shoulder to see if my dad is watching, because he'll scold me for messing around instead of paying attention to what's really important—racing—but I stop dead in my tracks when I see his finger pointed in his partner's face.

Vince's jaw flexes as my dad lays into him about something, his finger getting closer and closer to Vince's face.

"What's going on?" Noah, the second-oldest Halston sibling, asks while sliding up beside me.

"I don't know—"

"Stop it!" Tessa shouts.

Noah and I turn to see Graham pulling Tessa by her shirt,

and off we go—Noah to pick on his sister along with Graham, and me to end up in the middle.

I cough. My throat is dry, and my lungs are tight.

The ringing in my ear subsides, and I open my eyes, pulling myself out of an old memory. Something orange dances in front of my face.

What is that—

"Fuck..." I croak.

Flames flick with wild velocity, the heat of them creeping against my body.

My movements are slow, my limbs heavy. Breathing is difficult as sweat drips down the side of my face, the salty taste landing on my lips.

There are voices in my ear. An argument mixed with cries of panic.

Sirens sound in the distance, and I attempt to climb out of my mangled car.

Someone tugs me the rest of the way, my feet numb as I try to stand. A medic sways in front of my vision, his mouth is moving, yet I can't seem to hear what he's saying.

My helmet slides off my head, the cool air coats my blazing skin, and then, I collapse.

Chapter One

TESSA

BECK

Be honest...if I happen to go through a drive-thru and order a medium fry, put it in my hoodie pocket, and secretly eat them during dinner, do you think Mom and Dad would notice?

NOAH

Dad would smell the salt from a mile away.

GRAHAM

No way.

NOAH

You're only saying no because you want some too.

BECK

We all do. I'll order you one, Graham.

GRAHAM

VAN

Don't.

ME

Can you grab me a Diet Coke?

BECK

Only if you give me Quinn's number.

I ROLL my eyes at Beck's request and type furiously into my phone.

ME

She has a boyfriend. Bring me a Diet Coke!

NOAH

What is for dinner tonight? If it's salmon again, I want fries too.

BECK

Whatever it is, it'll be saltless and tasteless.

VAN

It'll be healthy and full of good fats which are vital for Dad's heart.

I click out of the group text and pull up my best friend's name.

ME

Beck is asking for your number again. I told him you have a boyfriend, so if anyone asks...you're unavailable.

I grab my keys and head out the door, my phone still in hand. Quinn messages back immediately.

QUINN

Is my invisible boyfriend at least decent looking?

I snort.

ME

Obviously.

Another text from the group chat pops up as I go to close my phone.

NOAH

Bring me fries just in case.

It's a short drive to my parents' house. They live ten minutes away, but the difference in our neighborhoods is unmistakable. Where their house sits high atop a luscious green golf course, the neighborhood hidden behind fancy gates and a security guard, mine has windows that allow the Las Vegas dust to slip through and neighbors that fight every single day only to make up each night.

I know that because of thin windows and walls.

My phone connects with my car's Bluetooth as I make a right turn. The womanly robot voice cuts through the click of my blinker to say, **"Van, in the group chat titled 'Four Bros and a Mistake dash Tessa' says, do not bring fries or a Diet Coke."**

My jaw drops in disbelief.

"Would you like to reply?" my car asks.

I grip the steering wheel tightly. "Yes!"

"What would you like to say?"

"Which one of you changed the group chat name again? Jerks!"

After my car repeats my text, I say *send* and work on unfurrowing my brow during the drive.

My bet is Beck.

He may be older than me, but he's the most immature of us all. Not to mention, he's been calling me a mistake for as long as I can remember.

I wasn't a mistake.

I was a surprise.

There is a difference.

"Noah, in the group chat titled 'Four Bros and a Mistake dash Tessa' says, not me."

I roll my eyes as the other texts come through, all of them denying the action or blaming one another until Van, my oldest brother, chimes in.

"Van, in the group chat titled 'Four Bros and a Mistake dash Tessa' says, will someone acknowledge my texts?"

My car comes to a stop as I pull up to the wrought-iron gate. I roll my window down, and Gabriel, the newest guard, steps forward and shoots me his best smile. "Another family dinner where I get to greet the most gorgeous woman I've ever seen."

Oh, Gabriel.

My brothers would skin him alive if they knew the forty-year-old divorcee was lusting after me.

"You make me blush," I tease.

Just as Gabriel rocks back on his heels to feed me another cheesy pick-up line, a text comes through my car's speakers.

"Beck, in the group chat titled 'Four Bros and a Mistake dash Tessa' says–"

I quickly reach forward and grip the volume button tightly between my two fingers, turning it all the way down.

"Have a great night!" I call over my shoulder, driving away quickly as Gabriel tries to make sense of what he just heard.

I turn down my parents' street, and to no surprise, Van is already here.

Always punctual, being the first born and all.

After parking my car, I angrily grab my phone and change the name of our group text.

The Queen and Her Peasants.

They all know I'm the favorite.

Well, besides Van, but that doesn't count because, again, he's the firstborn.

I skip up the porch steps and walk inside the home I spent my teens years growing up in. There's a light ocean-y scent in the air, followed by lemon and garlic. My nose crinkles, and I pull my phone out of my pocket.

ME

It's salmon again.

NOAH

Goddamnit.

I press my lips together and round the archway. I spot Van on the couch, who clearly reads the latest text and follows it with an eyeroll.

"Vivi," I sing-song. "Your bestie has arrived."

"Aunt Tessa!" Vivian climbs down from a chair pressed against the counter beside my mother and springs into my arms. Her little arms wrap around my neck, and I squeeze tightly before placing her back on her bare feet.

"Start it," I say to her.

She giggles. "Girls rule…"

"And boys drool!" I finish.

My dad, sitting on the couch next to Van, snorts.

"Remember that," Van echoes. "No boyfriends until you're at least thirty."

"Thirty!" Vivi shouts. "Daddy, that's so old!"

A laugh bursts from my mouth. "Yeah, Van. That's so old."

He turned thirty over the summer.

Van flattens his lips before catching my eye. "Are you waiting until you're thirty too? Considering you've never had a boyfriend."

I huff. "That's not true!"

"Sebastian doesn't count," Graham, who just arrived, says as he passes through the kitchen to get to the other side of the couch.

I cross my arms and glare at my brothers.

Sebastian was my boyfriend in elementary school.

I've had plenty of boyfriends since then. Only, I've kept most of them a secret because the moment I'm interested in a guy and my brothers find out about it, he suddenly disappears.

"And Patrick doesn't either."

I spin angrily at the sound of Noah's voice from behind. "Yeah, because of you!"

Van and Graham had already graduated high school by the time I entered for my freshman year, but Noah was a senior, with Beck just one grade below him.

Try having a boyfriend with two overbearing older brothers ruling the school.

Noah shrugs, heading for my mom, who's busy cutting vegetables for the salad.

"Don't date my friends, and we won't have any issues," he notes, leaning in to give her a kiss on the cheek.

She presses her face toward him. "Leave your sister alone."

With Vivian's back to me, I send my brother the finger. He repays me by pulling a French fry out of his hoodie pocket before shoving it in his mouth.

My eyes grow wide. *Betrayal.*

Knowing Beck, he's probably parked out on the street, piling his own fries down his throat before coming inside to *feign* hunger.

Speak of the devil.

Beck appears beneath the archway, wiping his mouth with the back of his hand. I casually walk over to him and give the air a sniff. He smells like the aftermath of a late night: grease and fast food.

We walk side by side toward the living room.

"Where's my Diet Coke?" I whisper.

"Gave it to your boyfriend," he answers, lowering his voice. "Oh, wait. You don't have one."

Graham coughs to cover up his laugh.

Van is engrossed in a conversation with Dad while Noah is still secretly eating his fries.

I silently snarl at all of them and disappear into the dining room to help Vivi set the table. And by help, I mean quietly going behind her to put the silverware in the correct spot.

Once we're finished and place all the food on the table, my mom whistles loudly–her signature dinner call when we were kids–and we all find our chairs. Vivian is in between me and Mom—*because girls rule obviously*—with my brothers across the table. My dad sits in his usual spot, at the head of the table.

"Lead it off, V," my dad says.

Vivian bows her little head and places her hands in her lap to pray. "Um...thank you for my daddy, and best friend, Aunt Tessa. Thank you for my uncles, and the best grandma and grandpa. And...thank you for this food...even though none of us really like fish. Amen."

I snort loudly, my hand flying up to my mouth to cover up a laugh.

My brothers, all except Van, refuse to lift their heads. Van, on the other hand, slowly raises his and sighs with a slight twitch of his lips.

I glance at my dad, his cheeks red from keeping it together.

After a second, he grabs his fork. "Well, she isn't wrong."

Laughter ensues around the table, which is the chorus of these dinners.

"Dad, what is that?" Beck points at the window behind my father.

As soon as my dad turns his head, a French fry sails through the air to land on Vivian's plate. Her eyes light up, and she quickly gobbles it up before my dad notices.

"Knock it off," Van snaps quietly to Beck.

He's the youngest of my brothers, though still older than me, and Van can't help but father him.

Beck rolls his eyes but then turns to Vivian and winks.

I take a bite of my salmon through a smile.

It's taken some time, but things are finally back to normal. Or...semi-normal.

After Dad had his heart attack during the height of our most competitive season and gave us all the scare of a life-time, we weren't sure how things were going to be moving forward. He hasn't been at the shop for the last several months, but our dynamic isn't that much different from before—other than the fish, of course.

"Kids." My dad puts his fork down on the table. "We need to talk."

I freeze with a piece of asparagus dangling in front of my face.

Did I speak too soon?

Van nods in my father's direction, and it's obvious he knows something we don't.

Graham runs a hand through his unruly dark hair. "What's going on?"

The asparagus drops from my fork, just like my stomach. "Is it your heart again?"

My mom whispers something in Vivian's ear. She nods excitedly, and they leave the table.

That means this is about Vanstone.

Shop talk.

"My heart will always be an issue, Tess." My dad shoots me a half-hearted smile. "But there's nothing new concerning it."

A crease forms in between Noah's eyebrows. "Then what's going on?"

He was probably the most affected when Dad had his heart attack. One second, he was going over two hundred miles per hour on a street circuit, and the next, Van was urgently telling him to pit through the headset because our dad couldn't breathe.

Silence settles over the table like some sort of warning. My spine stiffens with unease, and I brace myself for what's coming next.

Van sits taller in his seat. "Dad is taking a step back to reduce the stress."

"A step back?" I ask. "What–"

My dad puts his hand up, and I stop mid-sentence. "As of today, I will be the Chairman of Vanstone Racing...and nothing more."

No one says a word.

No one breathes.

The table freezes.

Naturally, I'm the first to break the silence. My lips slowly part. "But...what does that mean?"

With sad crinkles around his eyes, my dad glances at the five of us before answering. "That means the future of Vanstone Racing is in your hands."

Chapter Two

ROME

I'VE MANAGED to fly under the radar for the last two months, and it's been refreshing. In Montreal, I couldn't even go out with a baseball cap on without someone noticing me. But here, on US soil, not a single person has given me a second glance.

The strip is too busy to be noticed. Las Vegas is packed full of tourists, showgirls trying to make a buck, and a load of people who should check themselves into Gamblers Anonymous. Or it could be because no one expects to see me here unless I'm behind the wheel of my car.

Or worse, no one has noticed me because Rome Pierce is obsolete after the crash that left F1 fans stunned to the point of silence. It didn't take long for my spot to be filled.

My father came out with a statement shortly after the wreckage: *My son is recovering well, and he will be back to racing at the start of next season. The crash was due to a malfunction with his brakes, something the Pierce team is working diligently to avoid in the future. For now, my stepson, Beau Pierce, will be stepping in to drive. Thank you for your concerns.*

A malfunction with my brakes.

What a load of fucking bullshit.

I tug my hat down farther as I step out of the Uber in front of Vince Halston's home. It's not as big as I thought it'd be, but Vince never was one for flashy things.

I glance down both sides of the sidewalk, skeptical that this meeting is just the two of us.

Everyone knows that Vanstone is a family-run team. Vince is the owner, naturally, but all four of his sons work closely together with him.

Then there's Tessa Halston.

Vanstone's Princess.

I rap my knuckles against the door, my chest tight.

It opens within a couple of seconds, like he and Rose were waiting for me.

"Rome." Rose smiles, and it's quite honestly a slap in the face.

Beatrice, the woman who stepped in to be my mother just months after my own passed, has never smiled at me like this, with warmth and love.

Actually, I'm not sure she's ever smiled at me unless a camera was present.

"Mrs. Halston." I nod at her, my voice cold.

My guard slides into place. I'm on edge.

Rose's warmth stays intact as she ushers me inside their home. The door latches behind us, and I give her a tight-lipped smile before she leads me down the long hall. I take the opportunity to scan my surroundings.

Framed photos of every Halston spawn over the years line the wall, mocking me all the way to the dining room where Vince is waiting for me.

Our eyes meet, and he stands from the table.

"I'll leave you two to talk," Rose says, backing out of the dining room as quickly as she came.

I watch her go, only to turn to see Vince standing before me.

He sticks his hand out while the other grips me firmly on the shoulder.

Months ago, I would've flung his arm away.

But now? I let it rest.

With hesitation, I place my palm in his. Both being dominant men, our grips tighten as we shake hands. As soon as we make our point, we let go, and I take a seat across from him.

Vince drums his fingers on the table. "Well?"

I slip the baseball cap off my head and place it in between us. My jaw aches, the pressure of my teeth grinding giving me a headache.

Fuck, this is painful to admit.

I clear my throat. "You were right."

Vince doesn't bat an eye. He knew I'd confirm his claims, as if the wreck that nearly took my life didn't already.

"And?"

And what?

Does he want me to tell him how angry I am? Does he want me to vocalize how my own father risked my life to win, just to beat Vanstone Racing? He tampered with my car so I'd have a better chance at winning, just to prove that he's better than his former best friend.

I swallow the bitter taste of betrayal on my tongue and ask the one thing I've been wondering for the majority of my racing career. "Is this why you left Pierce Racing?"

Vince leans back in his seat, eyeing me closely. A slight

nod is the only thing I get for confirmation, and it's because he doesn't trust me.

Just like I don't trust him.

Not to mention, we were both forced to sign NDAs with Pierce Racing—even me, despite the fact that I'm blood.

"I promised myself that if I ever caught wind of your father cheating again, I'd make sure to stop it this time. Hence the altercation you heard on the radio."

I narrow my eyes as skepticism enters the conversation. "Why didn't you go to the FIA years ago if you knew he was cheating? An NDA can't legally stand when the FIA is involved in something like that."

Vince sighs, the answer already on the edge of his lips. "Because I chose to go with the settlement. There were strings attached."

I don't doubt it.

"Like?"

"Silence," he says. "And silence is survival in this business, Rome."

As much as I hate to admit it, I understand.

I've been tight-lipped since the wreck, and it isn't by choice. I know that if I speak up about what happened outside of the walls of our shop, there will be consequences.

A lot of backlash.

My own name soiled, my racing career down the fucking drain.

There are too many unknown variables.

I stare at Vince, and he stares at me.

So much has changed over the years, but he still looks the same despite a few wrinkles and, of late, a less-than-stable heart.

I went from considering Vince a second father one day to calling him my enemy the next, and that's how it has remained for the majority of my life. But now, I'm sitting at his dining room table with my heart pounding like a fucking racehorse, because this meeting isn't just to clear the air.

A stillness settles around us with words left unsaid.

He shifts in his seat and reaches for a manila envelope. It slides against the table until it's in front of me.

"Take your time," he says, getting up from the table. "I'll be on the patio when you're ready."

My throat tightens.

I wait until he's completely out of view before pulling the envelope the rest of the way across the table. My heart pounds harder when my finger skims the paper. I scan the proposal quickly, my blood running hot with each word.

The letters blur together, and it isn't until I reach forward to grab the pen that I breathe easily again.

What was it that Vince said?

Silence is survival.

I'll stay silent with Vince.

That is, until we win, fair and square.

Chapter Three

"SHOULD WE GET A SHOT TO CELEBRATE?" Quinn wiggles her eyebrows up and down with a glimmer of rebellion in her eyes.

I grin. "Just one?"

Quinn flips her auburn hair from her shoulder and turns toward the flirty bartender. "Three lemon drops please."

She peeks back at me. "*Each.*"

"You've got it, beautiful." He winks at Quinn and makes our drinks, despite the long line of men waiting to order.

I move off to the side and gaze around our favorite bar. It's not on the strip, so instead of the vast space being filled with tourists going wild while on vacation, it's packed full of UNLV students. I've lived in Vegas the majority of my life, unlike most of those on the strip and in the F1 world. It's unusual for an F1 team to reside in the United States, but leave it to my father to be the first.

As soon as he made the break from Pierce, off to the US we went.

We've been here ever since. He's built Vanstone Racing

from the bottom up, and as of yesterday, it's all up to Van, Noah, Graham, Beck, and me to keep things steady within.

My brothers' positions remain the same, but I've gotten an upgrade.

A promotion, if you will.

Tessa Halston, Vanstone Race Engineer.

It has a certain ring to it, doesn't it?

Beck nearly had an aneurysm at the table with my father's announcement, but I think that had more to do with him than it did with me.

My brothers and I know the racing world inside and out. People say it's in our DNA, but that's because it's truly all we've ever known.

The five of us are a walking encyclopedia of all things F1 related, but each with our own niche. Van is the main race engineer for Noah, who is one of the best drivers of his time—minus Rome Pierce, who I like to pretend doesn't exist. Beck is our reserve driver, and in his terms, that means he's not good enough. In reality, it means he's who will drive for Vanstone if Noah ever gets injured. Then you have Graham, who is an absolute wizard in the garage.

And last but not least, there's me.

Vanstone's Princess, as the media likes to reference me as.

I shouldn't complain.

It's a helluva lot better than what the other teams call me, which is *Pit Porn.*

Disgusting pigs.

But now, I have the opportunity to prove myself.

The only thing missing is a second driver, one more seasoned than Beck—something he is incredibly bitter about.

"Congrats, bestie." A lemon drop appears in front of my face, and I greedily take it.

The kick of liquor hits the back of my throat after the tangy lemon, and I finish it off by licking the sugar from the rim.

"And another." Quinn tips her head back and takes her second shot, and I follow suit.

By the third one, I'm wiping the back of my hand across my mouth, the burn of vodka settling in my lower stomach.

"To you, my little overachiever." Quinn bumps shoulders with me, and I laugh.

"I'm not an overachiever. Just the same ol' Tessa who spends her days picking through data and tweaking sims."

Quinn rolls her eyes. "You are too. In high school, you wrote your senior thesis arguing that women have just as much right to be on the racetrack as men do, and I recall you ending your presentation with a promise of being there one day."

I pause. *Okay, fine. Maybe she's right.*

"I prefer the term go-getter."

Quinn's mouth turns up. "A powerhouse."

"A prodigy."

A laugh-like snort leaves us both, but then she turns somber.

"How's Beck?" she asks.

I lift a brow. "You're concerned about Beck?"

My brother and Quinn have been neck and neck since the moment she and I became best friends. He constantly picks on her, even now that we're adults, and she religiously tells him to fuck off.

Their friendship, or non-friendship, has turned from childish pranks to Beck banning the entire senior class from pursuing her. Now, he constantly hits on her just to piss her off.

Beck is only nineteen months older than me, but he acts years younger.

I'm honestly surprised he isn't here, bouncing around from uni girl to uni girl. They're obsessed with him, especially when he tells them that he drives an F1 car for a living.

I have a hunch that he uses them to fulfill his need for adrenaline.

Beck makes reckless decisions, both on and off the track.

"I'm not concerned about Beck," Quinn argues. "I'm just wondering if we're going to have to drag him out of here as he drowns his sorrows from remaining the reserve driver."

I sigh. "There's a good chance."

Quinn grabs onto my hand and drags me onto the dance floor. "Enough about Beck," she shouts. "Let's dance!"

The alcohol sloshes in my lower belly, loosening me up just enough to follow after my best friend. She's always been the fun one of our duo, never hesitating to toe the line of rebellion, and on nights like tonight, I have a commitment to do the same.

After all, I *am* celebrating.

"Say it louder, Quinnnnnn. Enough about *Beck*."

Quinn and I turn abruptly toward the instigator himself. His pale-green eyes are glassy, and half of his drink sloshes over the rim of his cup, landing on the floor between us.

My shoulders drop. "Beck, you're wasted."

He scoffs. "You're the one who just downed three shots."

I narrow my gaze. "Are you spying on me?"

Beck's lazy gaze shifts to Quinn.

She crosses her arms. "He's probably spying on me. Did you already threaten all the men in here not to touch me with a six-foot pole? Making up some excuse that I have herpes or something?"

Beck's lip twists before he puts the cup of liquor up to his mouth.

"I hate you," she mutters before ramming her shoulder into his on her way past.

He stumbles and follows it with a chuckle, longingly watching her go.

I step closer to him and snap my fingers in his face.

He turns back toward me. "I'm not spying on you. I was here first."

"Yeah, I can tell." I laugh sarcastically. "How much have you had to drink?"

He hums. "None of your business." Then he bops me on the nose and grabs a random girl to dance with.

Ugh.

I weave in and out of the crowd and head for a quiet corner. I pull my phone out of my pocket and start a new group chat with my other brothers, sans Beck.

ME

911

As soon as I fire off the message, I change the group chat name to clue them in.

Sober Siblings Only

VAN

No.

I quickly text back with my location, and a **yes**.
Noah leaves the group.
No sooner does a huff leave me than Noah texts me separately.

NOAH

I'm not sober, so I can't be in that group.

ME

I switch back to the group text and see that the name was changed.
Another One Bites the Dust

GRAHAM

Do I have to? Can't you handle it?

I skip my eyes past my phone screen to search for Beck in the crowd. The last I saw, he was nuzzling some blonde's neck with his hands on her hips.
Come out, come out wherever you are.
After I come up empty-handed, I go back to my phone.

ME

If I have to go search for him and find him in the bathroom with some girl, I'm going to throw up the three celebratory shots I had.

Graham adds Noah to the group
Noah changes the name of the group
Two Drunk Siblings and Two Responsible Siblings
I look to the ceiling and sigh.

ME

Stop changing the name of the group text and get here to help me before Beck makes a fool of himself or worse…gets arrested!

The last thing our family needs right now is extra stress. Why can't Beck understand that?

GRAHAM

Fine. I'm on my way.

I sag with relief.

Thank you.

I slip my phone back into my pocket and look for Quinn.

I find her, but I also find Beck, and his hands aren't around that blonde's waist any longer.

Instead, they're around some guy's throat.

Chapter Four

ROME

THIS PLACE IS INFINITELY BETTER than the last. There aren't any cougars that smell of smoke, wearing thick eyeliner and whore-red lipstick, continuously scraping their nails against my chest while they go on about their divorce and how their ex-husband was lousy in the sheets.

This bar, miles from the strip, is more my style.

The women, though on different levels of life than I, are at least my age and don't reek of cigarettes. Instead, they smell of flowery perfume, liquor, and bad choices.

Right up my ally.

The best part about it? They have no idea who I am.

Out of nowhere, a chick with wavy, thick hair slips in front of me. "Hurry. Dance with me."

She wraps her fingers around my wrist and tugs me to the center of the floor. Confusion backs my every step, but who am I to deny a damsel in distress?

I could use a distraction—one that takes my thoughts of Vanstone Racing and pushes them all the way to the back of my skull.

The auburn-haired girl's hands land on my shoulders, but her eyes flit off in a different direction, like she's looking for someone.

Or hiding from someone?

I'm not sure which.

"What's your name?" I ask.

She briefly looks at me. "Quinn."

"I'm Ro…" I pause. "I'm Pierce." *Just in case.*

Quinn says nothing. Her attention moves past me to continue her search efforts.

I lean closer. "Who are we looking for?"

She scoffs. "No one important."

Well, alrighty, then.

I'm fine with being her cover for the night, I guess.

She stiffens in my arms, and pure revolution whisks over her face.

Oh, hell.

She's found her target somewhere behind me, and if I'm not careful, I may be caught in between a rock and a hard place.

A hand unexpectedly lands on me, and *yep, here we go.*

I spin around, prepared to talk myself out of whatever this is, but I'm met with a familiar face. It takes Beck Halston half a second to realize that I'm familiar to him too.

What are the fucking chances? Is this fate? Or maybe karma?

I signed a contract to race for Vanstone—which by default means I'll be working with the entire Halston family —no more than six hours prior, and now I'm face to face with the youngest son who has already made the headlines for his hot-headed, impulsive behavior.

This has to be some sort of test.

Beck bares his teeth at me. "Oh, hell no," he growls.

The heavy blow to my jaw is followed by a sharp sting. I reach up and grab my face, opening and closing my mouth a couple of times.

He must know I can't hit him back.

I should have amended that part of the contract.

"Beck! What the fuck?" The pretty auburn, clearly involved with Beck, puts herself in between us. She places her hands on his chest and shoves him backward.

"Do you know who he is?" He points at me with pure hatred in his eyes.

I'll eat that look for breakfast, thank you very much.

"Beck! Jesus Christ!"

My shoulders tense.

Tessa, the only Halston daughter, the girl who is no longer a girl, moves in between Beck and my dance partner. She gently pushes Quinn to the side and peers at her brother. "Can you get it together?" she shouts. "I really don't feel like bailing you out of jail tonight!"

I chuckle.

Beck glares at me while talking to his sister. "Do you know who she's dancing with?"

"I honestly don't care who she's dancing with!" Tessa snaps. "And you shouldn't either!"

Beck glowers. "Rome fucking Pierce."

A sick smile slides onto my face because, truly, I just can't help myself.

A decades-long rivalry between our families has embedded this behavior into my very bones, and although I'm part of the Vanstone crew now—something I'm beginning to think they're unaware of—it's hard to ignore.

"What?" Tessa turns around hastily, and we lock gazes.

Shock moves over her features, little worry lines digging into her forehead. She sucks in a sharp breath through her slightly parted, pink lips. Those big brown eyes of hers widen, and she blinks several times like she can't believe I'm standing in front of her.

She recovers quickly and moves into full-on manager mode.

"Quinn, take Beck outside and wait for Graham. He's on the way." She turns and looks at me. "*You* stay here with me."

"I'm not going anywh–" Beck's words fade with Quinn pulling on his arm toward the door.

With their departure, Tessa snaps at me. "Let's go."

She flings her hair out of her face and turns, expecting me to follow her.

That would just be too easy, so I keep my feet planted. "Where we goin', Tess?"

Her steps falter.

I get a quick glimpse of the side of her soft cheek as she glares at me over her shoulder.

"Do *not* call me Tess."

I lift my lip. "Why not? I thought you liked that nickname?"

She angrily faces me, and a rush of hot excitement fills my veins.

"Friends and family call me that…" Her finger pokes my chest, and it takes everything in me not to grab a hold of her small wrist.

"And you are *neither,*" she finishes.

I roll my lips and hum. "What about co-workers?"

A line of confusion works its way in between those perfectly shaped brows. "What?"

The music in the club shifts to some sort of techno song,

and the lights sync up with the beat. She stares at me, the shadows playing with the delicate features of her face. Her cheeks fill with air, and then she lets out an annoyed sigh. Her warm fingers wrap around my arm, and I let her tug me through the gyrating crowd.

We get to the hallway lined with mostly women who need to use the restroom and pass by each and every one of them. They look at me first, and then they move to Tessa's hand wrapped around my bicep. They share looks of envy and praise.

I chuckle to myself.

They think Tessa is leading me to a secluded spot to have her way with me.

How twisted would that be on Monday morning when I show up to work alongside her?

She'd probably strangle me with a tire gun hose, and depending on how good the hookup was, I might let her.

Tessa opens a door that reads *Employee Bathroom* and pulls us both inside. She lets go of me, and I glance at it to see if there's a mark left behind, but it's just my imagination.

The lock latches, but she makes no move to face me. "What are you after, Rome? Why are you in Vegas?"

I lean against the sink, the cool porcelain a bite to my palms. I wait patiently for her to turn around to face me. I'm not speaking to her backside, even if the view is sort of nice.

Eventually, she turns around in haste, her wavy brown hair loose behind her shoulders.

"Hello?" she says sarcastically.

I eye her closely, and the stuffy room fills with hot tension.

"Your father didn't tell you?" I'm casual about it, my head tilting to the side.

She crosses her arms defensively. "Tell me what?"

My smirk deepens, and I don't even have to say the words.

Tessa's horrified expression tells me she knows *exactly* why I'm here.

Chapter Five

TESSA

A MILLION THOUGHTS fill my head, crashing like waves in the ocean. One revolting thought after another. And for the first time, I don't have a solution to any of them.

My first thought is to accuse him. "You're lying."

Rome's brow hitches. "I'm a lot of things, but a liar isn't one of them."

I doubt that.

"My father wouldn't hire you." I say this more to myself than him. "You're a *Pierce*."

His surname rolls off my tongue bitterly. The taste left behind is as sour as the three lemon drops I had.

Rome's knuckles turn white, his grip against the sink firm with frustration. "And?"

I scoff, my arms tight against my chest. "And being a Pierce means you're shady...and entitled. *Arrogant*. That isn't how Vanstone Racing is portrayed." My lip lifts with disgust. "You and your father both think you're untouchable! Why do you think my father left?"

Rome runs his fingers through his dark hair, the same hand going back to the sink to hold himself up as he leans against it in the most superior way. His flexed jaw catches my eye, the edges of it sharper than a knife.

It's no wonder his face is on all the billboards.

Next time I see one, I should climb to the top and slash Xs over his eyes.

Rome hums, and I pull my gaze from his stupid, edgy jaw.

His eyes are fiery, like two blue flames driving into me. "So that's why you think your father left? Because we're arrogant?"

Silence bounces off the walls of the stuffy, dim bathroom. Remnants of Lysol and bleach surround us, which has to be the reason for my short breaths.

"I know that's why," I say. "So what are you really doing here? Did you come all the way to Las Vegas to snoop?"

I push off the bathroom door to eliminate some of the space between us. I straighten my shoulders but keep my arms crossed against my chest. "Or did you come here to intimidate my brothers? Thought you might try to fuck with their heads before the season starts so you have a better chance at winning?"

Rome's cheek twitches, and I want to smack him.

He shoves himself off the bathroom sink and is in front of me before I have a chance to spew any more reasons why he'd be here.

I raise my chin.

Rome Pierce's blue eyes alone are an intimidation factor, but I've never been one to back down from a scuffle. That's what having four older brothers will do for you.

Even as he reaches forward to wrap his large fingers around my chin, I remain steady on two sturdy feet.

"You know," he drawls, dropping his gaze to my mouth. "Vanstone's Princess shouldn't use ugly words like that."

I grind my teeth back and forth.

He clearly knows that label pisses me off. Rome Pierce, on top of his arrogance and haughtiness, is also observant.

Good to know.

When I say nothing, he chuckles darkly.

"Especially *fuck*," he says smoothly.

I bounce my eyes back and forth between his, my heart beating faster and faster with every passing second.

"That word alone may give a guy the wrong idea," he says, the smirk deepening on his annoyingly chiseled face.

My lips part.

His insinuation shocks me, but it's fleeting.

I take a quick step back and place my hands on his shoulders. I ignore the hard muscles beneath my grip and bend my knee.

It collides with his muscular stomach. He buckles at the waist, wheezing.

I should've aimed lower.

"I wouldn't fuck you if my life depended on it." I grip the door handle. "Now go back to where you came from. There is no reason for you to be in Las Vegas."

With a sick grin, he looks up at me, still crouched forward with his arm wrapped around his waist. "You sure about that, Tess?"

I swing the door open.

Of course I'm sure.

Pierce Racing likely got word that my father is stepping down, and that's why Rome jumped on a plane to Las Vegas. He's here to rattle his biggest rival. To apply pressure where it hurts most.

Unfortunately for him, Vanstone's Princess doesn't crack.

* * *

"We are not telling Dad."

All four of my brothers stare at me—Van from across his desk, Beck sitting on the edge of it, and both Graham and Noah in the chairs placed at the foot of the maple wood with their long legs stretched out in front of them.

I pace the office.

The office my father graciously handed over to Van.

"I agree," Beck says.

Graham rolls his eyes. "You only agree because you don't want Dad finding out you were three sheets to the wind and about to end up in handcuffs."

"I wasn't *that* drunk," Beck argues. "And even if I wasn't drinking, I still would've punched him."

"I think Dad should know," Noah interjects. "Even if he is somewhat removed from the business, he should know."

"Why?" I stop pacing and place my hands on my hips. "What's the point? Rome was here to screw with our heads. He knows that things are shifting within Vanstone, and he took the opportunity to play on it. It's water under the bridge as of today."

It wasn't on my bingo card to discuss Rome Pierce the morning of my first official day as an employee for Vanstone, so if we could wrap this up, that'd be great.

Plus, the sooner we get to work, the sooner I can figure out who is joining our team as our second driver.

One thing is for certain: it's not Rome Pierce.

"She's right."

Beck, Graham, and Noah give Van their attention.

Of course I'm right.

Beck jumps up from the edge of the desk. "You're siding with her?"

Van sighs but slowly nods his head.

It's eerie to see him behind my father's desk because they resemble each other so much. Both with light-green eyes and the same angular face with a faint scruff against their hard-lined jaws. The only difference between them is that my father has a light dusting of gray sprinkled throughout his hair.

"I knew this would happen," Noah says jokingly. "Tess is already taking over."

I lift a shoulder. "It's not my fault I'm smarter than the three of you put together."

"You're clearly not," Beck chuckles. "You can't even count. There's four of us."

"Van isn't included, idiot."

Van, busy staring at his phone, glances upward. He swings his attention around the office, stopping to look at each of us briefly. "Just got word that our new driver is here."

My heart skips a beat, and butterflies swoop low in my belly. "Are you going to spoil the surprise?" I ask eagerly.

His eyebrows rise at the same time he does. "I'm just as lost as you are. Dad wouldn't tell me who was joining the team, and I didn't want to press him."

Oh?

That's...conflicting.

Nothing but my brothers' footsteps follow as I walk over the glossy marble floor toward the lobby. Nerves eat away at my insecurities, and I pray that my father informed our new driver that I'd be their head engineer.

I can't imagine many men would be glad to know a woman is going to be calling the shots, especially in such a male-dominated sport.

Before I get too close to the lobby, I run my hands over

my teal Vanstone polo to smooth any wrinkles. I put a smile on my face and round the corner, only to slam into something hard—or *someone*.

My face collides with his chest, the scent of expensive cologne mixing with my senses. Two strong hands wrap around my upper arms to steady me, and I hear Beck's voice in the distance.

"You've got to be fucking kidding."

I snap to attention.

Two icy-blue eyes peer down at me, and a smirk that sends me to the red curves across Rome's lips. "Nice to see you again...*Tess*."

Chapter Six

ROME

THE SCENE UNFOLDING in front of me is so much better than I expected.

I stand back in the shadows of chaos as Vince slips in between Tessa and me, breaking us apart as soon as we collide.

The high points of her cheeks are pink with anger, her lips parted as a breath escapes.

Looks like she put on some type of lip gloss.

Just for me?

My cheeks beg to curve, but I quickly relax the muscles as Vince steps in to calm his raging children.

"Beck, act your age," he demands with a shake of his head.

Noah, who hasn't looked in my direction once without a scathing glare, elbows his youngest brother in the stomach.

Beck growls, his fists flexed at his sides.

Graham, easily one of the best mechanics in the industry, blows air out of his mouth, but he, too, remains quiet.

Heavy silence bounces from one Halston to the next,

each of them locked onto me with too many different emotions to name.

Van, the oldest and clearly still the most mature of the bunch, steps forward with his hand outstretched between us.

I take it, noting the firm grip.

"Welcome to Vanstone Racing," he snips, the words forcefully slipping through clenched teeth.

"Thanks," I say in return, squeezing his hand just as hard as he did mine.

"This is bullshit."

We all turn toward Beck.

"Beck," Van warns.

Beck points at me. "He's a Pierce, for fuck's sake, and now he's racing for us?"

Vince doesn't try to interrupt him. He lets him continue.

"You really think that low of me that you hired *him* as our second driver? Instead of me?"

I glance at Tessa, just for shits and giggles, and she has that glossy lip of hers trapped between her bright, white teeth. She nibbles on it nervously, bouncing her attention between Van and Vince.

"You're not ready," Vince stresses, looking at his youngest son.

He isn't wrong. Beck is skilled—I've never seen someone with so much passion and drive on the circuit. However, he makes mistakes, ones that simply come from not enough experience.

Beck remains quiet, but the look he gives me says plenty. His jaw flexes, just like his fists, and then he turns and storms the hallway with the echo of a slamming door in the distance.

And then there were five.

"He'll be fine," Van reassures Vince. "Let him cool off."

"I'll go talk to him." Graham turns and walks in the same direction as Beck.

Noah steps forward. "He might need back-up."

Tessa huffs and rolls her eyes.

Obviously, everyone wants to get the fuck away from this entire situation, and I don't blame them. Awkward doesn't even touch the uncomfortable energy in the hallway.

Van and Vince catch eyes, his oldest son inching his head to the left. Vince nods and looks at his daughter. "Tess, can you give Rome a tour? Van and I need to discuss some business."

She has an amazing poker face.

There isn't a single slight of refusal on her soft features.

Instead, she smiles and bats her eyelashes. "Sure, Dad."

"Thank you, sweetheart. Get to know each other while you're at it." He shifts to me. "After all, you'll be working closely together."

My eyebrows crowd.

Why does that seem more implied than before?

The moment Tessa and I are alone, the air in the hallway heats. She's in front of me before I have a chance to blink, and just like a few days ago, her warm fingers clamp onto my arm, and I'm being dragged behind her like a lost puppy.

"Where're we going?" I ask, humor lifting my words.

She throws a glare over her shoulder. "Shut up."

We push through a door, and it shuts sharply behind us.

Once the light is on, I realize we're in one of the sponsor suites. We have them at our headquarters too.

Had.

I'm no longer a part of Pierce Racing, so everything from

this point forward is in the past, a memory–or nightmare. One or the other.

Tessa lets go of me, grabs a remote from the center table, and points it at the glass-lined wall.

My mouth curves, and as if she can sense it, she snaps her eyes over to mine. Just the mere anger in the warm brown sends me through the roof.

"Privacy glass?" I tease. "What exactly are we doing in here, Tess?"

Her lips draw back in a snarl. "I told you that only friends and family call me that, and you're neither."

I casually place my hands into my pockets. "Sorry. With the privacy glass, I thought maybe we were about to become more than friends."

She shakes her head with irritation, and just like before, excitement zips down my spine.

Why is it so fun to pick on her?

Back before our fathers ended on shitty terms, I was the one who used to stick up for Tessa. Beck and Noah would chase her in the paddock and torment her, and I'd be there to smooth things over. But now, just after two instances, I'm the one doing the picking, and for some reason, her little scoffs and eyerolls feed me like I'm a starving man.

"What's your plan?" she asks tightly.

My plan is to get back at my cold-hearted father. But, of course, I can't say that to her. Not after dotting all the I's and crossing all the T's.

Vince was adamant his children remain unaware of what's really happening at my father's company for legal protection, which is exactly something a father should do–protect his family.

My father must've missed that in the parenting classes he never attended.

"Well?"

I drag my gaze from the shiny floor to Tessa again. With her hip popped and arms across her chest, she looks like a little spitfire, and if I'm being completely honest, the only thing it does is egg me on.

She watches me closely while I stride across the floor over to the leather couch. I sit down slowly with my legs stretched out in front of me. One of her gracefully arched eyebrows rises when I lift my hands and place them behind my head.

"My plan is to win," I say.

She snorts, and the gloss on her lips catches the shine from above. "Couldn't beat us fair and square, so you thought you might as well join us?"

I snicker but don't bother denying it. I do like to win. Whether that be in qualifying, on the circuit, or tucked away in this luxurious room with Tessa Halston.

"I know why you're here."

Oh, she's confident. But I'm certain she shouldn't be.

With a resolute stare, her chin edges forward. "You're here to take Vanstone Racing out from under us. You and your father probably have some grand plan to overtake the business because he can't stand the competition."

I chuckle and pair it with a quick shake of my head. "That would make your father pretty dense, wouldn't it?"

Tessa's mouth screws up, heat rushing to her cheeks.

I expect an argument, or some type of insult, but I get neither. The only response I get is cutting silence, which gives me the chance to notice how fast my heart is beating.

Tessa shifts on her feet, the rubber soles of her tennis shoes squeaking over the waxed floor. I place my hands on my lap and peer at her from across the room. The longer we stare at one another, the faster my blood pumps.

I can see why she's been labeled as Vanstone's Princess by the media. She's painfully gorgeous. Long, glossy brown waves for hair with warm eyes that match, though they're pretty cold staring at me. She has a body that begs for my—*a man's*—touch, the perfect size breasts, and hips that curve just below her slim waist.

Vanstone's Princess? More like the other title she's been granted over the last few years: Pit Porn.

Shit, stop it.

"Well?" My voice is edged with irritation.

"Well what?" she snaps back.

"Are you going to give me a tour of my new facilities, or do you have other plans?" I purposefully drag my gaze down her body, just to drive my point in.

Her rushed gasp catches my attention, and I stare at her mouth. Her pink lips pinch together, and her fists curl with anger.

I chuckle, and vexation flashes across her features.

God, this is too easy.

Her stomps across the room fill me with unmatched energy. I stand quickly to follow her, with humor following me.

"Keep up and pay attention," she barks over her shoulder. "I wouldn't want you to trip over your own feet by staring at my ass."

Her dig has me impulsively opening my mouth to spew a lie. "You don't have to worry about that." I peer down at her ass. "I've already looked, and I've gotta admit...I've seen better."

A growl rumbles out of her. "*Pig.*"

I smirk. "*Princess.*"

BECK HAS CHANGED *the group name.*
Four Halston Siblings and One Black Sheep

NOAH

Here we go.

GRAHAM

Day three and Beck is still butthurt.

ME

As long as you're sticking to the plan, baaa all you want.

After chaos ensued on Monday, we had an immediate sibling meeting where Van, with my encouragement and support, reminded the three stooges of the entire reason we are in the situation we're in: Dad's health.

Beck can have all the emotions he wants as long as he's keeping them under wraps around our parents.

I step onto the pavement in front of Vanstone HQ and shut my car door.

Rome's parking spot is empty.

Figures I'd beat him to work. He'll probably show up late because the almighty Rome Pierce doesn't need practice.

He's taken the last few days off to get settled in, securing a place to live—hopefully temporarily—and collecting his belongings from the moving company. It's given us time to recalibrate our high emotions, and it's given Beck a chance to cool down.

If the media hasn't caught wind of the recent changes within Pierce Racing, they're bound to find out soon. We have a meeting with the PR team this morning, and knowing Gia, she'll want to get back to posting on social media as soon as possible.

"Good morning, Tess." Ellis, our head security guard, nods at me.

I smile. "Morning, Ellis. How was your break?"

"Ah, I spent most of it in the nursing home with Mom, batting away all the old ladies."

I scan my badge and laugh. "I'm sure you hated the attention."

Ellis is a quiet, older man who is as stoic as a brick wall. He's been with the company from the beginning, following my father from Pierce Racing, which means he's seen me at my best and worst. From awkward haircuts, to braces, to finally filling out a bra and learning how to use a curling iron...Ellis has been there.

He's practically family.

"Loathed it," he says. "Got to spend some time with Ariel, though, so it wasn't awful."

My chest warms. Ellis rarely sees his daughter, and it kills him. After his ex left town with her, Ellis took her to court, which led to a nasty custody battle where he gained some of the visitation rights back.

I raise my brow. "Did you give her the present?"

Ellis grumbles. "Yes, and you were right. She loved it."

I smile. "I'm always right."

He chuckles and turns toward the shuffling of someone else approaching.

The air shifts, tight tension filling every open space there is.

"Name?" Ellis snips coolly.

I peer over my shoulder and bite the inside of my cheek to keep myself from laughing. Rome stands with his shoulders squared, a badge that appears small in his large hand.

"Seriously?" A line edges itself in between Rome's eyebrows, right beneath a lock of dark hair that hangs over his forehead. "You've known me since I was five," he reminds him. "And we already did this skit a couple of hours ago, Ellis."

A couple of hours ago? And who does he think he is using Ellis's first name like that? They aren't on a first-name basis.

"*Name?*" Ellis repeats.

I fail at keeping my laugh silent.

Rome snaps his gaze to mine, his blue eyes like icebergs, sharp and dangerous.

I sink my teeth into my lip.

Ellis eventually lets him through with the slightest glint of humor in his eye.

I quickly turn and continue on my way, but of course, my nemesis catches up.

"Nice of you to show up," he snips, zipping right past me.

Our shoulders brush, and my brown hair whizzes out of my face from the haughty air he carries. He's in dark slacks, a white dress shirt, and a casual suit jacket that hugs his arms like he's about to outgrow it.

I pause. "Excuse me?"

"You heard me."

I pick up the pace and step in line with his casual yet determined strides.

"I'm right on time."

He stops dead center in front of the elevator, his hand outstretched toward the button. "Oh? So you all wander out of bed and into work at this time on purpose?" His finger presses the up arrow. "Interesting."

I cross my arms.

He glances at me briefly and chuckles.

"What?" I snap.

The elevator door slides open, and Rome shoves his hands into his trouser pockets while stepping over the threshold.

I stay rooted in place. There is *no* way I'm going to share a tiny space with him.

"Nothing."

"No." I shake my head. "Say it."

He leans back, hands still in his pockets, and runs his attention down my body. "It's just that not much has changed since we were kids. You're still a brat."

The elevator doors slide shut with my jaw hanging loose.

It's official.

I can't stand Rome Pierce.

My glare stays glued to his playful eyes through the glass of the elevator. Even as I head for the stairs, I refuse to back down.

I'm making it to the meeting before him.

Even if I have to freaking sprint there.

He arrives on the second floor before I do, but with quick feet, I make it to the hallway just as he steps out onto the marbled floor.

Warm hints of his cologne fill the air, and it does nothing but make me angrier.

"Are you racing me, Princess?"

I stop dead in my tracks, but this time, I make an effort not to pop my hip and cross my arms. I wouldn't want him to call me a brat again.

"Stop calling me that," I say, voice chilled.

A few steps behind me, he asks, "What should I call you, then?"

I grin and peer over my shoulder. He's waiting with his eyebrows raised high.

"How about *boss*?"

His hot chuckle hits the back of my neck, and goosebumps rush to my arms. "Not a fucking chance."

Rome may think he has the upper hand when it comes to me—and probably all of us at Vanstone—but little does he know, I'm the one that'll be whispering in his ear, calling all the shots when the time comes, which makes putting up with his sharp tongue and irritating smirk worth it.

I brush away the warmth on my skin and wrap my fingers around the conference room door handle. "We'll see," I say.

I carry so much satisfaction from the interaction that I can't help but smile.

Gia, already sitting at the long table with her phone in one hand and a pen in the other, looks at me suspiciously. "Why do you look so happy?"

I place my purse on the table and take a seat beside her. "I'm always happy to see you."

Gia and I are close in age. We met last year after we

hired her for social media relations and have gone out a few times together. She's all business during the hours from 9-5, but when the sun goes down, she's your typical girl in her early twenties.

Rome walks in next, his eyebrows still furrowed. He lowers himself in the chair farthest away from me, the slight creases surrounding his squint filled with silent questions.

"God damn." Gia turns toward me with reddened cheeks.

"What?"

Her eyes grow wide. She inches her head in Rome's direction. "That's what."

I roll my eyes.

"Can you honestly tell me that you don't think he's one of the hottest men you've ever seen?"

Of course he is.

Until he opens his mouth.

Or until I remember who he is and where he came from.

What was my father thinking, hiring Lucas Pierce's son? How does he expect us to trust a man like him, who was raised to follow in his father's footsteps?

One thing is for certain: Rome Pierce may be utterly gorgeous, but I will never, *ever* trust him, and before the season is over, I'll uncover every last one of his ulterior motives.

Chapter Eight

ROME

I HATE MEETINGS.

It takes every ounce of energy I have not to let my head fall back for a quick nap. I used up the majority of my energy already, spending an hour in the gym, training, and then not losing my temper when it came to Ellis purposefully giving me a hard time.

I'm not sure what I expected.

Of course no one trusts me at Vanstone—no one other than Vince, but he's not here. Instead, it's the Halston clan, and they aren't exactly shy with their loathing.

They have nothing on my father, though, so if anything, their scathing glares are entertaining. Particularly Tessa. She may hate me even more than Beck.

Why does that give me pure satisfaction?

I stare at her from across the conference table. She's pulled her long, chestnut hair up into a bun held together with a pen, showing off her slender neck and heart-shaped face. Her eyebrows pull together as she stares at something on the other woman's phone–Tia? Clea? I forgot her name.

I glance at my watch.

My skin itches to get out of this stuffy room and into the simulator.

It's been far too long since I've gotten any practice, and the first Grand Prix is right around the corner.

"Are you logged into social media on your phone?"

I glance at another woman, who's been typing furiously on a laptop, and nod.

"Can we see it?"

Only if it speeds this meeting up.

I lift my hip and pull my phone out of my pocket. Tessa leans across the glass conference table, and out of pure instinct, I drop my gaze to her cleavage.

Her breasts are annoyingly perky.

I sigh and drop the device into her hand but not without skimming my finger against her wrist for fun.

She jerks her arm away with a blush creeping over her cheeks.

My palm tingles, and I lean backward in my chair to watch Tessa scan the contents of my social media accounts. She and *Mia?* huddle together, their faces side by side, to drink in everything on my profile.

Tessa snorts angrily and shoves the phone away.

I raise a brow. "Something wrong?"

She rolls those big, brown eyes in my direction. "Do these women really think they stand a chance, dropping into your DMs like this?"

For the record, they don't stand a chance, but letting on that their messages annoy me would mean that Tessa and I actually agree on something, and it's much too soon in our platonic relationship for that.

I kick my arrogance up a notch and shrug. "Can you blame them for trying?"

She rolls her eyes again, which only amuses me.

The other woman, *Leah?* blows air out of her puffed cheeks. "I don't think anyone blames them."

"Gia!" Tessa shrieks.

Oh. Gia.

A vibrating noise comes from my phone.

Everyone looks at it.

Tessa clears her throat.

When all I get is silence, I finally ask, "Well? Who is it?"

She slowly hands me the device, a glare fixed on her features. I look at the screen, and my shoulders tense.

Dad is calling.

Fuck.

"Answer it."

I snap my attention to Tessa.

My phone stops vibrating, only for it to pick up again a moment later.

He knows.

Either that, or he's ready to chew me out for being late this morning.

I've got news for him, though—I won't be showing up at all.

I hit decline and keep my expression void of emotions. Tessa tries her hardest to read me, her quick scan moving across my face.

We both look at my phone with another incoming call.

Beau is calling.

My chest tightens.

"Are we finished here?" I ask, voice edgy.

Gia clears her throat. "Yes. We'll send over the contract for permission to take over your social media account within the next few hours."

"Great." I hastily push my chair out with a good grip on my phone and head through the door.

I pull open the search engine, and I don't even manage to type my full name before an article pops up on GRID, one of the biggest news sources for Formula One: *Rome Pierce leaves Pierce Racing and heads for rival team.*

A wave of nausea hits my stomach.

I'm a grown-ass man, yet the fear of disappointing my father, instilled in me at a very young age, is too engraved in me to erase.

A cold sweat breaks out along my skin. I press my sweaty forehead to the wall and practice the breathing techniques I learned over the last few months.

I imagine my father is throwing shit in his office right now, with Beau taking the brunt of his anger. Not that I care much for my stepbrother. He's a prick—and a shitty driver too. He's also a mama's boy. In other terms, that means he's a fucking pussy.

My phone vibrates, interrupting my breathing.

Beau is calling.

This time, I don't ignore it. I press answer and put it up to my ear.

"Are you out of your fucking mind?!" he roars, not even bothering with a hello. "Did that wreck fuck your head up too? Because last I heard, it was just the flesh on your leg that was damaged."

The faded scar on my shin burns, like it has the ability to hear the insult.

"My head is perfectly fine." I remain calm. Though, from the way my ears burn, I know my blood pressure has risen.

"Then what the hell are you doing? Are you that bored that you want to cause a fucking uproar within the Pierce household? Talk about taking things too far, Rome." He scoffs loudly. "Your dad has every person imaginable trying to get those articles taken down."

My thoughts race. If he's trying to take care of the articles, that means he thinks this is a rumor.

"Where are you?" Beau asks.

I exhale deeply. "In Las Vegas."

There's silence on the other end of the phone.

I nod at one of Vanstone's many employees as they walk past. I wait until they're out of earshot to confirm the news. "I quit Pierce Racing."

"No, you didn't."

"I did."

He laughs, the menacing noise making the hairs on the back of my neck stand up. "You're fucking with me."

I'm done arguing with him.

"If that's what you want to believe, then I can't stop you."

There's more silence, and I imagine him in his office with his feet kicked up on his desk.

"If that's all..." I say. "I've gotta get to work."

The creaking of his chair catches my attention, and I know I'm right in assuming he's in his private office, away from the chaos likely ensuing down the hall.

"You just couldn't handle it, could you?"

I make my way to the elevator. "Handle what?"

Risking my life even more than usual every single time I rev the engine, obeying a man's ruling who would do anything to win? Like bend the rules and cheat his way to the top?

"You just couldn't handle that I was in the spotlight for once, instead of you."

I laugh, unable to stop it before it slips out. "Sure, Beau. That's *exactly* the reason I quit and came to Vanstone."

I know my stepbrother well enough to know he doesn't catch the sarcasm from my tone, and by the look of Tessa's face at the other end of the hallway as she eavesdrops on my call, she doesn't either. But neither one of them are privy to the real reason.

One assumes I'm here to take over and run Vanstone into the ground, and the other assumes I'm just an attention-seeking asshole with a desire to cause a ruckus.

Turns out, they're both wrong.

Chapter Nine

TESSA

I STAND BEHIND some of our most trusted engineers, their concentration steadily on the computer monitors while mine remains on the large screen taking up the majority of the wall. Rome is silent, continuously pushing himself in the simulator.

I bite my tongue, wanting nothing more than to jump in on the action, but today is all about letting Rome get comfortable with our technology.

A curse flies from his mouth. "It's too stiff over the bumps."

I glance at the monitors, then back to the screen.

He's braking early.

Another few times around the toughest chicane and I'm grabbing a headset and slipping it on my head. "Stop braking early."

His growl, deep and gritty, flows through the headset. "What are you doing here, Princess? Get out."

I roll my eyes. "Try brake bias two clicks forward on the next."

He forces the next turn, and I raise a brow. This is definitely going to take some time.

"You're not listening to me," I say.

"Because you don't know what you're talking about."

A choked laugh leaves me, and next thing I know, the sim is cut off, and Rome is disengaged.

I look at the other engineers. "Give us a minute."

They happily oblige, and I can't blame them. The tension from Rome alone is enough to send the hairs on my arms erect, and now that he's glaring at me from across the room, he's nothing but a tall, broad, dark shadow with tense shoulders.

"The fun is over," he bites out. "I need to concentrate."

I lean forward, pressing my hands on the table lined with monitors of various stats. "Are you saying I'm a distraction?"

His lip curls with irritation. "Not a good one."

He means it as an insult, but it doesn't faze me. "I grew up with four brothers, Rookie. Try again."

Rome jerks backward. "*Rookie?*"

I shrug. "You're driving like one."

Those blue eyes, icy and cold, narrow. I stay rooted in place, whereas he inches forward. The only thing in between us is a large computer screen, the pull from our bodies tight.

I stare at him, flexed jaw and high cheekbones. The first two buttons of his crisp, white shirt are undone, his hair a wavy mess from spending hours in the simulator.

"I'm not driving like a rookie," he says, slow and steady. "Your engineers just suck. My car is too tight, the tires drop early, and it's lazy on turn-in."

Some of that may be true, and adjustments will be made, but my heart is beating too quickly to agree, so I do the opposite, like I'm seven years old again and arguing with my brothers over something ridiculous.

"The car isn't too tight–*you* are. The tires are fine. The data proves it." I lean in even closer, my long hair whisking over the screen of the monitor, illuminating our faces. "And the car isn't lazy on turn-in...your driving is."

Something dangerously enticing flashes across Rome's face. His head tilts in a predatory way, and the air crackles with electricity. I've struck a chord, and it was way too much fun.

"You expect me to trust a single word Vanstone's Princess says about *my* driving and *my* car?" A chuckle rolls off his tongue. "You're good for one thing and one thing only, Tess."

My nostrils flare, a tinge of metal on the tip of my tongue from biting down on it.

Rome's face is inches away from mine. His hot, seedy breath does something to my stomach, sending it on a ride against its own free will.

He smirks. "You're nothing but pit porn, baby."

The insult is a slap across the face, but I don't so much as blink.

"So get out of the sim room, let the engineers back in here, and go home," he adds.

I pull my lips into a smile—something my opponent doesn't see coming. A line appears in between his eyebrows, his breaths short and sharp.

"The only engineer you need is already here."

I pull away from our shared space and take a seat in the head chair. I smooth my hair and place the headset on my head, adjusting the mouthpiece so it's lined up perfectly with my lips.

Rome peers down at me, the light from the screen deepening every angry curve on his face. "Are you trying to destroy Vanstone all on your own or…"

"I'm trying to keep you from destroying it," I counter. "Now sit down, and let's get to work."

He stands tall, his arms crossed over his chest. "I'm not driving with you in my ear. Go get my real team."

I click a few buttons on the monitor, the large screen behind Rome changing to mimic the adjustments I've made. He glances backward before spinning toward me with an angry brow.

"Better be careful insulting your head engineer, Rome."

Confusion blankets his face. "You're not–"

I show him my phone screen, another article from Formula One's most reliable source posted moments after the latest of him switching teams.

Vanstone's Princess takes on a new lead at Vanstone Racing.

Rome's lips split with shock, the color on his cheeks turning to an ashen gray.

"You've got to be fucking kidding," he mumbles.

"Get back in the sim. We have some adjustments to make."

* * *

"Well?"

I glance from my plate, the grilled chicken drier than the middle of the desert.

My dad's knife screeches as he cuts into his piece, Beck snorting quietly from beside me.

"How is he doing?" Dad asks.

He as in *Bastard*–I mean, Rome.

"It's good." The lie flows effortlessly. "We've been

working out the kinks in the sim and getting to know each other. He's starting to catch on to my terminology."

He hates me and disagrees with everything I say.

And if by getting to know each other means bickering the majority of the time, questioning adjustments made on his car, and driving me mad to the point that I had three Diet Cokes yesterday instead of one...then yeah, I'm telling the truth.

Van pipes in. "Good, because if you two show anything but a unified front tomorrow at the gala, the media will use it to their advantage, and Pierce Racing will have a ball with it."

I kick Van under the table.

He jerks, his eyes flying to mine.

No stress for Dad, remember?

"Daddy!" Vivian stresses. "You owe a dollar."

Noah chuckles. "Pay up, big bro."

Van pulls a dollar out of his wallet. It lands on the middle of the table, and Vivian smiles happily.

Beck leans toward her and whispers something in her ear. Her face lights up, the bright green color of her eyes filled with eager excitement.

Next thing I know, Beck is elbowing Graham, and Vivan's laugh fills the dining room.

"What the hell was that for?" Graham wheezes.

Beck high-fives our niece.

"Uncle Gam," she stresses, using the same name she's called him for years. "You owe a dollar too."

"There's our little go-getter." Dad chuckles and leans forward to ruffle her hair.

The doorbell rings, and surprisingly, he stands up first to get it.

"Expecting someone?" Van questions.

My mom begins getting a plate ready, the last piece of grilled chicken that none of us are sad to see gone placed in front of the chair next to Noah. He looks to it and then to the rest of us.

Dad's voice carries down the hall and into the dining room. "Come on in. Rose saved you a plate."

"Who is it?" Noah asks Beck, who is leaned so far back on his chair that the wood creaks beneath his weight.

"What the actual fuck," Beck whispers angrily.

"Uncle Beck!" Vivian shakes her head, the braids I gave her swinging back and forth. "Now you owe a dollar too!"

His chair snaps back to the floor, his fist clenched on top of the table.

My dad rounds the corner first, only to be followed closely by the very last person I want to see.

Especially at my parents' house.

For Sunday dinner.

"What the hell," I mumble.

Vivian giggles at me, but she doesn't tell me to put a dollar in the swear jar because *girls rule and boys drool.* Obviously.

"How is that fair?" Graham asks, ignoring the elephant in the room like the rest of us. "Tessa cursed, but you didn't tell her to pay up."

Vivian, with a scrunch in her nose, gazes at him. "Life isn't fair, Uncle Gam."

His jaw slacks. "Your father is really rubbing off on you."

She smiles happily but quickly turns her attention to Rome, who looks more tense than usual.

"Who are you?"

"Viv," Van stresses her name.

"Rome," he says flatly. "And who are you?"

"The language police," Graham mutters.

She nods. "I'm Vivian, and if you use a curse word, you have to put a dollar in the middle of the table."

Rome blows a breath out of his mouth. "That's good to know. Thank you."

Dad chuckles.

"We're already up to three dollars," she adds.

Rome keeps his attention on Vivian. "Who gets the winnings?"

Vivian smiles, proudly showing her recently lost tooth. "I split it with Aunt Tessa."

Rome slowly cranes his neck over to me. Our eyes snag, and unfortunately, the novelty of his blue eyes hasn't worn off. My pulse quickens, regardless if he's been nearly impossible to work with all week.

"Well, in that case..." he drags his words out, flicking a brow in my direction.

I fake a smile for the better of my father's health, but my body language tells a different story.

One that I'm certain Rome can read.

Chapter Ten

ROME

STEPMOTHER DEAREST IS CALLING.

Ignore.

Five seconds pass, and my phone vibrates again.

Stepmother Dearest is calling.

Beatrice is out of her mind if she thinks I'm going to listen to her whine about how ungrateful I am, or how I need to stop being a spoiled rich prick and come home. It's been days since my conversation with her son, and my father hasn't reached out since the first call I ignored.

Her name flashing against my screen tells me that he's still angry.

I wonder how many high-end pieces of art he's broken from throwing them across the house. It doesn't take much to think back on the times he's let his anger drive his impulsive actions. Glass from broken frames sprinkled throughout the foyer, vases crumbled with water and flowers in every other direction. The maid bent down low, cleaning up the mess he made, while Beatrice stood like a dictator to make sure she didn't miss a shard of glass.

I toss the valet my keys.

He fumbles with the catch, his youthful eyes saucers as he stares at my Lamborghini.

"Treat her right," I warn jokingly.

He perks up. "Oh, I will, Mr. Pierce."

I stop in my tracks, my black Oxfords pressing onto the red carpet. "Mr. Pierce is my father." My tone is heavy with irritation.

The valet shifts nervously. "Understood."

I put my back to him and shake off my sudden hostility. I scan the crowd and look for my new team. After yesterday's *family* dinner—that I was legally forced into from that ridiculous contract I skimmed and signed—the plan was set for the event. The Halston siblings would wait for me alongside the red carpet so we could showcase our unity together.

The idea of it makes me twitch.

There is no unity when it comes to the Halston siblings and me.

Particularly with Tessa and me.

We've been thrown together like oil and water. It's chaos in the sim, and her voice from hours of perfecting my car follows me well into the night as I toss and turn in a bed that isn't mine, in a house that's too modern and cold.

"Rome!"

Jericho, a driver from the UK, stands in front of me, wearing something much more elaborate than I am, with his hand outstretched.

Is that cheetah print?

He pulls me in for a bro hug, slapping me on the back with force.

"It's good to see you. How's the leg?"

It aches every time someone mentions it.

"Good as new," I say, placing my hands in the pockets of my slacks.

Cameras flash around us, and he shields his mouth. "Dude, I almost fell over when I read the headlines."

I give him a tight smile.

It's not like I didn't expect everyone to be buzzing over the news, but it irks me all the same.

"What happened? Fight with Daddy?"

I shake my head, preparing the lie I had constructed on the way over. "I just needed to make a name for myself instead of piggybacking on my father's legacy."

Jericho nods respectfully. "I knew I liked you."

I chuckle. "Unless I outrace you?"

He smirks. "Not this year."

Maybe not.

"I thought you left for other reasons," Jericho adds.

I lift a brow, my suspicions raised. My father is slick, his illegal modifications flying beneath the radar. But someone is bound to catch on eventually. And if they don't, I'll find a way to prove it without incriminating myself by breaking the NDA.

"Go on," I press.

"There's a rumor circling."

Cameras click again, but I'm too impatient to care.

"What rumor?" I ask.

Jericho turns his face, his hand going up to scratch the side of his cheek to shield his mouth. "That you moved to Vanstone to score the main prize."

"Isn't that what we all want?"

Jericho smiles deviously. "Not that prize..." He glances behind me. "That one."

I follow his line of sight over my shoulder.

My entire fucking body runs hot.

I clench my jaw tight, and I can't decide if I'm fueled with annoyance from Jericho's insinuation that I'm only with Vanstone because of a certain female that's a pain in my ass, or if I'm annoyed because she's turned every single head along this carpet by wearing a simple dress and flashy heels.

The slit along her leg is like a siren calling, and the closer she gets to me, the harder it is to breathe.

From annoyance, though.

Not from attraction.

So what if her dark hair is pulled away from her face into one of those sleek buns, highlighting her cheekbones? And her exposed throat with a delicate necklace wrapped around the bare curve of her neck doesn't put dirty thoughts in my head at all.

Fuck, I hate that she's so attractive.

Instead of greeting her like a gentleman, I force out an insult. "Nice of you to show up."

A hard line digs in between her eyebrows. The shimmery shit on her eyelids catches a glare from the flash of a camera, showcasing the vexation I've purposefully put there.

I put my arm out for her to take, like we planned the evening prior.

She takes it while placing a fake smile on her glossy lips. "Do you ever have anything nice to say?"

"I save my compliments for those who deserve them."

She huffs quietly. "Silly me to think your shit attitude was only reserved for normal business hours."

I turn my face, my mouth pointing directly at her ear with those stupid gold hoops. "I actually reserve it just for you, Princess."

Her bony elbow digs into my side, and I grunt, removing my arm.

"Stop whispering in my ear. People will get the wrong idea."

I snicker. "It's too late for that."

Her brown eyes catch mine questionably, and as if he knows what we're talking about, Jericho intrudes on our hushed conversation.

"Vanstone's Princess."

He bows like a nobleman in front of her, and it's hard not to laugh.

Tessa shoots him the same look she gives me every single morning. "Very funny, Jericho."

He stands up straight, his 6'3" frame enveloping her. "Rome thought so."

The wind from the snapping of her head in my direction is refreshing across my balmy skin.

"No one cares what Rome thinks," she seethes.

He whistles. "There's that feistiness that Vinny always talks about."

Irritation crawls up my spine.

How does Vinny Walsh know anything about her?

I'm the only one who should be privy to Tessa's fiery attitude. She's *my* engineer, not his.

My chest tightens from the sudden jealousy. I take Tessa's arm in mine again to pull her away from Jericho, and to my surprise, she goes willingly.

I glance at her, and it's obvious she's not fully in the moment. Her thoughts are elsewhere, and I'm pretty certain it has to do with Vinny.

I tug her toward her brothers, who just arrived.

"And here I thought your feistiness was only for me," I mutter.

Tessa doesn't so much as blink in my direction, which is sort of unsettling.

Beck, dressed similarly to me in a black suit and bowtie, curls his lip with disgust. "You two look like a couple."

That seems to get Tessa's attention.

She rips her arm out from mine hastily, nearly tripping over the red carpet.

"You good?" Van asks, looking at her strangely.

Noah laughs. "You need a Diet Coke?"

"I'm *fine*," she snaps. "Let's just go get this over with. I need at least ten hours of sleep in order to deal with this one and his lazy driving tomorrow."

Did she just call my driving lazy?

I watch her go, the dress hugging her curved hips like a glove, irritating me even more.

Noah, who I've rarely seen at HQ, as he stays in the other wing, practicing in his own sim, pats me on the chest. "Good luck with that one," he says, joining her in the photo backdrop.

Beck steps in line with his siblings but not before he flips me off.

Something I'm hopeful the cameras don't catch.

"Come on," Van sighs. "Let's get a quick photo and mingle before heading out. We're not ones to stay out and party like the rest of the drivers here tonight."

I've never really been one to do that either, knowing my father would go even harder on me the next day if I wasn't fully present or, worse, hungover.

But I just might stay out a little longer tonight.

Simply because I can, and maybe because I need a fucking breather from the Halston siblings.

Chapter Eleven

SILLY me to think there wouldn't be any drama because Pierce Racing wasn't on the invite for this particular brand sponsorship, but leave it to Walsh racers to prove me wrong.

Jericho's comment about Vinny hums beneath my skin, silently brimming the surface. My arms break out in goose-bumps, my gaze winding around the large area to spot him before he spots me.

Vinny crossed my mind while I was getting ready, and I should have taken it as a warning. Like the universe's way of throwing me a bone to mentally prepare for the testy run-in, as if my nerves haven't already been fried all week from the bane of my existence: Rome.

My neck still tingles from his hot whisper against my skin.

I'm apparently starved for a man's touch if Rome Pierce gets me going.

I growl quietly into my glass cup, the ice clinking together with the bitter taste of vodka on my tongue.

Rome did not get me going.

It was the action itself.

Not Rome.

"Is it time to go yet?" Beck whines.

I place my glass down on the cocktail table and look at him flatly. "We've been here for less than an hour."

He bristles, the curl of his lip showing his frustration. "I'm not even sure why I'm here. I'm not the one they want to see."

"You're a part of Vanstone too," I say. "Your time will come."

"Easy for you to say," he argues. "You've reached your goal."

I laugh bitterly. "My goal is to win a race as top engineer, and I'm not sure if you noticed or not, but Rome and I aren't exactly meshing well."

Beck follows my line of sight.

Rome and Noah stand side by side, a sponsor rep opposite of them. She says something, and Rome flashes her a grin—one I never see. Instead, I get arrogant smirks after he lands an insult or a scowl.

The woman touches his arm, her long, red fingernails stark against his black suit.

I curl my fingers around the glass cup.

"I'm stepping out for air," Beck says, leaving me alone at the cocktail table.

The last time he did this, I ended up in a position that sits like a secret in the back of my head.

I scan the room.

It's always nice to know where the threat is, and for once, I'm not referring to Rome.

Jericho stands tall in his suit and runs a hand through his hair as he checks the same watch the rest of the racers are wearing tonight. They've already taken a photo of Rome and Noah with theirs, which means we don't have much longer until we can head out for the evening.

"Looking for someone?"

I turn quickly, my movements jerky. I knock my drink over simultaneously and gasp.

Rome catches it with a cat-like reflex, placing it back on the table. "Too much to drink?"

I scowl. "Not nearly enough to deal with you."

His chuckle is gruff.

I pull my drink out of his grasp, and just to prove a point, I press the glass against my lips. Rome peers at me from his tall stance, his dark lashes outlining those stupid blue eyes. I sip the vodka into my mouth with ease, although the liquor burns my tongue.

Rome surveys my wet lips. His pupils grow when my tongue jolts out to lick the rest.

"See something you like?" I ask.

He snaps out of it before I manage a cheeky smile.

Our heated glares mimic each other. From the outside, I guarantee we look like we're going head to head, just like rivals do.

"And what if I said yes?"

He's toying with me.

I know he doesn't see something he likes. In fact, he can't stand me—especially when he's in a sim and I'm barking out demands.

Still, the question lands like a threat. It hits a little too close, sparking heat down my spine before I can stop it. I hate the way my body reacts before I'm able to shove the reaction aside.

But I do.

I bury it.

There is absolutely no way I'm letting him have the

upper hand—not at some sponsor gala, or at the office, and especially not at our first Grand Prix.

The sooner Rome gives in to my authority, the better.

My elbows press into the table. "Two can play this game, Rome. Don't even try to win."

He leans back, my glass now in his large grip. My lipstick stain on the edge touches his lips, and the rest of my drink goes down the hatch.

The glass clinks onto the table, and I'm both stunned and annoyed.

Rome's devilish glint drives into me in the tight space we've found ourselves in. "I don't have to try," he says with arrogance. "I'm a natural when it comes to winning, Tess."

I roll my eyes so hard I get dizzy.

I refuse to look at him any longer, fearful if I keep up this little back and forth we've found ourselves in, people will get the wrong idea.

We're too close.

Our faces a breath away.

If only everyone in this room knew that we were at each other's throats instead of the opposite.

"I told you that only friends and family call me Tess—"

"And I'm neither," he finishes for me. "I just can't help but call you that, though. Your angry face is my favorite."

I scowl and turn away, only to grow rooted in place.

My stomach curls into a ball of nausea with my gaze locked across the room.

Look at me! Letting my guard down because of Rome. I allowed him to distract me and rile me up to the point that I missed the moment Vinny walked into the room.

It's not that I long to see him.

Instead, it's out of protection.

"I'm ready to go," I announce.

"Already?" Rome tilts his head. "We just started having fun."

"If getting on my last nerve is fun, then sure."

I glance back to Vinny, who stands next to Jericho.

"Winning is fun," Rome drags out. "And it looks like I won this one, Princess."

Maybe, but only because I'm distracted by something worse than him.

I move away from the cocktail table and put my back to the gala. I long for the door like it's my savior. My ears ring, and the back of my neck prickles with the thought of every-one's eyes on me—especially Vinny's.

I want to poke his eyes out so he can't look at me and cut his hands off so he can't touch me. But more than both of those things, I want to beat him on the track just as badly as I wanted to beat Rome before he signed a contract with my father to join our team.

Chapter Twelve

ROME

I WATCH HER GO.

Not in a longing way, but instead with puzzlement.

These types of events are stuffy. In Canada, I'd have a few women I'd rotate through, bringing them with me as my "date" so I wasn't totally bored out of my mind, but tonight, I'm flying solo.

Which is probably why I couldn't help but toy with Tessa.

Clearly, we need to take a break from one another after the day we had. I thought the rivalry between Beck and me would be the most prominent within the Halston family, his jealousy impulsively throwing him at my throat, but I was wrong.

It's my little spitfire engineer.

We're supposed to be working seamlessly together, and we're not.

I didn't mesh well with my father, cautiously disagreeing with his shots on the track, and now I'm finding myself in the same scenario over at Vanstone.

If you asked me who I trust more, my father or Tess, it'd be her.

That's a secret I'll die with, though.

I turn back toward the mingling and look for the rest of my team. They're all still here, in various spots, each of us in our black suits. Jericho and Vinny, both decent drivers who I've never had beef with, break apart from conversation.

I watch Vinny sneakily head for the door, and after a few long seconds, I find myself following him.

Something is pulling me in that direction.

A magnetic force of sorts. A fuzzy thought. A tight knot in the pit of my stomach that switches between curiosity and protection.

Cool air brushes across my face, cooling my skin. The street is just as busy as it always is. Vegas never sleeps, the blurring headlights zipping past as Ubers park off to the side beside valet drivers in expensive cars.

Drawn like iron to a magnet, I find Tessa in that black dress that reveals just enough to keep me on my toes. Her chest expands, but it doesn't deflate, as if she's holding her breath.

I shift my attention, and my eye twitches at the sight of Vinny.

Heat surges through my veins from the way his arm finds her waist.

Does she like that?

A man like Vinny pulling her away possessively from the cameras and chaos?

I pause when she lifts her hand and slaps his arm away.

He grins and then whispers something in her ear.

My fists clench, but I can't look away.

"Sir?"

Vinny leads Tessa away, and my hackles rise.

"Sir, do you have your ticket?"

I glare at the valet, and he backs off immediately. I resume the show that I apparently have a front-row ticket to, but Vinny and Tessa are gone.

Unable to keep myself from chasing the fire, I weave in and out of the crowd, forcing tight-lipped smiles when needed, and round the corner.

My pulse skips at the sound of her voice.

The same voice in my ear that drives me absolutely fucking insane while we work tirelessly to fix the inconsistencies within my car.

"Vinny, back off."

He chuckles, and my nostrils flare.

Did he not hear her?

"How long are you going to hold out on me?" he asks. "You give me a little taste and then play hard to get."

"You *took* a little taste," she says, emphasizing the word *took*. "There's a difference."

My ears grow hot.

Vinny slips his hand down the front of Tessa's hourglass frame until he lands at her hip.

She grips his wrist. "Vinny."

"Tess," he murmurs.

His mouth moves to her neck, and rage mixes in with my rational thoughts.

She turns her head, panic evident. Our eyes snag, and for the first time, she doesn't look at me with disdain. Instead, she's looking at me with relief.

It fucks with my head.

I step forward, gravel crunching beneath my weight. "You speak English, yes?"

Vinny's mouth hovers over Tessa's delicate neck, and he

turns slightly to look at me. I shove my hands into my pockets to hide my flexed fists from both of them.

I feign a calm composure and wait for his answer.

"Can't you see that we're a little busy?" he asks, moving closer to eliminate any space between them.

It takes one quick helpless look from Tessa in my direction for my restraint to break.

I stride toward them, Vinny's edged jaw flexing the closer I get.

"Take your hands off my engineer."

His guard drops, and Tessa takes full advantage. With the slit in her dress, she's able to raise her knee and forcefully shove it in between Vinny's legs. He bends at the waist, and a guttural noise follows.

Tessa slips out from his grasp, and out of pure instinct, I grab onto her arm and move her behind me so he no longer has the privilege of looking at her.

I don't care that Vinny is incapacitated, I step in line with him and forcefully grab a hold of him. With my fingers digging into his arm, I shove him against the building wall. He flings my hand away but doesn't dare swing at me.

I'm bigger and better than him, and he knows it.

"Don't touch what's mine," I warn.

Shit, reel it in, Rome.

The last thing I need is a headline about how I got into a fight with another racer or, worse, that there's something going on between Tessa and me.

"Tess and I—"

I snap my hand forward, colliding with his neck. "Her name is Tessa," I seethe. "Only friends and family call her Tess, and from what I just witnessed, you're neither."

"'Fuck, fine," he forces between clenched teeth. "Chill."

For good measure, I press my thumb onto his windpipe before I let him go.

He gasps for air and reaches for his neck.

His glare makes me chuckle.

To my surprise, he begins to head in the direction of the gala but not before halting right beside Tessa.

I clench my jaw.

He's testing me.

He glances at her once before glaring at me over his shoulder. "See you on the track."

"Looking forward to it," I say, tone low.

Tessa waits until he's out of sight to face me. Her arms are crossed over her breasts, and if she wasn't glaring at me the way that she is, I may have offered her my jacket like a gentleman, but I can tell by the groove in between her eyebrows that whatever she's about to say isn't going to be a *thank you.*

I wait silently.

Her pretty brown eyes, full of fear moments ago, narrow with irritation. "I am *not* yours, Rome Pierce!"

I scoff. *See?*

Chapter Thirteen

TESSA

I'M NOT sure what I'm more perturbed about: the fact that Vinny crossed a line—again, Rome declaring that I was his, or that his proclamation gave me butterflies.

How dare my traitorous body?

Rome pushes his hands into his pockets, a faint chuckle slipping from his mouth. He appears so cool and calm after the altercation, as if his hand wasn't wrapped around another man's throat.

"I was referring to you being my engineer...my team-mate," he says, a smirk slowly appearing on his face. "But glad to know that's where your mind went, Princess."

I turn around hastily, my cheeks burning with embarrassment. The clicking of my heels echoes between the two buildings, mixing in with Rome's slow strides behind me. Before I'm able to step foot on the sidewalk, I'm pulled backward by Rome's hand around my waist.

Mid-gasp, he presses me against the brick wall.

"Not so fast."

A strand of Rome's dark hair falls onto his forehead. I

stare into his blue eyes—a mirror of the ocean, a mix of dark and light blue, full of life.

Oh my god, knock it off.

"What was that all about?" he asks.

I swallow. "Nothing."

Rome scoffs, and his hands land on his hips. "That's not what you silently told me a few minutes ago."

I cross my arms defensively. "I didn't silently tell you anything, and it's none of your business."

He pins me in place with a stern look, and my heart skips a beat. The air between us is charged, and he pushes right through it to end up inches in front of me. He grabs onto my chin and angles my face toward his.

I'm stuck, my chest refusing to take in a breath.

"Everything about my engineer is my business."

My stomach flips, like it's demanding I give in and tell him every last secret I've ever kept.

But then I remember that he's the enemy—new teammate or not.

"I don't trust you," I admit.

His dark chuckle gives me goosebumps.

"I don't trust you either."

His lip curves into a smirk, and he finally lets go of my chin. He walks toward the road but stops and glances at me over his shoulder. "It's fine. You don't have to tell me. I'll just ask your brothers."

I panic.

My heart jumps to my throat.

I rush after Rome and grab onto his arm. He willingly lets me drag him back into our hidden spot with a stupid, victorious smile on his face.

I uncurl my fingers to cross my arms angrily. "My brothers don't know, and I'd like to keep it that way."

Rome presses himself onto the brick wall and kicks one leg over the other lazily. His hands disappear in his pockets, and he looks like he's posing for an ad, showcasing the sleek suit he's wearing.

He's too talented as a driver to also be *this* attractive.

It's unfair to the rest of the male population.

"I'm listening, Princess."

I sigh loudly with a roll of my eyes. "It was at the prize ceremony. He had a lot to drink and got handsy. That's it."

"Got handsy?" he repeats. "How so?"

My face heats.

I'm downplaying the situation, and he knows it.

"You know..." My words fade, but he doesn't bite.

"I don't know," he says. "I've never gotten handsy with a woman who didn't beg for it."

I shift on uneasy feet, my thighs pressing together briefly.

"Maybe I begged for it at first," I say, lying.

He surveys me closely. "Did you?"

I look away. *Of course I didn't.*

He snickers. "That's what I thought."

"It's not a big deal. I put a stop to it before he got carried away," I add.

Rome's expression darkens. He's in front of me before I have a chance to take a breath, his arm winding around my waist possessively.

"It is a big deal," he says, tone low and slow. "And I have no problem making him pay during the race."

"You shouldn't be thinking about anything other than what I'm telling you while on the track," I remind him. "Leave Vinny and anything else out of it."

"I wonder what your brothers would think if I happened to slip up and tell them."

My nostrils flare. "Don't."

The smile that slides onto Rome's face makes me pause. *Oh God.*

"I'm really going to like having something to hold over your head...*Chief.*"

His chuckle mocks me as I follow after him down the alleyway.

"Rome."

"See you tomorrow," he says, not bothering to look at me. "I expect those changes to be made to my car before I get there in the morning."

My jaw drops. The audacity!

"You don't get to call the shots!" I shout after him.

He gives me one last look, eyes glimmering with mischief. "You sure about that?"

I follow his line of sight and land on my brothers, standing near the curb, waiting for their vehicles. I glance back at Rome, and his smile deepens, which irritates me like no other.

I get into my car and take off from the venue but make a left instead of a right.

As much as I don't trust Rome, I have a feeling he follows through on his threats, and if my brothers learn about Vinny's disgusting behavior, it'll do nothing but bring more drama to our team. And with Rome's recent presence stirring up a bunch of shit, I'm better off playing it safe.

So off to the office I go.

* * *

"Run it again."

"It's still tight," he snaps.

I can't help but laugh, which pulls on every one of Rome's tight strings. He jumps up from the simulator, his headset flying across the room. "Did you make the changes?"

Unlike the rest of the engineers in the room, I stand my ground. "You know I did. You just can't admit that they're wrong."

Rome's broad shoulders tense, his black t-shirt straining against his tight muscles. We stare—I mean, *glare* —at one another from across the room, and the longer I hold his eye, the faster my pulse races.

I'm thankful my dad is no longer showing up at HQ unannounced, because if he were here, I'd have to play nice to keep up with the charade that everything is *just fine* when, in reality, it's the opposite.

I keep my eye on Rome. "Everyone out."

No one argues.

The only one willing to go head to head with me is the devil across the room.

There's a faint brush against my hand, and I look up to see Dylan, one of the engineers we pulled from working with Van and Noah.

He peers at me with a worry line etched in between his eyebrows. "You sure you're okay being alone with him?"

I laugh softly. "I'm not afraid of Rome Pierce. But thank you for asking."

Dylan nods tightly and leaves the room.

As soon as the door shuts, Rome snorts. "Is there anyone at Vanstone who isn't related to you that doesn't want to fuck you?"

Hot anger surges through my body. "Excuse me?"

"Just making an observation," he states.

I scoff. "Well, maybe you should pay more attention to

your driving instead of worrying about my friendships with the employees of Vanstone."

"Friendships?" He chuckles. "Okay."

"Are you insinuating that they're something other than friendships?" I ask, rounding the computers to get closer to him. "Because if you think I would risk my career by fooling around with someone on my team, then you clearly don't think very highly of me."

Rome's edgy jaw levels out, his blue eyes as sharp as a knife. "I don't know if you would, but they sure would."

He drives me mad.

Every last nerve ending in my body is fried by the time we're done for the day.

The bantering is at an all-time high, and the quick-witted insults and fleeting glares are enough to set the entire room on fire. It's no wonder the rest of the engineers jumped at the opportunity to escape when given the chance.

"Get back in the car," I demand.

Rome shakes his head. "I'm done for today."

I glare at him. "It's only been an hour."

"Feels like an eternity."

My heart pounds.

This isn't working.

He doesn't trust me, and he thinks he knows better than I do.

I know it's because I'm a Halston—a female Halston, at that.

It makes me wonder why he left his father's side, and why mine was willing to hire him at the drop of a hat.

None of that really matters at the moment.

What matters is that something has to give, and if step one is proving to Rome that I do know what I'm doing as the leader of his team, then that's what I'll do. Step two is getting him to trust me.

"Fine." I stomp over to the computers and start to make the proper adjustments on the car.

"What are you doing?" he asks, clearly annoyed.

Unwilling to make eye contact with him, I continue staring at the bright screen. "If you're not going to do your job, then I guess I'll do it for you."

"What is that supposed to mean?"

I smile to myself. "It means it's my turn to drive."

Chapter Fourteen

ROME

I CHUCKLE.

Is she serious?

Tessa's hips sway with purpose toward the simulator. She stops right in front of it and flips her long hair over shoulder before climbing down into *my* seat.

"You're done for the day, right?" she asks, feigning sweetness.

I meet her fluttering eyelashes and coy smile.

It's a test if I've ever seen one.

She's baiting me and trying to manipulate me into dragging her out of my car so I'll keep practicing, but the only thing her fiery attitude is tempting me to do is throw her over my shoulder and plop her sassy ass on the desk to show her who's really in charge.

I flick the image away. "And miss out on proving you wrong?"

She scoffs, and I'm drunk on excitement.

"Let's see what you've got, Princess." I sit on the edge of the desk lined with monitors. I glance at the presets.

They're the ones she recommended yesterday. The same ones I argued with.

I should let her do her job, but coming from a different racing team, I have a wealth of knowledge that those at Vanstone don't possess, unless, of course, the cheating was going on for far longer than I realized and all the things I learned were skewed in a way that isn't possible.

The buzzing of the sim's engine pulls me back to Tessa.

Why does she seem so comfortable in my seat, as if she's born to do this?

She clearly trusts her abilities as a driver and engineer, which is what this is all about.

You have to trust your car...and your team.

As of right now, I trust neither.

Tessa takes off, and I sit back to watch silently, ready at a moment's notice to prove my point. Except, the longer she drives, the more agitated I become.

After the second chicane, I'm eating my words.

Fuck.

I glance at the monitor and then back to her driving.

The data proves it.

She's right.

Fuck me—she's *right.*

"Impressive, huh?"

I jerk against the chair, and Van comes into view.

When did he get here?

I lean farther back, and Beck is here too.

My body heats. I was so engrossed in Tessa driving that the rest of the world shut off. I no longer had control of my surroundings, kind of like when I'm in the middle of a race.

"She's alright," I say, refusing to fully agree.

"I heard that!" she shouts. "I'm better than alright, and you know it."

Beck makes a noise of frustration. "I'm glad she doesn't drive, 'cause she'd be the star driver of Vanstone instead of any of us."

Funny. I was wishing the opposite, because watching her drive like this is mind-blowingly hot.

Van clicks a few buttons on the computer, and sure enough, it improves things and completely derails my recommendations.

I can thank my father and the rest of Pierce Racing for that.

After she finishes, she jumps out of the sim and stares directly at me. I stay neutral, each muscle on my face steady and unreadable.

Nothing needs to be said.

She knows she won this one.

"Hey." Van stands up from the computer, his hands digging into his pockets. "I need a favor."

Tessa's shoulders drop. "Vivi?"

He rubs at his neck, something I do when I'm stressed too. "Yeah."

The angry lines on her forehead smooth, her expression softening. "I'll go get her. We're done here anyway."

Van's eyebrows dip. "You are? I was going to stay and work out some kinks in exchange for your help with Vivian."

Tessa shoots me a scornful look, and I know she's about to throw me under the bus, so I quickly beat her to the punch.

"Tess said she needed a break," I lie. "But I'm good to keep going."

Her jaw drops, hands flying to her waist.

Van doesn't notice. "Alright. Give me a few to grab the rest of the guys."

Her brothers exit the room, leaving me all alone with their sister. *Goody.*

"What are you playing at?" she snaps. "Don't you want to win?"

Is that even a question?

"Or are you just trying to sabotage Vanstone?" She huffs. "Why did my father bring you on to race for us? I don't understand! Is this some stupid test to see if I'm capable?"

It's a fucking test alright, but I'm not sure she's the one being tested.

Tessa stomps past me. "Figure your shit out," she grumbles. "We leave for the first prix in less than a week, and you're not ready."

I jut my hand in her direction, before she's too far away, and collide with her hip. She pauses, her chestnut eyes flinging to mine.

"The car isn't ready," I argue.

Her pretty pink lips flatten into a scowl. "You're wrong, Rome. The car is ready..." She shoves my hand away. "But we're not."

I force a hot swallow down my throat and watch her go.

She said *we're not ready*, and I'm not sure how I feel about us being grouped together like that.

The door slams, and instead of our spat putting me on edge with worrisome thoughts of our upcoming prix, I'm buzzing with energy. Arguing with Tessa is more exhilarating than it should be, and it's beginning to fill my head with all sorts of insane thoughts when, in reality, I should be thinking about how I'm going to beat my father's team instead of how I'm going to continue to drive my head engineer crazy.

Tessa's right.

I do need to figure my shit out.

* * *

I shift my Lamborghini into park with the sun still hidden behind the night sky and walk toward the office. The building is wider than it is in height, the sign that reads *Vanstone* mocking me the entire walk toward the door.

It's been weeks since I've joined my rival team, and where I should be getting more comfortable with them, it's only gotten worse.

Even after attending another Halston Sunday dinner, things are rocky.

But only at the office. At Vince and Rose's house, sharing another heart-healthy meal consisting of fish and a green leafy salad, the Halston siblings are on their best behavior. Noah and Graham discuss strategies with me, Van pipes in when his daughter allows him to, and Beck looks me in the eye when speaking instead of off into the distance like before.

Then there's Tessa.

She's all sunshine and rainbows. She helps her mom in the kitchen, teams up with Van's daughter on every subject, and makes sure the peace is kept while reminding her dad to take his medicine.

It's all very conflicting, and I leave their home envious each time, just like I used to do when we were younger and our families were still affiliated with one another.

The Halston family split from Pierce Racing and continued on with their happily ever after, whereas I remained with my father and stepmother, who only showed me love when I won a race.

I climb out of my car with a horn sounding behind me.

Another horn echoes in the near distance, and a spark of excitement pulls on my attention.

I peek over my shoulder to look for Tessa.

I knew she couldn't help but show up at the same time, just to further prove that she's as hardworking as I am.

Except, her parking spot is empty, with another that's taken.

My nostrils flare, and my fingers curl around the strap of my bag with tension.

He walks slow with purpose, clearly with the intent to intimidate me.

My heart beats right out of my chest, and as soon as he's within distance, I speak up. "What are you doing here?"

My dad's cheek lifts arrogantly with a smirk, and it's clear the apple doesn't fall far from the tree.

"Can't avoid me if I show up to your new place of employment." He cranes his neck to peer at the sleek Vanstone sign, nowhere near as flashy as the Pierce one on his building.

Modesty isn't his vibe. My father has too much money for his own good, and he never misses an opportunity to flash his wealth, even down to the sign on his building.

There's a hint of disgust lingering, and he gives me the same look I've seen each and every time I've disappointed him over the years. "Do you know how much shit you've stirred up?" he asks. "Do you know the rumors flying around because of your impulsive actions?"

I haul my bag up higher on my shoulder. "I don't know why I'm surprised that you flew all the way to Vegas just to berate me." I shake my head and sigh. "And I've read the rumors..."

There are speculations of something shady going on,

and I can only hope the FIA doesn't take them with a grain of salt.

"They're not really rumors, though, are they?" I ask.

He acts quickly. His fingers wrap around my shirt, and I'm suddenly pulled toward him with force. I flex my jaw and attempt to lean out of his space so he doesn't pull an old trick of his, like headbutting me.

"You won't last long here." His acrid coffee breath brushes against my face. "We'll beat you in Bahrain, and the next race after that, and the one after that too. Pierce Racing wins races, with or without you, Rome."

I look him square in the eye, shoving away any fear left inside my body that was purposefully put there when I was a young boy. "But is it really winning if you cheat your way to the finish line?"

The blue in his eye darkens. I prepare myself for the blow against my jaw, but nothing happens.

Instead, a hand lands on his chest.

Graham steps in between us, his glare steady on my father. "Leave, or I'll get the FIA involved."

My father, the arrogant bastard that he is, grins. He releases my shirt with a dark chuckle.

I take a step away, my anger following closely behind. I ache to hurt him, to make him bleed like he's done to me a thousand times over again.

"Never thought I'd see the day where a Halston protects a Pierce."

Graham shakes his head as he steps farther in between us. "I'm protecting Vanstone, Lucas. I know you're unfamiliar with such a thing as loyalty."

My ears ring from my father's coarse laughter as he walks toward his rental car.

"Loyalty?" He scoffs over his shoulder, shifting his gaze to me. "What a funny thing to bring up."

"Fuck you," I blurt.

Graham's shoulders tense, but he says nothing.

I turn away and stomp toward Vanstone's building with sweat trailing my spine. Ellis is there to open the door, but he doesn't look at me. He's too busy glaring through the glass at my father and his screeching tires as he peels out of the parking lot as quickly as I did out of his a month prior.

GRAHAM HAS CHANGED *the group name.*
Family Bond Fund 🏎️

ME

???

I park my car and huff at the sight of Rome's Lamborghini.

I may hate him, but I can't argue with his work ethic.

VAN

It's too early for this.

Six in the morning, to be exact.

NOAH

I agree. I haven't even had my coffee.

I notice that Beck hasn't chimed in, which isn't totally unusual, considering the sun hasn't risen, but with the change in group name, I grow suspicious.

> ME
>
> Is Beck in jail or something?

I have our media team on speed dial. We've already had a bajillion meetings regarding Rome and the recent speculations over why he's moved to Vanstone, so what's one more meeting about Beck being incarcerated?

That'll do wonders for my father's health.

> BECK
>
> I'm an angel. 😇

I snort and step out of my car with a Diet Coke in hand. I'm going to need about ten more of these to get through my day.

> GRAHAM
>
> I could've gone to jail today.
>
> VAN
>
> It's 6:04 a.m.
>
> GRAHAM
>
> I was a participant in a fight club at approximately 5:47 a.m.

I stop walking in the middle of the parking lot and glance at Graham's car and then to Rome's. My stomach somersaults.

Did they get into a fight?

> VAN
>
> You're on my nerves with the riddles.
>
> NOAH
>
> Same. I still haven't finished my coffee.

Beck changes the name of the group.
Mostly Nonviolent, Except Graham

GRAHAM

I didn't get into a fight, but I broke one up.

ME

Between who?

Rome and his other personalities?

My steps are slow toward Vanstone's doors. I'd rather be prepared when facing Rome this morning. What if he got into an altercation with Ellis? He does love to give Rome a hard time.

GRAHAM

You're not going to believe it...

I stare at my phone and wait for another text to come through.

Graham

Rome and his dad.

My heart slips. *What?*

VAN

Lucas? Where was this?

GRAHAM

At the office! In the parking lot. I was in my car and saw the entire thing go down. Once I saw Lucas grab Rome by the collar of his shirt, I intervened. He was about to clock him.

My fingers work overtime.

ME

Then what?

GRAHAM

Well…it ended with Rome saying fuck you to his dad, and then Lucas tore out of the parking lot faster than I could even wrap my head around what had even happened.

VAN

Why is Lucas even in town? We're all heading to Bahrain in two days.

I'm not sure I agree with the way my stomach twists with worry.

Surely I'm not worried about Rome.

I shake my head. Of course I'm not. I'm only worried about this messing with his head and distracting him.

BECK

I gotta say…it makes me hate Rome a little less, knowing he said fuck you to his dad.

I type, **Is Rome okay?,** only to delete it a moment later. I know my brothers well enough to know they'll take my words and twist them into something they're not–like implying that I actually care about Rome, which I do not.

I care about Vanstone and winning. Not Rome.

There's a difference.

I pick up the pace and walk toward Ellis.

"Busy morning?" I ask.

He frowns. "You could say that."

"So you saw?"

He nods. "I was about to step out there, but then I saw your brother take charge."

"Was it bad?" I ask.

Ellis's cheeks puff with a nod. "Seeing the way Rome's father treated him this morning makes me a little less skeptical of his reasons for switching teams."

Interesting.

I say nothing else and walk into the quiet, vast lobby. My phone continues to vibrate in my bag, but I'd rather speak face to face with Graham and get a good read on what's going on before finding myself alone with a testy Rome.

Music blares throughout the speakers when I walk onto the shop floor. The tall garage doors are open slightly to let some air in, with engine parts splayed over the floor next to each car. My brother has his back to me, his eyes set on the computer screen as he checks something.

"Graham!" I shout.

He doesn't move an inch. I try again, but still, he doesn't move.

I pull a pen out of my purse and chuck it at his head.

He turns around angrily, his brown hair falling onto his forehead. His jaw unflexes when he sees me, but that doesn't seem to deter him from bending low to grab the pen to throw it back at my face.

I move quickly, and the pen misses me by an inch.

He keeps the music on and points to a sign above my head. I turn and read it.

No girls allowed—only the word *girls* is crossed out with permanent marker, and instead, it says *sisters.*

I roll my eyes and wait for him to cut the music.

"How long have you had that sign up?" I ask.

Graham shrugs with a grin. "A while." He goes back to his monitor. "Do you need something?"

"Yeah," I stress. "Give me the tea! What happened?"

He glances over his shoulder. "What more is there to say? I already told you."

I throw my hands up with a scoff. "Did Rome say anything to you about why his dad was here?"

Graham shakes his head. "No."

"Did you ask?"

He squints. "Uh, no?"

I glance to the ceiling with frustration. "Did you ask him anything?"

Graham chuckles. "How could I? He stormed off into the gym and has been there since."

I glance at the large clock on the wall in the middle of the shop floor. "Still? That's way longer than usual."

Graham spins all the way around and eyes me closely. "Do you have him on a time limit or something?"

My spine stiffens. "What? No. I just...know his schedule."

Never mind the fact that he didn't exactly share it with me. It's just nice to know where the enemy is at all times.

"Well..." Graham walks off toward the cars to tinker with something. "He's still in there last I saw. Maybe you should go ask him all these follow-up questions."

"I guess I will—"

"But I'd do it at your own discretion," Graham interrupts me.

I pause. "What is that supposed to mean?"

He cuts the music back on and gives me a thumbs up. I scowl and leave the shop floor.

All drivers exercise to maintain high endurance and strength, mainly to handle the G-forces, so it's not unusual that he's training. Noah and Beck do the same, though later in the day. But Graham's warning rests quietly in the back of my mind until I spot him.

My steps falter. I wouldn't be surprised if the glass window didn't fog up from the rush of warmth to my skin.

The visual of a sweaty, bare-chested Rome will forever be embedded into my brain.

I hate that he's so damn attractive.

The dips of his toned stomach rise swiftly from his run on the treadmill, and not only can I see from the bulging of his muscles that he's been lifting weights, but the floor is scattered with dumbbells.

I step away from the glass, but my gaze doesn't lag. I follow him across the room as he hops off the machine and moves to the punching bag. He punches it several times before pushing off it to turn toward the window.

I stop breathing.

Our eyes lock, and he pauses.

Sweat trickles down the side of his flushed face, his dark hair sticking to his forehead.

Jesus.

My skin prickles with something I refuse to acknowledge.

He's worked his body to the brim of exhaustion, and just staring at him without a shirt on makes *me* exhausted. It's becoming harder and harder to deny that my body finds him attractive. My stomach flips each time he gets close to me, and a rush of heat slips down my spine whenever his hand lands on my hip.

I have to glance away.

It's too dangerous to look him in the eye right now.

I turn abruptly, which isn't obvious at all.

The door creaks open. "Now that you're done fanta-sizing about me, what do you want?"

And just like that, I want to smack him.

I turn and fling my hair over my shoulder. "You're supposed to be taking it easy. We have a race soon."

A bead of sweat drips off the end of his nose and onto the floor. "This is taking it easy."

I cross my arms. "You're usually done by now and posted somewhere in the lobby, waiting to tell me that I'm late or something. So, try again."

Rome blinks a few times, and I wait for him to spill about his father showing up, but instead, he pops his AirPod back into his ear and shuts the door in my face.

I gasp.

He did *not* just do that.

I stomp after him.

The gym is hot and stuffy, which doesn't help my already flushed cheeks.

I walk over to him, ignoring the rippling of his back muscles, and rip the AirPod out of his ear.

He turns and wraps his sweaty fingers around my wrist. The AirPod drops to the ground, and I try to jerk my arm back.

It doesn't budge, and Rome's fingers squeeze tighter.

"Why don't you just tell me why you're really here, Princess." His tone is low but smooth.

My pulse flies beneath my skin.

I swallow and raise my chin. "I came to check on you."

He squints, the blue hardly visible behind his dark lashes. "You came to ask questions."

He isn't wrong, but he isn't fully correct either.

Whether I want to admit it, there is a deep-rooted part of me that wants to make sure he's okay. Ellis's earlier statement presses on my mind, and I don't like it.

"That's not true," I argue. "Believe it or not, I care about my driver."

Something flashes over his face, but the moment passes quickly, and he's back to acting like the villain. His tongue jolts out of his mouth to wet his bottom lip. "Your pulse says otherwise."

I forcefully tug on my wrist again, and this time, he lets me go. I'm not expecting it, and I stumble backward. I lose my footing, but instead of colliding with the floor, I collide with something else.

Rome's bare chest.

His hand splays on my lower back, and he presses me to his firm body. I peer at him with wide eyes, and he gazes back at me with a knowing glint. "Careful, Tess. I might think you came here for something else if you keep looking at me like that."

One second, I'm staring at his mouth, and the next, I'm shoving him away. "Ugh! You are so irritating!"

His smile grows bigger, and I hate that it's such a nice sight.

I blow a breath out of my mouth in frustration. "You know what? I no longer care how you are. Hurry up and meet me in the sim. We have a full day of meetings starting at eleven, and then we're on the road to Bahrain."

He bends down to grab his AirPod off the floor. "Yes, ma'am," he mocks, sending me to the red.

I quickly scan his sweaty chest and huff. "And take a shower!"

"You take a shower," he counters, nodding to my shirt.

Tiny wet speckles dot the front of it from pressing against him. I groan and wrinkle my nose.

"You can join me if you want," he teases, voice sultry and hot.

Heat spreads over my cheeks at the mere thought. I turn around hastily, to avoid him seeing my unwarranted blush, and storm out of the gym. I let the door slam behind me and go directly to my car. I tear out of my Rome-infested shirt and throw on a wrinkly Vanstone sweatshirt instead, as if removing the thin scrap of cotton is going to hide the way my body burned when pressed against his.

Chapter Sixteen

ROME

EVERY DRIVER IS anxious before a race. Some stay that way even with the tires moving beneath them, while others grow calm from the familiarity of it. I'm typically the latter. Even with a nagging voice in my ear and competition surrounding me, a sense of home settles.

Probably the only home I've ever known.

The rest of the race weekend fucking sucks, though.

Especially now, since I'm in the spotlight—and not for the right reasons.

Never mind the fact that Tessa is the first female engineer in our sport. The media has completely blown past that milestone to focus on why *Rome Pierce switched teams, no longer driving under his father's command.*

"Remember what we rehearsed," Gia whispers, popping her head in between Tessa and me. "And act like you two get along. If other drivers suspect you two are at each other's throats, like you've been since arriving in Bahrain, they'll use that to their advantage and twist it to fit their narrative."

Tessa pats Gia's arm, the dainty gold rings on her

fingers catching the light. "Relax, Gia. We've got this." Her soft expression switches like a flick of a light when pointed at me. "As long as you let me do the talking."

I snort. "Not a chance."

Frankly, I'd rather skip out on this entire press conference and let Vanstone's Princess do what she does best—keep the peace. But then that would mean I'd have to give in to her control, and in case she didn't notice by now, I like to be in charge.

"I need a drink," Gia mumbles.

Someone with a headset calls over to us. "They're ready for you."

I nod and let Tessa go first.

She hesitates, and I'm positive it's because she's confused by my nice behavior.

The cameras are rolling, though, and you never know who's watching.

Once seated, I do a quick sweep of the room. A few rookie drivers linger in the back behind the camera and a cluster of journalists, along with Gia, who gives us an energetic thumbs up.

I exhale.

No sign of my father.

Yet.

"Rome," a man garners my attention. "How confident are you heading into this first weekend after the long break?"

I put on my best persona and lie straight through my teeth. "As confident as someone who's been racing since they were able to walk," I pause. "Maybe even before then."

There are a few chuckles here and there, and then comes the next question.

"How does it feel to race again after the season-ending crash last fall?"

My leg twitches beneath the table, a phantom pain burning the skin. "I've crashed plenty of times, so I feel the same. The only difference this time was that the world was there to witness it, but that's just part of the job. I think most racers can agree."

Tessa shifts in from beside me, her tan leg that I noticed right away when she showed up in a sporty-looking skirt brushes against mine, to distract me.

The journalist clears his throat, and I quickly snap back into the present, except I only catch the tail end of his question.

"—dynamic with your new team versus your father's?"

My heartrate spikes. "I'm sorry, can you repeat that?"

Tessa's leg brushes against mine again.

Fuck, stop it.

"How would you describe the dynamic with your new team versus your father's?"

Think fast, Rome.

I lean back in my chair to seem more comfortable than I am. "It's been different..." I glance at Tessa, who sits poised with her high ponytail, the hairstyle pulling my attention to her soft, slender neck. "Obviously."

The crowd laughs again, and Tessa smiles—only, I know it's fake.

I've seen her real smile, and it's much prettier than the one she's giving the media.

Prettier?

"Tessa? Would you like to comment?"

She leans over and grabs the microphone from me, our fingers brushing along the way.

"I grew up with four brothers," she says, deadpan. "I can handle Rome Pierce as my driver."

Her driver?

I grumble under my breath, something only Tessa hears.

This time, her knee knocks into mine on purpose. With an instinctive reflex, I grab a hold of her thigh with my free hand, the tablecloth hiding our battle from the rest of the room.

Laughter rings around us from her answer, but it's muted from the pounding in my ears. My skin sparks when my palm collides with her smooth leg. Something deadly simmers just beneath the surface, and it's so distracting I almost miss the new addition to the crowd.

My father stands alone with his arms crossed, a glare fixed in my direction. Arrogance seeps from his pores, the energy in the room awakens, and like a moth to a flame, everyone turns to catch a glimpse of him.

"We only have time for one more question," someone says, their voice barely reaching my ears.

"Is there anyone you're particularly eager to measure yourself against?"

Silence covers the room like a blanket.

The hand on Tessa's leg grows heavy, and I can't seem to pick it up.

I swallow and try to tie words together to make a decent sentence, one that can't be twisted to fit someone else's narrative of the weekend.

The microphone is still in Tessa's left hand. I see it out of the corner of my eye.

I turn to look at her, and for the first time since coming to Vanstone, she isn't glaring at me. Her eyes are soft around the edges, the brown color full of warmth. Then, her right hand falls to mine, still glued to her leg. She gives it a gentle squeeze, and it completely derails me.

We make eye contact for a second, maybe two, and that's all it takes to bring me back to the present. Instead of taking the microphone from her, I lean close, her perfume engulfing me.

"Myself," I say. "At the moment, I'm my own competition. It's the reason I left Pierce Racing and came to Vanstone. I'd like to hone my skills in a different light and see how I do away from all I've ever known."

"Like a challenge?" the reporter asks as a follow-up.

Tessa, sensing my ease, begins to pull her arm away, but I wrap my fingers around hers to keep her hand in mine—like some sort of security.

What the hell am I doing?

"Exactly." I nod. "I love a good challenge."

The words have never rung truer than they do in this exact moment.

Chapter Seventeen

TESSA

"HOW ARE YOU FEELING?"

I shift the phone to my other ear, something I've done three times since my dad called.

"I feel like I could throw up," I say honestly.

He chuckles, and my mouth lifts into a small smile.

My stomach has been in knots since arriving in Bahrain, and it has nothing to do with the deep-fried Khanfarooshes I have been indulging in.

Rome has been laser-focused since arriving on Monday yet still arguing with me every step of the way. It wasn't until the press conference that he began to loosen the reins a little. I assumed the track walk would mimic a WWE showdown between us, but to my surprise, our thoughts aligned, and we were able to make the changes to his car and get in a few practice sessions.

He's still quiet, though. Watchful. Definitely keeping his eyes on his dad and anyone else sporting Pierce's red and yellow colors. Then there's the whole thing at the press conference. What started out as us silently fighting beneath the table turned into something else entirely.

Or maybe I'm reading too much into it.

Either way, right now, we're all business.

Rome is out in the paddock, surrounded by media, with Gia close by to make sure he doesn't say anything that he'll regret. I stand back with the rest of the engineers, preparing everything for the race.

Rome did not qualify as well as we'd hoped.

Though my brother Noah didn't either, so there's that.

Dad's coffee mug clanks onto the counter through the phone.

"Aren't you supposed to sleep in when you're retired?" I ask. "It's, like, four in the morning there."

His familiar chuckles soothes me. "Can't teach an old dog new tricks."

Mom's voice is faint from somewhere nearby. "He hasn't slept a wink since you kids left for Bahrain!"

"He's been up for hours!" Vivian echoes.

What the heck is she doing awake?

My parents watch Vivian when Van is on the road, but that's becoming trickier as of late.

"Dad, we totally have it under control. We were basically born on a circuit."

Taking a step down is supposed to ease his worries for his health, and here he is, still wound up.

"I know, it's just—"

"It's just nothing," I cut him off. "Go play Barbies with Vivian. I have a race to win."

"Barbies? Since when has she ever played with dolls?"

I smile and continue to stare into the paddock. The crowd is thinning, and the majority of the racers are heading into their own pens to prepare. We have twenty minutes until the national anthem, and then it's go time.

"Hey, uh, before we get off here...is Rome near?"

No, but it sure feels like it.

He's standing next to Noah, and from the sharp edge of his jaw, they must be talking about something intense. His race suit hangs loose around his waist, unzipped, with the tight fireproof underlayer hugging his toned arms beneath—the same toned muscles that are engraved into my brain from walking in on his intense gym session the other day.

"He's in the paddock with Noah."

As if Rome knows I'm gawking at him, he snaps to me from across the crowd. I instinctively take a step backward, like he's standing in front of me instead of several yards away.

Gia walks over to him with her headset perched on top of her head. He leans down to hear whatever she has to say, her mouth inches from his ear.

An abrupt—and totally uncalled for—rush of something hot shoots down my spine.

I pause, barely able to register the words leaving Dad's mouth.

Did I just get jealous? I must be more cagey over this race than I thought.

"Just tell him I said to stay focused and remember why he came to our team."

"Yeah, okay," I say.

It isn't until we get off the phone that I fully register what he says.

Remember why he came to our team.

But that's just it.

Why did he come to our team? And why is my father so adamant that he help Rome succeed?

Or is it about helping me succeed?

After hanging up with my dad, I place my headset on

and purposefully keep my back to Rome so I can ease my thoughts.

It isn't just the racers that have to concentrate, but the entire team.

This isn't my first time calling the shots, so it should be easy-peasy. I've had to take over a time or two when things got hairy with Dad's health, except...this is the first time I'm doing this in my new position and with a driver who is at the very center of the media as of late.

All eyes are going to be on him.

"What's going on over there?"

I peek upward at Van, who has made his way over to me. He's staring into the paddock, his own headset still around his neck, and I hesitantly look in the same direction.

My eyes widen, and I quickly jump into action.

I click my headset, turning it to the right channel. "Gia, get Rome."

She hisses in my ear. "If it's not Beau, it's Vinny. I can't keep up."

Rome, standing entirely too close to Vinny, says something with a cocky grin. Vinny stiffens, and I hold my breath. Gia slips up beside Rome and grabs his arm to gently pull him away so it doesn't look obvious to any lingering cameras.

"Tell him I said to leave Vinny alone and get focused."

I feel Van's attention on my face, but I stare at Rome instead.

Gia covers her mouth with the clipboard, so no one can read her lips, and repeats what I've said.

His mouth twitches, and he says something back to her that I can't hear through the headset no matter how hard I try.

She sighs loudly.

"What did he say?"

Rome casually walks toward his pen, like the rest of the racers.

Noah is already tucked away in his, meditating or doing whatever he does to get centered.

"He said, 'Vinny would be happy to know that you, of all people, are standing up for him.'"

I grit my teeth and glare at the back of Rome's head on his way toward the pen. With the door opened, he peeks over his shoulder at me and winks.

As much as I want to flip him off, I don't, because I know there are too many eyes around, and they're definitely watching us.

Chapter Eighteen

ROME

INSTRUMENTAL MUSIC PLAYS through my AirPods. I close my eyes with the thought that the alarm on my phone is ticking too quickly.

The race is about to start, and my head is fucking spinning.

Why did I pick a fight with Vinny?

Is this what it's like to self-sabotage?

I have my father scowling at me, with my old team backing him every step of the way, and now I have two racers who want to eat me alive on the track.

Vinny *and* my stepbrother.

I mean, I love a good competition, but I'm all over the place, even if on the outside I appear as confident as I always do. The truth of the matter is, my life has been turned upside down, and I don't know how to handle it.

Some will say it was my choice to leave Pierce Racing, but was it?

I exhale and pinch the bridge of my nose. The piano in my ears is background noise to my winding thoughts. My pulse is sky-high, and I can only pray that when I'm seated in my car, the familiarity will calm me enough to focus.

I open my eyes, and a breath catches in my lungs.

Tessa stands inches in front of me with her long, brown hair flowing out from underneath her Vanstone hat. She peers at me like she has something to say.

I lazily skim her body, hesitating on the hem of her skirt. It hits mid-thigh, and I'm instantly reminded of the way her leg felt beneath my palm. Sweat prickles the back of my neck, a rough swallow moving down my throat.

Fuck me. I need to get laid.

Anger zips to my fingertips.

I pull my earbud out and fling a glare at her.

I'm not sure if I'm pissed because she's in here while I'm trying to get in the zone, or if it's because she was able to cut through my messy thoughts and center them all around her.

"Out." It's a single word, but my tone packs a punch.

Tessa crosses her arms. "You have two minutes to get out there and onto your spot for the national anthem or you get fined," she scoffs. "Which means *Vanstone* gets fined."

My eyebrows draw together in annoyance. "You're my engineer, not my handler."

I stand from the couch and shake myself into the rest of my race suit. I zip it up and brush past her, bumping into her shoulder for good measure.

Her sharp gasp cuts through the tiny room.

"I'm not your handler?" she questions from behind, her tone full of sarcasm. "If I didn't have Gia intervene when you were talking to Vinny, what would've happened?"

I head toward the other racers with Tessa hot on my heels.

"You seem awfully protective of him," I say.

"And you seem awfully jealous."

My steps falter.

Me? Jealous?

I don't get jealous, and especially not where it concerns her.

I'm too close to my opponents to say anything else, so I keep my mouth shut. I walk over and stand beside her brother, who doesn't even look in my direction.

He's clearly focused. Unlike me.

I don't note a single verse of the national anthem or notice the cameras zooming in on my face. My heartbeat drums inside my ears instead, even as I pull my helmet on and get seated in my car.

It isn't until her voice filters through, wrapping around my head like a relentless weed, that I can hear again.

"Radio check. Can you hear me?" she asks.

I clench my jaw. "Unfortunately."

She scoffs, and I chuckle inside my head.

I wiggle my fingers.

In and out.

In and out.

In and out.

I keep them outstretched when I realize my stretches are mimicking her breathing through my helmet.

"Stop breathing so hard."

She growls. "You are unbelievable."

My lip twitches. "I've heard that many times, especially in the bedroom."

Her loud, exasperated sigh derails my nerves. But only for a second.

"Take off the way we did in practice," she reminds me.

I remain silent.

5...4...3...2...1.

Breathe.

By turn one, I'm already down two positions.

I'm tense, my body tight, and I know Tessa is holding her tongue on my shit take-off, but I would almost rather her say something instead of the deafening silence.

"Car to the left and right. Hold your line."

"Which cars?" I ask.

"Doesn't matter. Focus."

My jaw locks.

Two cars touch, and carbon fiber scatters in the front line.

"Fuck," I curse.

Someone locks up, and I'm forced off the racing line. I avoid the spin and cut a curb, still managing to get back on track despite the minimal space.

I lose a spot, which pisses me off.

"Whoever the fuck that was just pushed me off. There was no space."

Tessa's voice, calm and steady fills my helmet. "Stay focused."

"It's a little hard when some drivers are purposefully pissing me off." I laser my vision in front.

I'm able to maintain my spot, but I'm on edge, especially when I see a blur of green from Vinny's car.

"Who was it?" I know she'll catch my drift.

Tessa's voice is the only one I hear. "Focus, Rome."

"Was it him?"

There's a pause, and then sure enough, I hear Tessa's sigh. "Copy."

Fucking asshole.

Of course Tessa would understand who I'm asking about.

"Your little boyfriend is about to lose his position."

"Call him my boyfriend again and you'll regret it," she stresses. "And pay attention! He's driving aggressively in the gray."

The corner is up next, and those are second nature to me. I do what I need to do, and yet, someone runs me wide, squeezing me toward the grass.

Vinny swerves late, and I'm hopeful a penalty appears.

"I swear to God," I grit.

"I see it, Rome."

Why does it calm me when she says my name like that? Like a breath floating effortlessly from her mouth, almost as if she's giving in to me.

Vinny does it again, and I curse for the third time since the race started.

"Dangerous," I mutter to myself.

Things are dangerous on *and* off the track at this point.

After pitting, Tessa comes back on the radio. "Be vigilant. He's behind you now."

Good. He's right where he belongs.

"Where are the others?"

"Not your concern," Tess says.

I grumble, but she's right.

I want nothing more than to race better than Beau, but he isn't going to race dirty or try anything with the recent drama involving our teams. It'd be too obvious—and too derailing.

"You're doing well," she says.

"Not well enough."

"You're welcome for the compliment."

"And you're welcome for making you look good on the job, Princess."

I'm positive she rolls her eyes.

"Lots of chatter on the radio," she adds. "He's angry,

and he's coming for you around those corners. Stay focused. Don't let me down now."

Never.

"Then keep talking," I order.

There's silence.

"Don't go silent," I demand. "I need you in my ear, Tess. I'm trusting you."

I can't believe I just admitted that.

Either way, my pretty little engineer understands the assignment.

She's in my ear for every corner, her tone smooth and calm, even when Vinny slips past.

I rush the detection line, and her voice comes next. "DRS, Rome."

The rear wing flap drops, and I fucking fly.

Tessa gasps excitedly, and like I'm a starving man, it feeds me.

I'm at my top speed and move ahead of him at the last second.

Vinny tries to catch up, but the DRS has already done the damage. He backs off, knowing that if he has contact with my car, he'll be at fault, and given the way he's raced today, the FIA won't let it slide.

"Yes! Good job, Rome!" Her excitement is...cute.

She grumbles next. "He's a fucking asshole."

I slow the car and hide my amusement behind my helmet.

"I hope our radio feed doesn't get aired on national television. What would your boyfriend do if he knew you called him such a name?"

She hums under her breath. "I don't know. What would your little girlfriends do if they heard you say that you liked me whispering in your ear?"

My eyebrows furrow. "I did not say that."

There is no way I admitted that, right?

"And what girlfriends? I don't date."

The radio cuts off, and I'm still left wondering if I admitted that I liked her voice in my ear.

I didn't, right?

Chapter Nineteen

TESSA

WE DIDN'T GET FIRST, second, or third, but I'm still going to celebrate because the race ended so much better than I thought it would. It started rocky with Rome unfocused and agitated, but the more the car moved beneath him, the smoother things became.

Vinny's reckless driving didn't deter Rome but, instead, encouraged him. It's nice to know that he can manage his temper when it really matters.

I swipe out of the overly encouraging texts from my dad, his attempt at making sure I know he's proud of me regardless, and move back to the sibling group text.

Beck changed the name of the group: **It's BahRaining Shots**

BECK

Uber is arriving in 5 minutes.

I quickly type while shoving my foot in a heel.

ME

I'm not ready!

My stomach knots.

I exit out of the group text and pull up a number I was forced to save in my phone. I click on Rome's name.

Just when I think we've turned over a new leaf, he goes off and does something like this?

I clench my jaw.

I'm sweating.

I grab a tissue and blot my face to keep my makeup in place.

After the race, there's usually some type of sponsored party exclusive to the drivers and their teams, including any plus-ones. It's frowned upon if you don't show, even if you perform poorly.

However, we're all about to skip it if my brothers know about Vinny's unwelcomed groping. It won't end well, and I'll be damned if the very first race without my father in charge, one of them gets arrested or, worse, *fined*.

> **ROME**
>
> I didn't say anything, but I love having something to hang over your head.

> **ME**
>
> 

> **ROME**
>
> Better watch it...I could always tell them if provoked.

> **ME**
>
> You watch it. Your career is in my hands every time you step onto the track.

> **ROME**
>
> And their careers are in mine. What would they do to him if they knew that he touched Vanstone's Princess?

He makes it sound like I wanted him to touch me, which was not the case.

I switch back to the family group chat and quickly get caught up on the messages I missed.

> **GRAHAM**
>
> Better not be trying to impress Vinny. He drove like a rat today.

> **NOAH**
>
> I don't know. My brotherly senses are tingling.

VAN

What did I miss?

BECK

Everything, Van. You miss everything.

NOAH

Vinny is always staring at her.

GRAHAM

Everyone stares at her.

I type aggressively while I pace my room in heels.

ME

I am not trying to impress Vinny!

Beck adds Rome to the group.
I stop breathing.
What the hell is he doing?

BECK

Welcome to the Halston sibling group chat, Rome. We still don't trust you, but I have a question.

I can't swipe out of the group text fast enough.
I click on Rome's name.
He beats me to the punch with a message.

ROME

For Christ's sake.
The group chat has messages coming in one after another.

NOAH

I have a question too.

BECK

Is there something going on with our sister and Vinny? I saw you two exchanging pleasantries before the race. Then Vinny looked over at my sister like you two were discussing her.

Beck is much more observant than I give him credit for.

My stomach is on the floor as I wait for him to respond.

To keep myself busy, I snap a picture of the dress Quinn forced me into buying, and the new shoes to match, and fire it off to her. I'm in desperate need to talk to someone who shares the same chromosomes as me for stability.

QUINN

DAMN YOU'RE HOT 🔥 🔥 🔥

I smile and swipe her message away.
Rome is typing, and I'm dying a slow death.
My phone vibrates, and I stop pacing.

ROME

Vinny was giving me shit for stealing a girl out from under him a while back. He's still bitter.

I make a face of disgust.
I go back to our message thread.

ME

Is that true?

ROME

Why? Jealous?

I roll my eyes and go back to the group message.

My lips flatten.
Really, Noah?

Rome types, and I have half a thought to storm over to his room so he can see me roll my eyes instead of sending the eye-roll emoji over text message.

I move over to our own text thread and type: ***The feeling is mutual!***

I really don't like the idea of Rome becoming friendly with my brothers.

He's already practically adopted into the family, and now my brothers are starting to kid around with him?

What happened to none of us trusting him? Sure, we

work together, but that doesn't mean we have to trust him off the track.

ME

I'm riding to the bar alone. You're all jerks.

Rome texts me separately.

ROME

You're not getting into an Uber by yourself in a foreign country.

I snatch my purse and head to the door.

ME

I don't know if you realized this or not, but I'm a grown woman who can make her own decisions.

I order an Uber for myself and head toward the elevator.

ROME

Trust me, Princess. I've noticed.

What does that mean?

I thrust my finger onto the button and wait while the numbers climb. Once the elevator arrives, I step inside with my heels clicking after me. I press L, but before the doors fully close, a hand jolts in between them.

No.

His spicy cologne fills the tight space, and I glare at his mischievous glint in his eye.

My lips part with annoyance. I cross my arms and growl quietly, looking elsewhere.

Out of the corner of my eye, I watch his head bob as he drags his attention down my body.

I'm in a simple, long-sleeve black dress with see-through mesh for the arms. It hugs my curves, but the length hits several inches beneath my butt.

It's classy but still hot.

At least that's what Quinn said.

Rome snorts.

I whip toward him with warm cheeks. "What?"

If I thought he was attractive in a race suit, then what on earth is this? He has the first three buttons of his dress shirt unbuttoned with the sleeves rolled up to show off his incredibly toned forearms, likely from manhandling his car. His black slacks are a perfect fit, likely professionally tailored for his long legs, and instead of his hair being messy from his helmet, it's styled with gel yet still looks effortless.

I catch him eyeing me up and down once more.

"You're definitely not riding in an Uber alone while wearing that."

I look at my dress. "What's wrong with what I'm wearing?"

He turns to face the door instead of speaking directly to me. "I'm half tempted to throw my jacket over your body to cover you up."

The elevator dings.

I step out into the lobby. "I'm wearing more clothes than half of the women you are found taking pictures with."

"Have you been looking me up online, Princess?"

I shoot him a look of disgust. "Absolutely not."

He gets closer to me, a grin etched into his chiseled face. "You're a terrible liar."

I flip my hair over my shoulder and ignore him. I glance past some members from other teams and ignore each and every one of them.

My brothers have probably already set off on their way without Rome and me, but I've got news for Rome. He's not riding with me.

I wave to the red car up ahead and step forward.

For good measure, I glance behind me with my hand outstretched toward the handle and grin, only for it to be swept away a second later.

"How does it feel to be on the losing end, brother?"

Beau Pierce stands with half his team, all who share the same arrogant smirk, in front of Rome.

His fist flexes beneath the suit jacket draped over his arm. "We're not brothers."

I put my finger up to the Uber driver and move toward Rome. I latch onto the end of his sentence. " —and even if you win, you still lose."

Beau steps forward, about to start something, but I quickly dart in front of Rome. He immediately grips my waist and pulls me backward, away from his stepbrother.

Beau's eyes flare with excitement, but it fades quickly when one of his crewmembers tugs him away.

Rome vibrates with anger behind me, his hand still locked onto my hip. He makes no move to stop glaring in the direction of Beau, so I grab his arm to pull him toward the Uber.

"Looks like you're getting your way," I huff. "Get in."

Chapter Twenty

ROME

TESSA TEXTS FROM BESIDE ME.

Her fingernails click against her phone screen, but I'm afraid if I look over at her, it'll push me clear off the edge.

What was she thinking stepping in between Beau and me like that? What if he had lunged at me and she was the casualty?

My father, Beau, and apparently Vinny, don't seem to understand that all actions have consequences. Beau would have plowed right through Tessa to get to me, and that's because he has never been held accountable for anything in his life. The thought probably didn't even cross his mind.

I lift my hip and pull my vibrating phone out of my pocket. It's a text from the Halston sibling group text that I was added to without my consent.

TESS

We will need all hands on deck at Lush.
Beau is already starting tiffs with Rome, and
the night hasn't even begun yet.

I slowly turn to stare at my little culprit. "I don't need help defending myself, Princess."

She tucks a piece of hair behind her ear but keeps looking at her phone. "Just like I don't need a bodyguard because of my choice of clothing."

First, she's wrong.

And two, this is completely different.

"I watched three bellhops stare at your ass while we walked from the elevator, one man stumbled over his own two feet because he couldn't look away, and..."—I point at the driver—"he can't stop looking at you in his rearview mirror."

He quickly averts his gaze when he makes eye contact with me from the backseat.

Tessa crosses her arms. "God, you're worse than my brothers!"

I shrug and rest my back along the seat. "You were the one who said my career was in your hands. Keeping you close and untouched means I'm keeping my career safe."

Close?

Untouched?

I'm out of my fucking mind.

We pull up to the bar, the Lush sign vibrant in the dark with a line of people wrapped around the corner.

Tessa's warm breath fills the backseat with her loud, exasperated sigh as she reaches for the door handle. I quickly lean across her, the scent of her flowery perfume tugging on my attention.

"Nuh-uh." I shake my head.

She pauses with parted lips.

I can't stop staring at them.

"Are you going to make me wear your jacket into Lush? Because if so, I'm not going."

Maybe I should.

"It'd make me look bad if I let you open your own door," I say.

She narrows her brown eyes, rimmed in some kind of shimmer.

"Fine."

I chuckle.

She acts like she had a say either way.

I slide out of my seat, open my door, and wait with my hand outstretched. On instinct, I glance at the space in between her legs. "Careful when you step out of the car." I curl my lip into a smirk. "Wouldn't want to flash everyone your panties."

She peers up at me to flutter her long eyelashes. "You think I'm wearing panties?" Then she giggles while bypassing my hand. "How silly of you."

The door of the car remains open as I stand there, frozen.

What?

I watch her walk confidently past the patrons with her chin held high. She finds Gia waiting by the bouncer, leaving me standing near the curb with all sorts of dirty thoughts swarming my head.

Before I shut the door, I bend down toward the driver. He's staring after her with a sick grin on his face.

"Forget you heard that," I snap, slamming the door shut.

I'm waved in by some of the other engineers on our team, the ones that work closely with Tessa, leaving her to deal with me.

Dylan holds out a long-neck beer. "To celebrate your first race with Vanstone."

I take it, and we all clank the bottles together before

slugging them backward. The malty foam relaxes me enough to chat with Dylan and the rest of the guys about the race, until I snag a glimpse of Tessa and Gia as they walk over to the bar.

Even though half of the establishment was reserved for us, the place is still packed. Tessa slips through the crowd, and I down the rest of my beer so I have an excuse to head that way too.

"I'm going to get another one," I say.

Beck and I catch eyes as I move past the dance floor. He's dancing with some dark-haired woman he hardly knows, with the rest of the Halston siblings off to the side, talking with Alejandro Suarez and his team. So far, no sign of Beau or Vinny, but I know they'll show up eventually.

My phone vibrates.

It's a new group text called, ***Earn Your Keep.***

BECK

You're up, Pierce.

I flick my eyes to him. He's grinning in my direction, still with one hand on the woman's hip, the other on his phone.

ME

What?

NOAH

Great idea. We're off duty.

What are they going on about, and why am I suddenly roped into it?

VAN

We're never off duty, and we're never not representing Vanstone.

Per usual, they ignore Van and his words of wisdom.

BECK

Tonight is your initiation, Rome. You're in charge of Tessa.

GRAHAM

Tessa is in charge of Tessa. If anything, maybe he should be in charge of you.

I move toward the bar and pick an open spot a few feet away from Tessa.

BECK

Tessa likes to take advantage of our distractibility on nights like tonight. She'll likely sneak off into the dark with some guy, and one of us will have to interrupt before it gets out of hand.

NOAH

Or some guy will follow her without her consent, and we'll have to set him straight.

Where were they the night that Vinny did that?

ME

And if I don't want to participate?

Oh, but you will, won't you?
I grit my teeth with the thought.

BECK

> Then I guess we still won't trust that you have Vanstone's best interest at heart and assume what Tessa assumes—that you're either here to 1. Ruin Vanstone's image or 2. Overtake the team completely before running back to your daddy.

They're so damn oblivious to the truth, and for the first time since joining Vanstone, I want to tell them everything.

As if I trust them.

ME

> Challenge accepted.

I glance over my shoulder at Beck, and he nods while grinning like a fool.

"A Jack and Coke, please."

Her voice naturally snags my attention through the bass of some song.

As soon as there's an opening beside her, I take it. Our arms brush, and I'm already buzzing.

A second passes and then another.

My lip hitches when she pretends to ignore me.

"A Corona," I say to the other bartender.

Tessa laughs under her breath and mutters, "Weak."

"Excuse me?"

She tracks the bartender with watchful eyes. "Nothing, it's just...a weak drink."

Or a safe one.

After all, I'm sort of on duty.

I say nothing but continue to stare at her. The shimmer on her cheeks draws attention to her face. Even from the side, she's alluring.

"Do you need something?" she finally asks.

"Just keepin' an eye on my engineer."

This time, she turns to face me. Her eyebrows draw together, an angry line in between them. "Did my brothers put you up to this?"

I squint. "I have no idea what you're talking about."

The bartender places a cup on the bar in front of her. "Jack and Coke."

Tessa switches like the flick of a light. She turns to him, smiles sweetly, and thanks him.

He eyes her for longer than he needs to, and a hot streak of something unrecognizable slashes at my back.

To steal back her attention, I reach forward and grab her drink.

With wide eyes, she gasps. "That's mine!"

"And now it's mine." I wink. "Enjoy your Corona."

I force myself back toward Dylan and the team, some of them near the bar and some of them joining Beck on the floor with strangers.

I rest against one of the reserved high-top tables and sip on Tessa's drink with my focus impenetrable, doing what I do best: observing.

I have Tessa in the forefront of my brain, with her brothers whispering in my ear, and in the back of my head, there's Vinny and Beau, who just so happened to walk in the door.

Chapter Twenty-One

TESSA

UNBELIEVABLE.

Instead of four sets of eyes on me, now there are five. How is that fair, and why does Rome even care what I do when we're not at work or on the track?

Ugh.

"I thought today went well," Gia notes from beside me.

She's sipping on Rome's Corona because I learned that the saying *'Beer before liquor, never been sicker. Liquor before beer, in the clear'* is the cold, hard truth.

"It went better than I thought it would," I admit. "I didn't think we'd get first. Not yet, even if Rome is extremely skilled–" I pause. "Do not tell him I said that."

Gia smiles with the beer bottle up to her lips. "I don't think Rome needs any ego-boosting. Your secret is safe with me."

True.

I grab my *new* Jack and Coke and take a sip. "Once we work the kinks out, I think he'll be right up there with Noah."

"Once you two trust each other, you mean."

I eye Gia from the side. "Same thing."

She laughs. "I'm going to take some content. Are you good over here?"

"I'll keep an eye on her," the bartender says from behind, his accent thick but his English well pronounced.

Gia glances from him to me, and I wink at her, giving her the okay to leave me.

I'm a big girl, even if my brothers think otherwise. What more do I have to do to prove to them that I can handle myself? I'm paired with Rome Pierce, for goodness' sake, and we somehow still finished in the top five today.

I'm fully capable of surviving the real world.

"Aren't you supposed to be working?" I ask, turning around to face the bartender.

He's a handsome guy—tall, with a black t-shirt that hugs his toned biceps. He shakes a drink with a sexy grin. "I am, but as long as you stay right there, I can make sure no one hits on you."

I eye him closely. "And what if I think you're hitting on me?"

He stops mid-pour and glances at the faint grin on my lips. "What if I am?"

I think about it for a second, and knowing my brothers and Rome are behind me, likely plotting some grand scheme to interrupt any type of fun I want to have, I fix my small smile into a larger one. "Then I guess I'll stay."

His smile grows, and it's a nice one. He has bright, white teeth that stand out against his tanned skin with scruff lining his jaw. "Then drinks are on me."

Butterflies flutter as I tip my drink back and swallow the rest of it.

I know my limit, and I won't go beyond it, so when he

puts another drink in front of me, I drink it slowly while chatting in between his drink orders.

Rome saunters up beside me at one point, ordering another Corona.

I keep my fingers wrapped around my drink and pretend he doesn't exist. Even when his gruff chuckle hits my ears, I stay angled away from him.

It isn't until I hear a girly voice ask him to dance that I give in. Her hand falls to his chest, and I can't help but turn my nose up at her. I don't know why the reaction comes, but he doesn't notice because his eyes are too locked in on her cleavage spilling out from her low-cut dress.

I focus on my burly bartender.

He's much more interesting.

Right?

A Corona slides next to my Jack and Coke. "Can you watch this for me?"

I turn and gape at Rome with irritation.

"I'm going to dance, and since you've sat here most of the night, I don't see you getting up anytime soon."

A devilish smirk curves onto his face, and I scowl.

He lets the woman pull him to the dance floor, and my face heats. I jerk back around and focus on the bartender.

"Hey, Sully? You good to take your break?" another bar tender asks.

Sully turns to me with a knowing grin.

"Yeah," he calls back to him.

One second passes, then another, before he's edging his chin to an area that leads to the back.

I nod subtly, but before I go, I down the rest of my Jack and Coke, all while leaving Rome's Corona alone on the bartop.

I weave through the crowd, ping-ponging my eyes at

each of my brothers. They're all busy talking, mingling, and dancing. Rome's back is to me with the woman's hands wrapped around his neck. Each team is split into different sections throughout the bar area, and I've kept a close watch on Beau, who hasn't done so much as look in Rome's direction. Vinny is too swept up in the women with barely any clothing on to cause a scene, so I take the bait and push through the swinging doors into the abyss.

It's dark and stuffy, but his manly cologne gets stronger the farther I step.

"Sully?" I whisper.

His hands find my waist, and desire sweeps me off my feet. I clasp my fingers around his neck, and he pulls me in close.

"Is this okay?" he asks, gruff and low.

"Mm-hmm."

His mouth hovers over mine. "Can I kiss you?"

Instead of answering him, I press my lips to his. Our tongues move against each other in a slow, intimate way, a little whimper leaving me from the pressing need I've pushed away for months now.

It isn't easy to act on.

Not with how much time I've been putting in at work and with my brothers always near.

Rome's face pops up in my head, and I bite down on Sully's lip.

A sexy growl rumbles from his chest, and he guides me against the wall. "I've never seen such a sweet face before, but damn you kiss like you know what you're doing."

I go in for another before breaking away. "That's because I do."

His hand travels up my leg, his calluses scraping against

my smooth skin. I hook it around his waist, and he squeezes my thigh.

Rome pops into my head again—the brief memory of his hand splayed on my thigh during the press conference days ago.

"When is your break over?" I ask, hoping to continue this so I can rid Rome from my brain. He takes up all the space lately, and I'm desperate for a break.

"Now."

My heart stalls, and if it weren't for Sully's mouth pausing over my neck, I would've thought Rome's voice was in my head.

Except, it's not, and he's standing less than a foot away from me.

Chapter Twenty-Two

ROME

MY SLOPPY DANCE partner doesn't smell right.

It's not floral or sweet. It's too strong and musky, like a spice you'd throw in some fancy entrée.

It's not like Tessa's perfume at all.

Fuck, get out of my head.

I turn Nadia around so I can check in on Tessa at the bar. She's been there most of the evening, flirting with the bartender. Occasionally, someone from our team would go talk to her while waiting for a drink, and Gia was with her for a little while, but now she's all alone, and he can't stop smirking at her.

It's been irksome, to say the least.

Almost as irksome as Beau and Vinny being in the same vicinity as me, but they've been quiet, which has only given me more space to focus on my task.

If the Halston siblings are testing me, then so be it. I already lost once today, and I'm not about to do it again.

I panic when I see Tessa's spot at the bar is empty.

She's missing, and so is the bartender.

The only thing left is my untouched Corona.

Damnit.

Her brothers must not know, because I haven't gotten any texts. They wouldn't let an opportunity like this slip to give me shit.

"I gotta go." I unwind Nadia's hands from around my neck and push through the crowd.

I head to the bathrooms first.

The line is long for both the men and women, and Vinny stands amongst the group with a bored expression on his face.

There's no way he watched Tessa and some guy disappear together. The jealousy would eat him up. Sort of like it's doing to me right now.

My pulse pounds.

Gia comes into sight, and I pull her aside. "Where is Tessa?"

Her eyes grow wide, but I don't miss the shiftiness of them. She locks onto two swinging doors, and I move her to the side.

She calls after me. "Leave her be, Rome. She never gets to have any fun."

I ignore her and stride toward the doors casually. I wouldn't want to alarm anyone by full-on sprinting.

And by anyone, I mean her brothers.

I picture her on the back of some stupid motorbike with the guy's helmet on, headed to his place. The feeling eats me up inside so quickly I push on the doors with force and move inside with my heart pounding violently.

It's dark.

I can't see shit.

But I can hear just fine, and her hot little whimper sends me to Hell and back.

"When is your break over?" she whispers.

"Now," I grit.

She gasps.

The kissing noises stop abruptly.

Against my better judgment, I pull my phone out and shine the light in their direction. Piping-hot anger races through my bloodstream, but I'm rational enough to know that it's completely uncalled for.

Why am I acting like this?

I want to rip his head off his shoulders.

I want to pull her away and bark that she's mine.

"What are you doing back here?" she hisses, face flushed and lips swollen.

God. Fuck. Don't even look at her mouth!

"Doing my job," I answer.

"Your job?" the man asks.

Someone knocks on the swinging door. "Sul, break is over. Wrap it up."

"So is this a common thing for you?" I ask. "Taking some innocent woman back here and fucking her on your break?"

"Innocent?" he chuckles. "There is nothing innocent about the way she was kissing me, mate."

My fist clenches.

I'm going to lose my mind.

Actually, I've already fucking lost it.

"Well, it was fun while it lasted." He grabs her chin sweetly and rubs his thumb over her lip. "You should probably go first, and take your bodyguard with you."

Tessa huffs. "Bodyguard! He's the one who's going to need a bodyguard after I'm through with him."

I chuckle darkly, mainly to hide my aggression. "Lead the way," I say to her.

"I hate you," she seethes on her way past, that floral perfume pulling me like a dog on a chain.

"I hate you too," I sneer.

Or do I just hate the fact that I *don't* hate her?

I follow closely behind as she weaves through the crowd. Vinny is up ahead on the left, and he eyes her before snapping over to me. One look in my direction and he's turning away with a scowl.

He's learned his place. *Good.*

We step outside, and Tessa immediately wraps her arms around herself from the cool temperature.

I pull my phone out to request an Uber.

"What are you doing? Reporting to my brothers that your job is finished here?" She scoffs and puts her back to me, wrapping her arms tighter around her body.

I shrug out of my jacket. "I called us an Uber, brat."

I step behind her and place my jacket over her shoulders. She freezes, her spine going ramrod straight, and then she flings it off. The thick black material lands on the pavement in between us.

I keep my chuckle on the inside, but I can't help but be amused.

"I'm not riding in an Uber with you," she snarls.

I press my lips together in an attempt not to laugh at her jerky movements as she snatches her phone out of her purse, angrily tapping on the screen to call for her own Uber.

Once she's finished, she shoves her phone back into her purse and tugs on the hem of her dress. It's ridden up higher from her little escapade, and just like that, I'm back in the red from the thought.

Her Uber pulls up first, and although I want to climb inside with her for more reasons than one, I don't. I need to put some fucking space between us before I do something stupid.

I'm all over the place.

I follow closely behind her and open the door. She whips her brown hair over her shoulder and shoots me a dirty look before sitting down and pulling the door shut.

My Uber comes right after hers, and I quickly get in so I can keep an eye on Tessa's car up ahead toward the hotel.

I shoot off a text to her brothers.

ME

Package secured. Tessa has arrived at the hotel.

BECK

Alone or did some lovesick fella follow her there?

Besides me?

ME

Alone.

Beck changes the group name: ***Welcome to the Family***

I shake my head and put my phone back into my pocket. My Uber pulls up right as Tessa's is driving off. I quickly scramble out of the car and jog toward the revolving hotel doors in search of her.

If I follow the line of steam from her anger, I'll probably find her a lot quicker.

I'm playing with fire.

I know I am, yet I can't stop.

The elevator pings, and she steps inside.

I do my best not to run.

If the doors shut before I make it over there, then I'll

take it as a sign, but when I shove my hand in between the doors, they open right back up.

Unfortunately, we're not alone.

There are a few hotel guests crammed inside the tiny area with Tessa absolutely fuming in the back corner. I make my way toward her and place my hand in the pocket of my pants with my jacket resting over my other arm—the same jacket she threw to the ground.

The air between us crackles, and I think everyone in the elevator can feel it. They share looks with each other, and when the door opens on their floor, they rush out, leaving Tessa and me all alone.

The door closes, and my heart skips a beat.

I angle my head toward her slowly, and she's glaring at me with a fire brewing in her brown eyes.

"Are you going to follow me to my room and put me to bed too?" she asks, annoyed.

I lift a brow. "That's an enticing thought. Maybe I should."

Her cheeks turn red, and I chuckle.

Then, out of nowhere, her finger presses onto the emergency stop button.

"What are you doing?" I ask.

She pushes off from the wall and stands way too close to me. "Did you go to my father and ask to join our team, or was it the other way around?"

I pause and repeat the question in my head before ultimately giving in, since it's not necessarily a secret. "I asked."

Her gaze narrows. "Why?"

I give her the same answer I've been told to give the media. "I wanted to see how I'd do on my own, away from my father."

She shakes her head. "That's either a blatant lie, or it's only half the truth. There's more to it. I saw the way you acted when your father showed up at the press conference."

I swallow. "So?"

"So, tell me," she orders. "I think I deserve to know why you're really here, since I'm your head engineer!"

I can't argue that.

But I still can't tell her.

"I can't tell you."

She fixes me with a confused look. "You can't, or you won't?"

"Can't."

She looks away, and for some reason, I want her eyes back on mine, so I give her a little more to chew on.

"It's in the contract."

Her posture stiffens. "What?"

I take a step away from her and rest against the elevator bar. The tension between us does nothing but amp me up. "The one your father had me sign."

Tessa looks me up and down, clearly not believing me. "And what else does it say in that contract? Does it say you have to keep Vanstone's Princess from getting laid?"

My mouth twitches. "It says I can't lay a finger on your brothers."

"And what does it say about me?" Tessa pops a hip, waiting for my answer.

On instinct, I rake my eyes down her body. *I wish it said something about her.*

I push off from the wall and erase the empty space between us. Tessa stands her ground, angling her chin to peer up at me. "It says nothing about you, so I guess that means I can touch you if I want."

She's calling my bluff, but she really shouldn't.

My body is acting in a way it shouldn't from having her in this tight space with no real exit. The tips of my fingers ache to grab a hold of her, and I can't stop teetering the line that is very obviously drawn between us.

Her mouth opens, and I stare at her moving lips. "Then maybe you should finish what you interrupted."

I think she's messing with me, so I throw it back in her face. "Careful what you wish for, Princess."

A look of uncertainty flashes across her face. "You wouldn't."

It's almost like she doesn't know me.

"It sounds like you're challenging me." I move quick. I snake my arm around her waist and pull her in close.

I can't help but notice the way her breasts press against my chest with her sharp inhale. I also can't help but notice that she isn't necessarily pushing me away.

She does look at the emergency button, though, like it's going to save her.

"Go on," I urge. "Hit it. It won't change things."

We're head to head.

The air in the elevator crackles with hot tension, and if she doesn't push me away in the next three seconds, I'm going in for the kill.

Fuck, I should stop.

We're letting things spin out of control.

The rigid pull between us is tighter than ever, like a rubber band about to snap at any second.

Tessa pushes the button quickly.

There's a dare in her eye.

She thinks I won't do this, but I'm not backing down where she's involved.

I grab her face and smash my lips to hers. She's startled

at first, her body snapping into a rigid posture, but then she gives in.

What started off as a bitter kiss turns into a thrilling ride. I deepen the kiss, my fingers getting lost in her brown waves. Her tongue moves over mine languidly, each stroke going straight to my dick.

Damn, she does know how to kiss.

I swallow each and every sexy noise coming from the back of her throat and push her against the wall so I can feel more of her body against mine. I grip the back of her knee and wrap her leg around my waist, pressing myself in between her legs.

She's warm and needy, rubbing against me like I'm no longer the villain who broke up her earlier romp at the bar.

Jesus Christ—

The elevator dings, and we both freeze.

Our eyes snag, and as if just now remembering who I am, she shoves me away and pulls her dress down.

The door slides open, and I recognize the man right away.

He's on Vinny's pit crew.

His focus slides from me and my rising chest to Tessa and her flushed skin.

A fleeting smile crosses her face, and then she darts out of the elevator, even though it's the wrong floor.

It takes everything in me not to follow after her, but I don't.

I can't.

What the hell was I thinking?

Chapter Twenty-Three

TESSA

NOTHING TO SEE HERE.

Shame?

Who is she?

Guilt?

None of that.

Humiliation?

Absolutely not.

Every time I look in the mirror and think about Rome, my cheeks ripen with heat, but that has nothing to do with what happened in Bahrain.

In fact, Bahrain did not exist.

I've deleted the entire trip from my brain.

I'm half-tempted to miss out on Sunday dinner and blame it on jet lag, but then that would mean I was affected by Rome's kiss, and I would rather die than give him that satisfaction. My plan is to treat him the same way he's treating me: like nothing happened at all.

The next morning, we didn't utter a single word to one another. Which isn't unusual. No one paid any mind to our silence.

On the plane, I slipped my eye mask over my eyes and put my headphones over my ears. Sleep came quick, mainly because I paced the entire night prior, fretting about what happened in the elevator.

I've never acted so impulsively before.

I'm the least impulsive out of my siblings—even Van, who knocked up a random woman, resulting in Vivian.

I'm responsible and driven by success. Not a mouthy, F1 driver whose kissing made my toes curl and stomach bottom out. He pushed me right up to the line, and I crossed it with him.

I gulp the rest of my Diet Coke and climb out of my car.

Besides Van, it looks like I'm the first one here. My plan is to escape with Vivian somewhere in the house to avoid Rome. Maybe play hide-and-seek and get lost.

I walk inside and scrunch my nose at the scent of Brussels sprouts. I'm happy my parents are continuing their healthy eating for my dad's health, but pizza and beer, like we used to do after a weekend race, sounds so much better.

"Tess! Quick! Help me!" Vivian, with her long hair in messy braids, slides on her socks to meet me in the foyer.

"Help you what?" I ask sneakily. "Is Grandpa playing hide-and-seek with you already?"

She shakes her head and tugs me alone. "No! Rome!"

I stop mid-pull. Excuse me?

"Rome?"

She tugs me harder. "Yes! Now, come on. Daddy said he went into the backyard, but I've already looked everywhere! Dinner is almost ready, so we have to hurry!"

There is no getting out of this. Vivian is as headstrong as they come—something Van is struggling with.

"Hmm," I hum under my breath and stand on the back patio, looking for a good spot that Rome would hide in.

Who would've thought I'd show up to my parents' for dinner, and he'd be playing hide-and-seek with Vivian? Maybe he had the same thought as I did and is trying to avoid me as long as possible too.

Actually, scratch that. Knowing Rome, he'll hold this over my head and blackmail me with it, because he would've had to be blind not to feel how into his kiss I was.

"Did you look in the tree?" I ask.

Vivian peers at me. "The tree?"

"He's athletic. He probably climbed it."

She runs down the steps excitedly and onto the thick, luscious grass. With her hands on her hips, she gazes up the side of the large mesquite tree, and a huge smile overtakes her face.

"I found you!" she shouts.

A moment later, he hops down on agile feet and bends in front of her. With a backward Vanstone hat on his head, I get a good glimpse of his proud smile. "You're a good seeker, V."

She giggles. "I know."

Rome tugs on her braid and stands up, both of them about to head toward me.

I quickly turn to avoid them.

I've never seen him so playful before, and I don't like that it softens him.

I wait until Vivian gets close to step in line beside her, leaving Rome in the dust.

Whatever happened to *girls rule and boys drool?*

Is Rome's plan to get everyone in my family to like him before sweeping the rug out from under all of us?

I'm tempted to shut the door in his face when Vivian and I step inside, but his presence behind me is like a weight.

"Cheater," he whispers, the word landing on my neck. "I know you told her where I was."

He sweeps past me, and I'm left standing there with goosebumps blanketing my arms from his warm breath against my skin.

Instead of annoyance coming to mind as I stare after him, it's something else entirely, and I do not like the way my body is reacting at the moment.

* * *

I yawn dramatically.

"Whew," I sigh tiredly. "I'm beat. The jet lag is really getting to me."

I purposefully ignore my brothers because they'll see right through my bullshit.

"I think I'm going to head home," I add.

My mom's face softens. "Do you want to stay here? I don't want you to drive if you're tired."

"It's just down the street," I remind her. "I'll be fine."

I yawn again for good measure, and Noah snorts. Once Mom gets up from the table to make me a to-go plate that'll probably stay in the fridge for weeks until it gets moldy, I kick him under the table and bare my teeth at him.

Sitting at the table, across from Rome, is going to put me in a mental hospital.

If I let my guard down, even in the slightest, I find myself looking in his direction.

It's like he senses it somehow because, each time, his eyes flick to mine, and my stomach flops.

There's a pull between us that's been there from the start, but now there's an ache that follows it.

A pining.

Or hunger.

Something that makes my body warm.

As soon as I get home, I can breathe again.

I flop onto my couch and pull out my phone to see numerous text messages lining the screen from the new-and-improved group text with Rome included.

BECK

That was the fakest yawn I've ever heard in my life.

VAN

I have to agree.

NOAH

I never would've gotten away with that.

GRAHAM

There's no way she's tired. She slept the entire plane ride.

ROME

She's trying to avoid me. I've made her angry.

I sit up abruptly, my hair flying out of my face.

He won't tell them, right? How could he? It would make him look just as bad as it makes me look. Unless that's his righteous plan—to turn us all against each other and disrupt any order we have on the team.

BECK

What gave you that idea? 😏

NOAH

Was it her red cheeks of anger that gave it away every time she looked at you?

It wasn't anger, but we'll go with that.

GRAHAM

Better you than us.

NOAH

Or maybe it was the way every compliment
our Dad gave you about your driving was
met with her pointing out something you
screwed up. 😣

I mean, if the shoe fits.

ROME

It's your fault my head engineer is angry
with me.

BECK

Who, us?

NOAH

No one forced you to treat her like a child at
the after-party. That was all you, bud.

GRAHAM

Yeah, no one said you had to make her
leave after catching her in the act.

So they're all in on this?
My blood pressure is rising with each chime of my phone.
I type a scathing message.

ME

For the record, I AM tired. I'm tired from
dealing with you five all week. And you can
all have your laughs now, but next week in
Spain, I'll find a way to have my fun without
any of you intervening. Even if that means I
have to sneak off with some guy to the
beach to have sex!

I purposefully added the sex part in there because I know my brothers will shiver from the thought.

> **BECK**
>
> I just threw up.
>
> **NOAH**
>
> Same.
>
> **GRAHAM**
>
> The word sex and sister should never share space in my brain.
>
> **VAN**
>
> I'm just wondering what I did to get grouped into this fight between all of you.
>
> And please don't have sex on the beach. You never know who's watching. You could end up on the front page of GRID.

He's right.

GRID is the TMZ of the F1 world.

Gossip. Rumors. Inside drama.

It's the last place any F1 driver, or their team, wants to be on.

> **BECK**
>
> I've been featured on GRID before. It's not that bad.
>
> **NOAH**
>
> Rome is always on there, aren't you? 😏
>
> **ROME**

Curiosity creeps into my head like a twisted vine until it wraps around my fingers, forcing me to type GRID into my phone's browser.

Right there, at the top of the website, is a photo of Rome from this past weekend in his race suit, all hot and sweaty, and then beneath it, is a photo of *me,* in the paddock with my headset resting around my neck.

I read the headline so quickly I'm dizzy. I sink back to the couch and open up a separate text to Rome and send him my address.

ROME

Is this a booty text? Or are you planning on murdering me?

ME

It's an emergency! Please hurry.

ROME

On my way.

I toss my phone off to the side and pace my living room.
This is bad.
This is *really* bad.

Chapter Twenty-Four

ROME

THERE'S a dead cactus on the porch in a blue pot, and it very well could be a sign for me to turn back.

My foot hovers over the faded welcome mat as I rethink my choices, but before I have a chance to back out, the door opens. Tessa aggressively grips my hoodie with her fingers and pulls me into her house.

"Someone is eager," I mumble.

She slams the door and turns to face me. She's adorably frazzled, with her hair in some crazy bun on the top of her head, fallen tendrils of brown framing her face. The high points of her cheeks ripen with heat, but instead of saying anything, she tugs on my arm until we're in her living room.

Her palms are on my chest, and I'm forced backward. I land on her couch with my legs spread wide and peer at her from below as she stands with her hands on her hips. If I were to reach forward even in the slightest, I could pull her onto my lap. My fingers twitch at the thought.

"You sure this isn't a booty call—"

I lean backward with her phone outstretched into my

face, ending the words on the tip of my tongue. I scan the screen quickly.

Ah.

I see.

An inside source reveals that Rome Pierce joined Vanstone Racing for a reason no one saw coming– Vanstone's Princess, Tessa Halston. The two were caught cuddling up during their weekend race in Bahrain.

"Well?" she huffs.

Tessa's brown eyes are wide with worry, and she's looking at me expectedly, like I can do something about it.

For her, I might.

I clench my jaw. Scratch that. No, I will not.

"Well, what?" I shrug. "It's just a rumor site."

Tessa clicks her phone off and throws it to the cushion beside me. "But it's not a rumor!" she screeches, clearly panicked.

"Technically, it is." I trail her as she paces over the large, colorful woven rug. "We weren't cuddling."

"You're right!" she shouts. "What we did was *far* worse!"

"Wait."

Tessa stops her nervous pacing and looks at me with hope in her eyes.

"We did something in Bahrain?"

If I were in reach, I think she'd slap me.

My lip twitches at the utter shock on her face, and it sends her in a spiral.

"This isn't good," she mutters, continuously pacing the living room. "People are going to think the only reason I became head engineer for the almighty Rome Pierce is because he's fucking me!"

Can she not put that thought in my head?

I've already had a hard time pretending this weekend didn't happen, when the truth is, I can't stop thinking about it.

Kissing her put a pause on reality. The world faded; my thoughts seized. I think maybe my heart might have stopped beating for a moment too, and if I let myself have that again, I'll probably become addicted.

I can't do this with her.

She's my head engineer, the team owner's daughter, and my former rival.

Things could get messy...*fast.*

I exhale and clear my head. Tess's pacing is unrelenting, and at some point, she shed her sweater and now stands in tight leggings and a tank top that hugs her in all the right places.

"Dad won't see it," she mumbles. "He's never on those sites. But what about everyone else?" She pauses with a deer-in-the-headlights look on her face. "What if one of his old friends calls and tells him?"

She needs to take a breather.

I watch her for a few more seconds and can't take it any longer. I stand from the couch, and stride to her. She's so in her head that she doesn't even notice, or maybe she doesn't feel my presence as much as I feel hers. My hands snap outward, and I grab onto her hips. The rushed gasp from her lungs pulls my attention right to her mouth.

"Take a breath, Tess."

Her long lashes flutter, but her breaths remain short and sharp.

I back her up to the wall and slowly grab a hold of her wrists, guiding her hands to my chest. "Breathe with me."

I inhale, ignoring the hints of her perfume, and then exhale slowly.

Eventually, she does the same. Our breaths begin to match, our chests rising at the same time. Those perfect, round breasts of hers call my name with each inhale.

"There." I make myself stare into her eyes instead of elsewhere. "For a second, I thought I was going to have to give you mouth to mouth."

Tessa glares, but I know her glares well enough now that I can recognize the crumb of humor behind the annoyance.

"What a shame that would be, huh?" I ask.

I smirk, and she slaps my hands away from her waist.

"I can't stand you," she snips.

"Funny, you seemed to stand me just fine the other night." I wink because I just can't help but get a rise out of her.

I crave it.

"Rome!" She crosses her arms in a huff. "Stop it. This is serious."

I sigh and force myself back to the couch. "It isn't that serious. Everyone around us knows we bicker like an old married couple. No one will believe the rumor."

"But there are people that will." Tessa's tone drops, and I'm not sure I like the way my chest squeezes from the hint of melancholy within it.

"No one saw us. Right?" she asks.

"Can you sit? You're making me nervous."

And I can't stop staring at you.

Surprisingly, Tessa abides by my demand, which really doesn't help my thoughts. She chooses to sit right beside me, the cushion dipping just enough to where our arms brush.

"It was Vinny," I say. "One of his guys walked onto the elevator after..."—I swallow and look away—"we kissed. He must have sensed something, told Vinny, and then Vinny's way of getting back at us for beating him was to do something like this."

"That fucking asshole," Tessa growls. "He's just jealous I didn't want to kiss him!"

My lip twists into a cocky grin. "Does that mean you wanted to kiss me?"

She doesn't have to answer or admit it.

I know she did.

"Of course not!" she exclaims.

I chuckle, and my smirk deepens.

She crosses her arms with her plump bottom lip plopped forward into a pout. "What are we going to do to fix this? I'd like a plan before Gia finds out."

"*We're* going to do nothing," I say. "I'll fix it."

Her scoff fans across my face. "And you expect me to trust you?"

I smile again, with another insinuation of our kiss on the edge of my lips.

Her perfectly arched eyebrows cave inward. "Don't!"

I turn away to hide my amusement and give myself space to take in her house.

It's small and cozy. Much homier than anywhere I've ever lived. But given the inviting feel of her parents' house, and the warmth you instantly feel when walking inside, it's not really a surprise.

The walls are a creamy tan with random pops of color sprinkled throughout the room. Three thousand comfy pillows rest against the couch, and there are flowy drapes covering the windows that face out onto the street. I'm surprised she hasn't closed them in fear that someone is peeking at us from the outside.

My mind wanders the longer we sit in silence.

What does Tessa Halston do on her nights off?

Does she cuddle up on this couch, swallowed by pillows, and watch some show on TV? Or does she open up a book and read until her eyes get heavy? Knowing her, she probably rewatches past races so she can learn every little thing about aerodynamics.

Or, what if she goes out with her friends and ends up bringing some random guy home?

My shoulders tense, and I quickly launch into a plan to ignore my last thought. "I'll bring a plus-one to the next media-packed event. Problem solved."

A sarcastic laugh bellows from her mouth. "And have everyone think that you tossed me to the side after one *cuddly* weekend in Bahrain? Absolutely not."

I slowly tilt my head toward her. "Do you have a better plan, Princess?"

She nibbles on her thumbnail, the thin, gold ring catching my eye. "I'll bring a plus-one instead."

My ears burn.

"No," I blurt.

The word is abrupt, and I don't really care how my refusal looks.

Tessa angles herself toward me on the couch and raises a brow. "No?"

Fuck. Think fast.

"How are you going to get your brothers to let you bring some random guy? If you haven't heard, they're awfully protective over you."

She scoffs, and those warm brown eyes roll in the back

of her head. "I'll just tell them the truth."

My shoulders tense. "The truth?"

Her lips flatten. "Not *that* truth. I mean that I'll tell them someone started a rumor, and I'm squashing it."

"You mean, *we're* squashing it," I add. "If you're bringing a plus-one, so am I."

She rolls her eyes again. "Fine."

"Glad we got this figured out," I say.

I stay planted on the couch after she stands abruptly. I watch the way her hips sway toward the door. She opens it and sends me a pointed look. "You can leave now."

"I could, yes."

But damn, I really don't want to.

"So..." She wafts her hand out into the open, as if to usher me through the door.

"I kind of like seeing where you live," I admit. "And this couch...it's awfully comfy."

"It is, and I have plans to spend my evening on it. *Alone.*"

There's a comeback ready to go in the back of my throat, but the vibrating of my phone catches me off guard. I pull it out of my hoodie pocket, and my flirty mood instantly disappears.

BEAU

You left a winning team for some Pit Porn? Can't say I blame you, but what happens when you get tired of her like you usually do? Toss her aside and still be on a losing team?

My shoulders tense, my phone creaking underneath my tight grip.

I'm not sure what I'm angrier about: the fact that he's

completely disregarding the truth of how corrupted his team is or that he's referring to Tessa in this way.

I click my screen off, shoot up from the couch, and walk over to the door, completely lost in my thoughts. The pressure of Tessa's hand on my arm stops me in my tracks. She looks to my phone, then to my face, a clear window of worry in the different hues of brown.

I look at her mouth, craving to shut the world out, if even for a second, but instead, I walk past her and get into my car.

Beau's text came at the perfect time—even if I fucking hate him.

Chapter Twenty-Five

TESSA

GIA CLAPS HER HANDS EXCITEDLY. "This is huge! The sponsorship isn't just for Rosa Negra Couture, but also for their partner liquor launch too! They want you to be a part of their European debut."

Rome isn't paying attention at all. He's holding a pen horizontally between his thumb and pointer finger and wiggling it like he's back in elementary school. Noah is hiding a paper football in the palm of his hand, waiting for Gia to turn her head so he can flick it across the table at Beck.

The drivers are required to sit through this meeting because they're representing the brand.

Well, we will all be representing the brand in Spain, but they're arguably the most important.

"First, there will be the red carpet and photos, where you are required to wear a piece of Rosa Negra Couture, then you'll move onto cocktail hour, where there will only be Rosa Tequila available."

Beck chants quietly from his seat. "*Shots, shots, shots.*"

Van shushes him.

"Then the product-unveiling moment, maybe a speech or two from the representatives, and mingling before heading back to the hotel for the rest of the week's festivities."

Meaning the track walk, qualifying, and the race.

Sponsorships are important, but the race even more so.

"It's also required for you to bring a plus-one."

I sit up a little taller in my seat, and the pen in Rome's hand stops wiggling.

"Perfect," Noah chimes. "You two can work on fixing your reputations."

Gia purses her lips. "It's only required for the drivers to bring a plus-one, but–"

"I'm bringing one too," I blurt.

A laugh shoots out of Beck's mouth. "Like who?"

I turn my nose up at my brother. "None of your business."

Noah attempts to hide a smile. "Vinny will be there. Maybe you can take him."

The pen clatters on the table. Rome's eyebrows draw together. "No."

Van's phone goes off, interrupting the tense moment. His eyebrows furrow after looking at the screen. "I have to take this."

"The meeting is basically done. I'll send the rest of the details via email," Gia says.

My brother can't escape fast enough. Beck's chair is still spinning by the time he darts from the door, leaving me and Rome to walk out together.

It's not as if we're not going to the same wing of head-quarters, but even after spending so much time with him over the last few days during test set-ups, sim work, and refining lines, being alone with him makes the skin of my chest itch.

I try to slow my steps to lag behind, but he notices and does the same.

Then I try to speed-walk, which only results in him chuckling from beside me.

I glare up at him, and he's showing off his famous smirk, the one that makes his icy-blue eyes seem a little less intimidating.

"So, who are you taking as your plus-one?" he asks. "You got someone in Spain lined up? Or are you bringing someone?"

I eye him closely. "Why do you care?"

His hands disappear into his pockets after hitting the button for the elevator. "I don't. Just curious."

I refuse to ask who he's bringing, because I'd rather jump from this balcony than have him think I care.

"You're just going to have to wait and see," I say, smiling.

He angles his head and squints. "You don't have a plus-one, do you?"

I laugh and play off my nervousness. "Of course I do. I have a long line of men I can choose from. I'm just trying to remember which one has the biggest dick."

A tight-lipped smile carves into Rome's tense jaw, but he recovers quickly when the elevator door opens up. Neither one of us steps forward.

I'm not sure I can stand to be in that tiny space with him again with the remnants of the last time we were in an elevator together in my head.

"Go ahead." He holds the door. "I think it's best if I get the next one."

I'm wary but slide past him into the empty space. I

reach forward to hit the button, and he removes his hand. Our eyes meet in the middle, and he grins. "Wouldn't want to have a repeat now, would we?"

I suck in my cheeks, knowing the pink color is likely giving me away.

He raises a brow.

The door shuts, and I exhale in relief.

How we can go from working tirelessly together, surrounded by the rest of our team, tweaking lines, and analyzing data, and then to *this* a breath later is beyond me.

I pull out my phone and text Quinn.

ME

I need a date for an event in Spain. ASAP.

QUINN

I'll be your date.

ME

Find me someone that'll shut Rome up, and you can come too.

QUINN

Are you going to make me go with Beck?

I don't answer her, and yet, she agrees.

QUINN

Fine. I'm in. I'll send you potential dates shortly.

I smile to myself.

Perfect.

*   *   *

"Wow."

My face flushes. I look down at the red gown, the color of wine, and run my hands over the silk material.

"It's the only one that fit me." I shrug shyly.

"And this is the only one that fit me." Quinn's red lips flatten.

My date, her cousin, gives her a onceover. "What's wrong with it? It looks fine."

"Exactly." She huffs. "You lose your breath at the sight of Tessa…" She glances at me and winks. "Rightfully so. But then you say I look *fine*?"

Jasper throws his hands out. "You're my cousin. What do you want me to say?"

Quinn pushes past him, mumbling under her breath. Jasper and I peer down the hall of the hotel and watch as she raps her knuckles against the door.

"This ought to be good," he mutters, grinning at me.

I shake my head. "They're destined to kill each other before the night ends."

"And you're destined to kill me in that dress, Tess." He eyes me up and down. "You grew up."

"You mean, I'm not that same tween girl with braces and wild wavy hair?" I laugh. "Thank God."

When Quinn found out that her cousin was going to be in Spain at the same time we were, it was a no-brainer for her to ask him to accompany me. He jumped at the opportunity. Getting to spend the evening with F1 drivers at a fancy venue in the middle of Madrid with endless amounts of top-of-the-line tequila…*hell yeah* was his response.

But now that he's staring at me like I'm his next meal, this night might not be as dreadful as I think. It's just an added bonus that I get to prove to Rome that I'm not dateless like he teased me about *all* week long.

I haven't seen him since before we got into Madrid.

Mr. Arrogant was finally able to get his private jet brought down from Canada, so he and whoever he brought as his plus-one flew in a day after us.

Down the hall, Beck opens his door. He steps out halfway and leans against the doorframe with his white dress shirt half-unbuttoned. "Yes?"

Quinn places a hand on her hip, the dark-green satin of her dress moving slightly. "When you see me, what is the first thing that comes to mind?"

My brother eyes her up and down longingly. His mouth curves up on the side, and I'm certain whatever comes out of his mouth is going to piss Quinn off even more than Jasper saying she looks fine.

"The word that comes to mind is..." He leans in closer to her. "Mine."

Jasper glances at me. "Are they a thing?"

Quinn's voice rings through. "I am not yours, Beckham! Not even for tonight."

"You're my date, so you kind of are."

"Date, yes. Plaything? Never." She throws her long, auburn hair over her shoulder and pushes Beck back into his room. "Hurry up and get dressed. I don't want to be late."

He follows after her, grinning like a fool, and shuts the door.

"Well, that answers that," Jasper says.

A laugh falls from my mouth, and Jasper grins at me.

I gaze at his handsome smile and vibrant green eyes, hopeful a spark will appear, but nothing happens until I hear a door open up behind him.

My body buzzes before I even see him.

The air in the hallway shifts, and I can't flick my attention back to Jasper. I'm glued to Rome, desperate for some type of sign that he's looking for me too.

Which he shouldn't be.

Neither one of us should be looking for each other.

Not in a near-empty hallway or a crowded venue space.

The *only* time either one of us should be searching for the other is on the track.

And yet, somehow, we find each other anyway.

JASPER.

More like Casper.

He's paler than my white dress shirt, and he gelled his hair like he's afraid a tornado is going to rip through and destroy it.

"Over here, Rome." I turn, along with my date, toward another camera on the red carpet.

My hand hovers over Rebecca's lower back.

I can't seem to touch her in the way that I usually do, considering the entire reason I brought her was to end the rumors of something going on with Tessa and me.

Maybe it wasn't the entire reason, but it was part of it.

I thought bringing Rebecca would get my mind back on the straight and narrow, away from this back and forth with Tessa, but here I am, gaping at her as I walk past her and her date posing for a photo.

And that dress.

Who the hell was in charge of the wardrobe? Surely Rosa Negra Couture's line had dresses that were a little less revealing.

Tessa's entire back is exposed.

I've already pictured myself breaking her date's hand for brushing his fingers across her spine.

"Thank you, Rome. You're free to go on in."

Rebecca and I are ushered off the carpet, making room for Beck and his date.

I recognize her from that first night in Vegas, at the bar, which seems like a lifetime ago. If I remember correctly, she's Tessa's friend.

Rebecca stops walking on our way to the bar area. "You look amazing in that dress," she says to someone. "Like it was made for you!"

I already know without looking that she's referring to Tessa.

Even on the days when Tessa is at HQ for more than twelve hours, she looks amazing—not that I'd admit that to her. But tonight? She's downright irresistible.

"Oh." Tessa shifts awkwardly, and it's obvious she's avoiding me. "Uh, thank you."

"Told you," Jasper whispers loud enough for me to hear. "That dress is going to kill me tonight."

Not if I get to you first.

The rest of cocktail hour is spent mingling with Rosa Negra Couture's top performers, potential sponsors, media representatives, and my other personality that can't seem to get it together where Tessa is involved.

Every slight brush of Jasper's hand on her back, or hip, or even his hungry gaze in her direction, makes me twitch with jealousy, and that's not something I'm used to.

I'm desperate for it to disappear.

"Are you okay?" Rebecca peeks at me over the rim of her glass cup. "You seem tense."

Rebecca has been to a handful of events with me and

plays her part well. She never misses out on an opportunity to attend as my date, because the more the media focuses on her potential relationship with me, the less they focus on her actual relationship with her much older modeling agent.

It'd be a scandal in the modeling community.

Just like anything between Tessa and me would be a scandal in the F1 community.

Ethics and all of that.

"I'm fine." I adjust my bowtie. "I'm just worried about the race."

I am worried about the race, because as of late, I'm having a difficult time concentrating on the actual skillset I possess to win.

"You're under a lot of stress." Rebecca's eyes soften around the edges. "I'm sure your father is beside himself from you up and leaving Pierce."

Funny.

I haven't really thought much about my father.

Our attention is pulled to the front of the room, where a man and two women wearing dresses similar to Tessa's stand in front of a microphone. "Ladies and gentlemen, if you will find your seats."

"Unveiling moment," I mutter. "Come on."

This time, I force my hand to Rebecca's lower back. I guide her through the moving crowd to our table with my heart pounding a million miles a second, hopeful that Tessa is at the same one.

Why? Because the thought of her being near makes me downright wild.

It doesn't take me long to spot her.

Her long brown hair is pulled back into a sleek bun, showcasing her shimmering cheekbones. There's a piece of silk from her dress that wraps around her neck, and the only thought that comes to mind when staring at it is what would happen if I untied it.

I pull out a chair for Rebecca, purposefully leaving the one next to Tessa empty, and scoot her closer to the table.

"Thank you," she says quietly.

I linger behind Rebecca's chair, playing Russian roulette with my choices.

Left or right?

I eye the empty space on the other side of Rebecca, and I know it's where I should sit.

Yet, my body has a mind of its own as I sink down into the seat beside Tessa.

I'm aware of every little thing she does.

Her breaths.

The effort she makes to scoot closer to her date.

The fleeting glances out of the corner of her eye, like she's trying not to look at me.

I reach forward and grab the bottle of exclusive tequila. My leg brushes against Tessa's bare leg, that high slit in the side of her dress drawing my attention. The exposed part of her dress shows how her ribs expand, and they don't deflate until I settle back in my chair, no longer touching her.

Interesting.

"Good tequila," I say to the table but really to Tessa.

Anything to get her to look at me.

Jasper leans past Tessa to nod in my direction. He reaches forward for the bottle and pours some into Tessa's empty glass and then pours a much larger amount into his own before downing it in one swig.

I chuckle. "Better slow down, Casper."

Tessa flicks her eyes to mine with her eyebrows drawn together closely. "Casper?"

My mouth twitches with humor, and I turn away.

Quinn and Beck make it to the table just as the speaker is garnering the room's attention. Beck whispers something in her ear, and she shushes him, causing Jasper to snicker loudly.

Tessa shifts in her seat again.

Her date is pouring himself another drink, and out of the corner of my eye, I see him down it just as quickly as the first.

The room erupts in a round of applause when the curtain opens up to a line of Rosa Negra Couture formal wear that the majority of us are dressed in tonight, courtesy of the event. Jasper moves toward Tessa, his mouth hovering over her ear. My chest constricts, but I keep my focus up front.

"You should be the model for their line," he whispers, except it isn't a whisper at all. "'Cause you look smokin' hot in that dress."

Quinn turns around and shushes him with her eyes alone.

Tessa clears her throat, and I swear she moves closer to me.

Rebecca elbows me gently.

"He's drunk," she mouths.

Clearly.

It isn't until he reaches across Tessa again that I act.

I grab the bottle of tequila and move it out of his reach. My leg brushes against Tessa's again, and this time, I let it linger longer than last time.

Jasper scoffs in my direction, but I ignore it.

I'm cutting him off.

I may not like him, and I'd prefer it if he got so drunk security had to remove him from this event, especially because his hand has crept onto Tessa's thigh, but I refuse to let him embarrass her by getting belligerent.

Tessa sits up higher in her seat, and if I'm not mistaken, she's angled herself toward me.

It isn't evident to the rest of the room, and maybe not even her, but that's just the thing lately—I notice everything when it comes to her.

Like how her breathing hitches when I press my leg against hers again, or how she drops her hand to her lap to grab onto Jasper's.

I lean back in my seat and casually look below the table.

Tessa's fingers are wrapped around Jasper's wrist, and every time he tries to move his hand farther in between her legs, she shoves it away.

A faint growl slips from my throat.

I glare at his hand, like I have the power to stop it.

She hears it, and so does he.

I glare at him and calmly shake my head no.

He has the audacity to smirk at me.

My fists flex.

Tessa glances at me and then to him.

Sensing what's going on, she tries to shove his hand away again, whispering something so low, I can't make out what she says.

The next five seconds move in slow motion.

He grumbles something and removes his hand from beneath the table, only to reach across Tessa for her untouched glass of tequila. Except, instead of getting a good handle on it, he fumbles it.

The sharp smell of liquor fills the air, and Tessa's rushed

gasp cuts across the space between us. The liquid spills over the table and onto her legs.

"Oh, shit," Jasper says loudly.

Van, from the next table, glares at us with a silent warning.

I do the same, but it's directed at one person only.

Jasper.

Chapter Twenty-Seven

TESSA

TEQUILA DRIPS in between my legs and onto the floor, splattering against my brand-new heels. My mouth hangs open in shock. I quickly scoot backward in my chair and pray no one is watching the scene unfold throughout the very prestigious unveiling occurring in the front of the room.

"Ah, sorry, Tess." Jasper's words are slightly drawn out from the amount of tequila he's consumed in the last hour. "Here."

He gathers the cloth napkin in his hand and starts shoving it in between my legs to *help*, only he doesn't get very far. Rome wraps his fingers around Jasper's wrist, and from the sight of his white knuckles, I'd say he's squeezing pretty hard.

"Don't even touch her," he snaps.

Jasper lets go of the napkin as soon as Rome releases his grip. I take over, perfectly capable of cleaning myself. I quickly wipe away the excess from my thighs so it doesn't bleed onto my dress. I move the silk aside to reach my ankle but stop breathing when Rome shifts beside me.

His callused palm gently touches my calf, and he lets it linger there for a few seconds. His fingers slowly wrap around my leg to scoot it closer to him beneath the table. I force myself to swallow and stay perfectly still. The soft touch of the napkin slowly brushes across my ankle with Rome's hand traveling down my leg to hold it still.

His fingers are warm and careful, yet I have goose-bumps challenging my thoughts.

I relax into his touch because it feels good. My heart beats harder the longer he dabs away the mess, and it's the only thing I hear inside my ears. His finger traces a line around the clasp of my shoe, and a shiver runs down my spine.

It's the faintest of touches, and yet I'm putty in the palm of his hand.

The room erupts in another applause, and it shocks me, like I'm caught red-handed.

I hastily pull my leg out of reach and stand on wobbly legs. "I'm going to finish cleaning myself up in the bath-room," I announce.

Jasper tries to follow. "I'll help you—"

"You absolutely will not!" Quinn hisses. "I'm walking you up to your room so you don't cause another scene!"

"Nice try, Quinny. I'm the older cousin. You can't tell me what to do."

"What are you? Five?" she snaps. "Let's go. Now."

I leave Quinn to deal with Jasper and search for the bathroom or, at the very least, a moment alone to gather myself.

Between Jasper's behavior, getting a drink spilled all over me, and Rome's touch lingering a little too long, I need a second. Or a shot. I should've grabbed the bottle of tequila on my way out the door.

It's pretty desolate outside of the venue room, and without any directions at all, I have no clue which way to go.

I choose to go left, because it's farthest away from the entrance.

The click of my heels echoes around the empty hall as I rush toward a door that I hope leads to a bathroom. I vaguely hear Quinn's voice as she scolds Jasper, but like a beacon of light, a bathroom appears.

Thank God.

I slip inside and press my back against the door. I exhale, and stare at myself in the mirror. The pink flush on my cheeks spreads all the way to my neck and down to my chest. I think of Jasper, and then Rome, and quickly reach up to loosen the silk wrapped around my neck.

I'm suddenly feeling very suffocated and sticky.

I gather a few paper towels and wet them with water. In the midst of cleaning my legs, the door opens.

I turn around in a rush. "Sorry! This is occupied."

Rome steps inside and locks the door behind him. "I know."

My breath catches, and fight-or-flight kicks in. I search for a way around him or another exit, knowing very well that there isn't one.

I don't really want to leave, though. I just know I should.

"Wh—what are you doing here?" I stammer. "Did anyone see you follow me?"

His blue eyes flick to mine. "No one saw me."

"Well..." I glance at the wet paper towels dripping onto the floor. "What about your date? I'm not so sure she'd be happy to know you followed me out of the venue after glaring at my date the entire night."

Rome scoffs. "Nice choice, by the way. He can't even handle his liquor. And Rebecca doesn't care where I go. She uses me as a cover just as much as I use her."

I eye him closely. "What do you mean?"

Rome's throat bobs up and down, like he's forcing himself to swallow. "She's in a committed relationship with someone she shouldn't be."

"Oh."

I act quick and cross my arms defensively so he doesn't notice the way my shoulders loosen from relief. "Well, you shouldn't have followed me. If someone saw you, then what's the point of either of us bringing a plus-one?"

Rome leans against the door and shoves his hands into the pockets of his trousers.

It's frustrating how attractive he is, especially in an elite suit. The dark navy brings out the color of his eyes even more, as if they weren't already the most vibrant blue I've ever seen.

I raise an eyebrow and wait for his answer.

He drops his lazy gaze down my body, and my face warms again.

I mindlessly take a step backward to fight whatever is happening between us.

"We each brought a date to fool everyone into thinking there's nothing happening between us," Rome mutters.

My stomach flips. "There is nothing happening between us."

Rome tilts his head and stares at me from across the small space.

I take another step backward and bump into the sink.

Why is it so warm and cozy in this bathroom? Does everything have to be so romantic in Madrid?

"You look flushed," he says.

My spine straightens. "Drinking tequila makes me warm."

His lips flatten. "But you didn't drink any."

"How do you know?"

Rome's tongue slips out of his mouth to run it over his bottom lip. "Because I watch you, Tessa."

It's so quiet I know he hears the way my breath catches.

He blinks. "And I know you've felt me watching you."

There's something extremely dangerous lingering in the air that I've only ever felt with Rome. At first, I thought the tension between us was because our rivalry between our teams ran bone-deep, but right now, the ache in my lower stomach is full of lust and hidden urges.

In every quiet moment, I think about the kiss we shared until I realize what I'm doing. And when I look at him from across the room, I pretend I don't feel the yearning. Every time he brushes his leg against mine, my skin prickles, and I tell myself it's from irritation.

But it's not from irritation at all.

It's something much worse.

Rome shifts against the door, and I quickly try to cover up my thoughts.

"Of course I've felt you watching me, and I know it's because you're waiting for me to mess up so you can tease me about it later on."

I'm giving him an out.

I'm giving him a way around this so he doesn't feed into it the same way that I am.

All he has to do is make some stupid remark to offend me, turn around, and leave me be.

For the first time, I'm willingly giving him the control.

His sexy chuckle echoes. "Is that why you think I'm watching you?"

I stare at him, my heart pounding a hundred beats a second.

With the damp paper towel still in my grip, I push off from the sink and walk toward the door, careful not to touch him with my hand resting on the handle.

His jaw is tight as he peers down at me.

Even with my heels, he's still taller than me.

"It better be the reason." My whisper slices through the tension.

He nods slowly, his temples flickering with every bob of his head.

I pull on the door handle, thinking he'll move out of the way, but he doesn't.

I stop breathing when his arm winds around the front of my body.

"And what if it isn't, Tess?"

Chapter Twenty-Eight

ROME

MY HEART PUNCHES the inside of my ribs with my arm around her waist. Hints of her floral perfume swirl around me when she pauses instead of pushing me away.

I don't know what it is about her that I can't seem to resist. At first, I thought it was the urge to make her angry, to irritate her until she was seething in my direction, because it was entertaining. But now I wonder if I was poking at her because I *liked* her looking in my direction.

It wasn't until she calmed me during the race that something shifted...and then came the kiss.

Now I'm hungry for it.

"Rome."

My name sounds like a beg, but I'm pretty certain she meant for it to come out as a warning.

"We can't do this," she says quietly, staring at the door instead of me.

And yet, she hasn't pulled on the door handle.

"I'm just here to help you clean up from your sloppy date spilling tequila all over you."

I make a deal with myself mentally.

If she pulls on the door handle for the second time, I'll let her go. But if she doesn't, it's game over.

It could be good to get this out of our systems. Maybe loosen the pull between us.

Or make it tighter.

With my one arm still wrapped around her stomach, I take the other from my pocket and reach for the towel in her hand. Her fingers tighten around the handle, but still, she doesn't open the door.

"Let me help you." I mean for it to come out as a question, but instead, it's a demand.

Tessa lets go of the towel, and I take it while slowly pushing her back to the vanity. I stare at the way her ribs expand with each quick breath through the mirror, and instead of cursing the open back of her dress again, now I'm praising it.

I turn the water on to wet the towel again. The squeak of the nozzle makes Tessa jump against the hard porcelain.

"Relax, Princess," I whisper into her ear. "I'm just going to wipe the tequila from your legs."

She shivers and grips the edge of the counter.

I bend at the knee and stare at the open slit of her dress.

I nearly shiver too.

My blood heats, and my fingers ache when I push the silk fabric off to the side, revealing more of her bare leg. A shaky breath slips from her the moment I place the wet towel onto her inner knee. Her knuckles turn white as she grips the counter harder.

"You're just as affected as I am, aren't you?" I mutter.

I watch in awe as goosebumps race up her thighs, disappearing beneath her dress.

Tessa says nothing.

I peek at her from below, and she has her bottom lip trapped beneath her teeth.

She's trying to hold herself together, just like me.

I move to the other knee, and dab her skin there, and then slowly drag the towel up farther. She inhales sharply, and her warm breath cascades below from the heavy exhale.

I reach the outer part of her panties with the towel, and I'm desperate to get a glimpse. I try to move her dress out of the way, and to my shock, she takes the silk into her hands and bundles the material around her waist.

Black lace panties stare back at me, and my tender cleaning grows rushed.

I clench my teeth and move to the other leg, wiping the damp towel over her groin harder than the previous.

She shifts against the vanity, and her hips move forward a fraction.

The towel falls to the tiled floor, but I keep my hand in between her legs, rising to full height.

I stare at her with a silent question.

Those brown eyes, usually fiery, turn rich and doe-like, and I plead my case.

"It's just us," I whisper against her lips. "No one on the other side of the door knows we're in here, and no one has to know."

Her lips open slightly, and I hold my breath.

Have I ever wanted someone so badly before?

The tiny gap that lives between our mouths is there one second then gone the next. She relaxes into me, sinking her hips to meet my hand between her legs with a sexy noise. I kiss her long and hard. My tongue works quickly to memorize every single inch of her feisty mouth.

I love her lips. I love her taste, and I love having her like this.

I toy with her over the lace, rubbing my finger back and forth softly, until she whimpers against me. I grip the back of her head to keep her lips pressed to mine and pull her panties to the side.

"Needy," I mutter against her mouth. "And I fucking love it."

I slide a finger inside, and her head slips backward with a faint moan. My other hand gets lost in her dark strands of hair, the pinned pieces loosening from my grip as she unravels from my touch.

"That's it," I say with a strained voice.

Seeing her like this is life changing. Having her all to myself, hatred and teasing aside, is going to kill me in the end.

I add another finger and watch her closely. Euphoria washes over her features, the apples of her cheeks pink, her lips parting with a whimper.

"Right...th–there," she moans.

My dick pulses as quickly as my fingers move in between her legs. I rub her clit, and her hips jerk from the touch.

Fuck, I think I'm in love.

I bury my head into her neck and tug on her earlobe littered with gold studs. "Show me what you look like when you come, Princess."

Her breaths are hot and sharp. I tug farther on the silk fabric around her neck, lowering it to give me access. I flick my tongue against her warm skin and press my lips there next.

"Ro–Rome." My name is a breathless sigh falling from her mouth.

It's like I already know what her body needs. I suck on her skin gently, nipping her with my teeth. Her hips move back and forth, meeting my fingers, and then she dips her head backward, giving me even more access to her neck to nibble on.

One more nick of my teeth, and she's a goner.

I'm desperate to watch, so I force myself to lean back and gaze at her thirstily.

Tessa is wildly tempting when she glares at me or rolls her eyes in my direction, but watching her come undone from my touch alone is an entirely new level of obsession.

I care about nothing else at this moment, except for when I'm going to get to watch Tessa unravel again.

Our eyes meet after her high, hers dazed and sated, mine fiery and hot.

"Now what?" she asks, voice raspy, eyelashes fluttering.

I readjust her panties, my fingers wet from her arousal. I gaze at her as I trace a line down her inner thigh, a dampness lingering behind.

"Now we go back out there and do what we set out to do." I reach up and re-tie the silk sash around her neck, hiding the faint mark that I hope she finds later.

"What did we set out to do?" she asks, still dazed from the orgasm.

I step away, and she watches me the entire way to the door. "Proving to the media that there's nothing going on between us."

The realization comes back to her, the flush of her skin slowly disappearing.

"But Tess?" My hand rests on the door handle, and I gaze at her over my shoulder. "There's definitely something going on between us."

Chapter Twenty-Nine

TESSA

A PHOTO of Rome and Rebecca comes through with Beck's text, and a surge of jealousy comes with it.

I quickly swipe it away, irritated at my reaction.

Firstly, I'm not the type of woman who gets jealous of other women. Secondly, they're not even a thing. And lastly, who am I to get jealous of *Rome's* date?

He gave me an orgasm and maybe made the night somewhat bearable after the disaster with Jasper, but that's it.

I was happy to see that we both acted completely normal the next morning and days following.

Just like when we kissed.

We have a job to do, and there is really no room for anything else. Not even an argument from the faint hickey on my neck that I've had to cover up with makeup.

I told Beck it was a mosquito bite, and that's what I'm sticking with.

VAN

Ressa?

I roll my eyes. Get with it, Van.

BECK

Tessa + Rome = Ressa

GRAHAM

This is unimportant. We're thirty minutes out from the race.

Nervous jitters fill my stomach.

I'm testier for this race than I was for Bahrain, and Rome actually qualified well yesterday. The need to succeed is stronger than before, and I can't figure out why. I'm always eager to please. The competitive nature all Halstons possess has been there since my first breath, but it's more pressing today.

I search the paddock for Rome. I don't see many drivers lingering; most are already in their own private tent areas, preparing.

Quinn, tucked behind our pit wall, catches my eye and waves a Styrofoam cup in front of her face.

I point to myself. "For me?"

She nods with a smile.

I rush through the crowd, eager for my Diet Coke, when a golf cart zips past. I come to a sudden halt and grab onto my headset before it falls to the ground.

The golf cart slams on the brakes the same time I send a glare in its direction.

This asshole!

Beau, in his half-zipped red-and-yellow race suit, twists

in the passenger seat with a nasty smile on his face. "Watch where you're going, Halston."

"You watch where you're going!" Quinn shouts.

I bite my tongue instead of feeding into it. Having words with anyone on Pierce Racing will do nothing but make my heart race faster, and that's the last thing I need right now.

Beau snaps his eyes to Quinn, who stands with her hand on her hip. Beck comes up behind her and puts his arm over her shoulder.

The golf cart takes off again, and Quinn flings his arm away.

I finish walking toward them and take the Diet Coke from her hand.

I sigh. "I love you."

I wrap my lips around the straw and take a huge swig of soda.

Quinn glares at Beck. "I had it under control."

He grins. "I know. I just wanted to touch you."

She rolls her eyes and turns back to me. "Are you okay? What a dick."

"That's Rome's stepbrother." I look down the paddock, and Beau is completely out of sight. "They hated us before, and now that Rome is on our team, they *really* hate us."

Quinn raises a brow. "Enough to run you over?"

I wouldn't put it past them.

My text tone goes off, and I glance at Beck with a flat expression because *of course* he told the group that Beau almost ran me over.

BECK

That stepbrother of yours is a real piece of shit, Rome. He nearly ran Tessa over with a golf cart.

Graham pops up from below the pit wall. "What?"

Out of the corner of my eye, I see Van lean forward from Noah's pit area.

Instead of saying anything, I sip on my Diet Coke and shrug. I click my phone off, ready to silence it for the race, when I get another text.

Except, Beck's phone doesn't go off.

Only mine does.

ROME

Where are you?

Just seeing his name on my phone, in our own private message thread, speeds up my pulse.

ME

You know where I am.

ROME

Come to my tent.

I move my attention across the paddock, and sure enough, the makeshift Do Not Disturb sign is taped to the front of Rome's tent.

ME

There's a Do Not Disturb sign on your tent. Does that no longer apply to me?

"I'll be back," I say to Quinn, handing her my drink.

On my way over, I notice that the paper sign is hanging in a different spot. When I get closer, the words become clearer. The Do Not Disturb is still in bold, but beneath it, there is a set of parentheses with slanted, messy handwriting inside.

Do Not Disturb

(Does not apply to Tess)

My lips twitch into a small smile.

"Since when do you call me Tess?" I ask, knowing he can hear me.

His hand cuts through the thin opening of the thick fabric, and he grabs onto the lanyard hanging from my neck. I stumble forward and stop when I hit his chest.

Rome's eyes bounce back and forth between mine, his hands wrapped around my waist. "Since you gave me a taste."

My mouth dries, and I try to speak through my tied tongue. "You're breaking our rule."

Rome tilts his head with his dark brows knitted together. "What rule?"

"The one where we don't talk about what happened," I say quietly.

I'm hyperaware of every move he makes. His firm jaw tightens and then loosens as soon as his eyes drop to my mouth.

Nervous and jittery, I step away from him. "Shouldn't you be meditating or something? You have to be out there in–"

"Sixteen minutes," he finishes for me.

My pulse flies. Rome and I are all business when surrounded by the rest of the engineers or on the track, but when we're alone, something simmers between us. The air crackles, and the tiny hairs on my arms stand upright.

"What did you need?" I ask.

I assume some type of last-minute adjustment, or maybe he had a breakthrough while being alone with his thoughts and needs to discuss a last-minute strategy.

Rome's chest expands with a heavy inhale. He holds it

for several seconds before clenching his eyes shut and exhaling.

Is he nervous for the race?

I take a step toward him. "Hey, talk to me. What's going on?"

He opens his eyes a breath later, the blue so bright I freeze mid-step.

"I just needed to see you," he mutters, like he doesn't want anyone to hear through the thin walls of his tent. "I wouldn't have been able to race if I didn't lay my eyes on you."

My shoulders slowly loosen. "Is this because of Beck's text?" I roll my eyes. "He's dramatic. I'm fine."

Rome says nothing.

His fists are clenched by his sides, the veins on the tops of his hands pumped full of anger.

The ground feels unsteady beneath me, and I know it's because we're alone in this stuffy tent.

"Find your center," I remind him. "You're about to be driving two hundred miles per hour, and now I really expect you to beat Beau." I give him a small smile in an attempt to loosen him a little.

His neck bobs up and down with a slow swallow as I step backward toward the tent opening.

"You've got, like, ten minutes to clear your head," I say.

I'm less than a foot away from the outside when I turn away, my heart pounding inside my ears. My fingers brush against the tent briefly, my stomach tangled with flutters.

But then, there's a shift in the air, and I'm tugged backward.

Chapter Thirty

ROME

THIS CAN GO EITHER WAY.

Tessa can refuse to cross the line for the third time, or she can give in to the only thing I think capable of clearing my head.

I've been on my best behavior where she's concerned; my focus stable, my qualifying solid, and then Beck's text came through.

Maybe it's because I know my father's watching me every single second he's able, with Beau glaring at me from across the paddock and very carefully dropping subtle threats when I'm within earshot, but I'm wound up. If I don't get it under control, it'll bleed out onto the track.

Tessa peeks at me through her thick lashes, a soft breath escaping through her parted lips. With one arm wrapped around her lower back, I press her tighter to me and grab a hold of her chin.

"What are you doing?" she whispers.

I swallow.

I hate admitting I need help or showing weakness in any way, but I can't seem to hide when it comes to her. I'm desperate to tell her every thought in my head, share every secret I've been asked to keep.

Is this what it's like to trust someone?

"I'm clearing my head."

I grip her chin hard and kiss her.

Life flows back into me, energy surging down my limbs. I make a guttural noise, and I know it's because I've had to suppress every last thought of her and shift my focus to the race and each sharp corner of the track.

I can't get her out of my head.

Tessa gets past her shock, her tongue sliding against mine. Blood rushes to my groin, and I tug her with me to the couch, our mouths never separating. I slip my hand beneath the thin athletic skirt she's wearing, and I cup her ass to pick her up.

I sink onto the couch and take her with me.

She straddles me, her long brown hair falling around us like a veil as she leans backward. "What are we doing?" she mutters before going back in for another kiss.

We're on borrowed time.

Kissing her was supposed to calm me for a second, but now my dick is throbbing, and I'm itching to touch her everywhere.

I slide my palm up the inside of her thigh, and she shivers. Heat pools in between her legs, and I'm right at the crease of her panties when she stops me. Her fingernails cut into my skin, and she drags my hand out from in between her legs.

"Don't deny me now, Princess," I groan.

I'll beg if I have to.

"Shh," she shushes. "Stay quiet."

I quickly glance around and remember where we are.

Shit, what am I doing?

Tessa pulls on my attention like I'm a puppet on a string. Her hesitant fingers slide underneath my long-sleeve top and move over each ab carefully until she reaches the top of my boxers.

The touch alone makes my dick jerk.

My stomach pools with desire, watching her slide off my lap.

She lands on her knees. *She isn't–*

Fuck. *She is.*

I flex my hips, and she pulls my half-zipped race suit down to my thighs, the rest of my pants and boxers going next. My cock is hard as a rock, but it doesn't deter my naughty engineer in the least. Her tender hand wraps around it, and all the blood rushes to the tip.

"Tess," I say her name like a plea for her to put me out of my misery, and she does.

Her lips wrap around the tip, and she slides me inside her mouth slowly.

My adrenaline spikes, like I'm out on the track instead of inside this tent with her.

I ease my head backward and white knuckle the sides of the couch because I'm afraid if I don't, I'll grab the back of her head and choke her with my cock.

"Fuck." I bite down on my lip.

Tessa sucks me harder and faster, those pretty lips perfectly wrapped around my dick. Her eyes peek at me through thick eyelashes, and I thrust my hips.

It's too much.

She's too fucking much.

My head spins, and part of me wants to get her to stop sucking me off so I can fuck her instead.

Tessa flicks the bottom of my dick with her tongue, and my orgasm shoots out of me without warning.

"Shit," I grunt.

I attempt to pull out of her mouth so I don't drown her with my cum, but she doesn't let up.

My phone alarm goes off.

It's time to go, yet I can't stop watching her swallow every last drop. I'm devastated from the sight.

Once she's done, she stands, and I quickly tuck myself back into my pants.

"Looks like we're out of time," she says, running her fingers through her hair. "Is your head clear now?"

I blink through my daze.

She holds her hand out for me, and I take it, standing full height above her. In the midst of getting myself situated and zipping my race suit, I lock eyes with her. She tries to act casual, as if she didn't get down on her knees in front of me, but the longer I look at her, the more her mouth tries to curve into a smile.

"We gotta go," she stresses.

There's still a slight glimmer in her eye that I can't help but chase.

"Why are you looking at me like that?" she asks over her shoulder on her way to the opening in the tent.

She knows exactly why I'm looking at her like that.

I follow after her, but before she leaves, I grab her from behind and press her back against my chest. My mouth hovers over her ear, "I expect you to be in my room after this race, Princess."

Her voice is quiet. "I think that depends on how well you race, don't you?"

I grimace, and she winks at me over her shoulder.

With pink-dotted cheeks and swollen lips, she muses behind a grin, "Good luck."

I don't need luck when it comes to her. My perfect firecracker engineer is the biggest motivator I've ever had, and if my race performance is any indication of whether or not I'll have her in my bed later, I'm going to push every single limit on that circuit.

I've never had something worth it waiting for me at the end of a race, so the thought of her being off limits doesn't cross my mind twice.

It isn't until the light turns green and I hear her soft breaths in my ear that I try to suppress the dangerous thoughts of her naked.

Her voice switches from sultry to professional as quickly as it takes me to get up to speed, and by lap fifty, we're like a well-oiled machine.

She's calling the shots, and I'm abiding by them.

However, when she's in my bed later, I'm going to make damn sure that the roles are reversed.

Chapter Thirty-One

HE DID IT.

He beat Beau.

He didn't get into the top three, but neither did our rival.

Noah came in first, so Vanstone Racing won the race regardless, with Rome taking fourth. Beau came in fifth, and the end of the race was just as exhilarating as before the race—where I did something unthinkable in Rome's tent.

I have no idea what came over me, but looking at him from across the paddock with his triumphant attitude, a gush of heat settles in my belly.

He's mid-interview, fans surrounding him from every angle, yet his eyes meet mine.

My heart stops, but I quickly shake myself out of it and send him a thumbs up. He grins, still answering a question with his mouth lingering over the microphone.

Gia appears next to him and drags him off to a different journalist. Rome glances at me again, but this time, his eyebrow flicks upward.

I roll my eyes and suppress a cheesy grin.

I know, I know. You beat Beau.

Quinn elbows me. "Did you two just have a silent conversation?"

I rewind a few seconds, and oh my God, we did.

My cheeks warm, and I deny the accusation. "Absolutely not. That would mean Rome and I are on the same page, and that's only happened during a race. *Once.*"

I know Quinn can see right through me, but she doesn't press. All she says is, "Right," in a curious way.

I distract myself by picking things up and helping the rest of the team get everything gathered since we leave early tomorrow morning for Italy, when my phone buzzes in my back pocket.

I expect to see "Dad" flashing on the screen, knowing he'll want to congratulate us on the race, because there's no way he didn't stay up to watch it. Vivian probably tried to but likely fell asleep right beside him on the couch.

Instead, it's Rome, and I don't miss the way every sense becomes heightened.

ROME

368. 10pm on the dot, Princess.

I chew on my bottom lip, my heartrate instantly rising.

ME

Who said you raced well enough for me to come to your room?

ROME

I think the smile on your face after I climbed out of my car was enough of an indication.

ME

You think that smile was for you?

I search for him in the crowd, wondering where he is that he's able to text me back and forth, but I come up empty handed.

> **ROME**
>
> It better be for me.

I grab onto my stomach to force the flutters away and quickly shut my phone screen off. I have to finish going over the data with Dylan and get things back in order before any of us turn in for the night to prepare for an early flight.

Or in my case, convince myself that going to Rome's room is a terrible idea.

* * *

I pace back and forth in front of the bed.

Quinn left in an Uber an hour ago to catch her flight, and as soon as I was alone, I started mentally listing everything that should prevent me from walking three doors down.

We can't do this.

We were rivals no more than a couple of months ago, and now we arguably work closer than anyone else in the business.

The head engineer and driver need to have a seamless relationship, and that does not involve crossing lines with each other. I'm much more responsible than this. Tessa Halston doesn't make impulsive decisions. I was voted most responsible in high school by my graduating class, so what am I doing right now with Rome Pierce?

The clock reads 9:59.

My heart beats twice as fast with each second that passes.

I changed out of my Vanstone apparel and into my pajamas, hoping it'd make me crawl into my bed instead of toward the door, yet I stand gripping the handle with the little devil on my shoulder, encouraging me to open it.

Like Cinderella on the night of the ball, the clock strikes, and I panic.

I back away from the door with my heart in my stomach, but with every step comes disappointment. I rush back over, open the door, and stand there with one foot out in the hallway.

The polished marble floor shows the reflection of a flushed-faced woman, drawn to the very line she's about to cross. I'm hungry for trouble, caught in the middle of a serious yearning for Rome Pierce and his irritatingly hot smirk and skillful hands.

A noise sounds at the end of the hall, and I quickly jerk backward, letting my door slam shut.

My phone pings.

ROME

You're late.

I stare at the screen, the words blurry the more I read them.

ROME

Didn't take you for someone who chickens out, Princess.

He strikes a nerve, and he knows it.

ROME

Bawk, bawk.

Did he seriously just bawk at me?

ME

I'm not a chicken.

I fight, tooth and nail, to ignore the way my legs want to move toward the door.

ROME

So, you're just late? I guess every minute you keep me waiting is another minute I'll tack on to not giving you that orgasm I owe you.

Heat settles between my legs.

I open the door again to let the hallway air wash over my warm skin.

ME

It's funny you think you have control over when I do and don't come.

ROME

I bet I can get you to come without even touching you.

Yeah, right.

ROME

Should we make a bet?

My bare foot unknowingly creeps out onto the glassy floor.

ME

Only if you want to lose.

The door latches behind me, and I open up the hotel key on my phone to escape back into my room, only to swipe it away when Rome's next text comes through.

ROME

> If you prove me wrong, I'll give you my private jet. You can fly to all the races around the world, and I'll be stuck on commercial flights with your brothers.

I freeze, my trek to his room abruptly stopping. He can't be serious.

ME

> What's the catch?

ROME

> If I can get you to come without even touching you, for the rest of the season, you accompany me on my private jet to every race.

A challenge brews between us.

I give in to the pull and stomp over to his room, ready to prove a point.

Or better yet, win a bet.

I raise my fist to knock, but the door opens before I get a chance.

Rome stands there in nothing but low-hanging black sweatpants, damp hair fresh from the shower, and a dangerously enticing smirk.

"I knew you couldn't resist a challenge," he murmurs.

I place my palm on the center of his bare chest and push him out of my way. "Hope you're ready to part ways with that private jet of yours."

His dark chuckle chases me all the way to the center of his suite, and the way my breasts tingle from the sound alone tells me this is going to be a little harder than I thought.

Chapter Thirty-Two

ROME

ALL IT TAKES IS the door latching to wake my dick up.

A need like I've never experienced brushes against my skin with my gaze trained to her ass in those cute little pajama shorts, stomping across my hotel floor. Tessa's long brown hair sways past her face with her abrupt spin, her arms crossing over her chest to hide the way her nipples poke through the thin fabric.

"By the looks of you, I'm already on my way to winning." I drop my attention to her breasts, a smirk ghosting my lips.

"I'm cold," she snips, turning her nose up in my direction.

I take a step toward her and chuckle. "Not only are you late, but now you're lying to me too?"

With every step I take, she takes one in the opposite direction.

I stop and mimic her stance, crossing my own arms. "What's the matter, Tess? Afraid you'll lose the bet?"

Blood rushes to my dick at the sight of her tongue

sliding across her bottom lip. She scoffs, and the only thing that does is turn me on further.

Staring at her, all alone in my hotel room, makes me wonder when our tension turned into sexual tension.

"There is no way you're going to get me to come without touching me." She's beaming with confidence, and her mouth lifts on one side into a cute grin. "Maybe if you were that bartender from Bahrain...but–"

I advance on her, and she stops mid-sentence. Her back hits the wall, and her dainty chin juts forward. Instead of grabbing her like I'm desperate to do, I place my palms on the wall beside her head.

She's caged in, and my heart races with how close we are.

"Your mouth drives me fucking crazy," I admit, staring at the perfect bow shape. My pulse flies from the heat coming from her body, and I shut my eyes when I lean in close, because her scent is intoxicating.

I line my mouth next to her ear, careful not to touch her, and whisper low, "Everything about you drives me crazy. Your mouth, your eyes, this body..." I blow a hot breath over her neck, and she shivers in front of me. With my hands still beside her head, I back away and peer at her through hooded eyes. "You on your knees with my cock in your mouth..." I shake my head. "The way your chest rises when you're turned on, like right now."

Tessa sucks her bottom lip into her mouth and chews on it.

"I'm not turned on," she finally says.

"Prove it," I demand.

"How?"

I flick my chin to her hand. "Well, since I can't check... you're going to have to."

Her pupils dilate, but she remains unmoving.

My desire is at an all-time high. I'm shaking with need, because I know *she's* shaking with need.

"If you're telling the truth, you have nothing to worry about. Right?" I ask with a tilt of my head.

Her eyes dart across the room, and she knows she's stuck.

"Or do you have something to worry about?"

"I don't!" she stresses.

I move my mouth over her other ear. "Liar."

Goosebumps cover her arms, and I ache for her.

She gulps and eventually uncrosses her arms. I take a step away, uncaging her from in between my arms.

Her confidence wavers with my sights set on her, but she's much too proud to back out of this. With hesitancy, she slips her hand beneath the waistband of her thin sleep shorts, and I can't decide if I should look at her face or the spot between her legs.

I opt for above the shoulders, and I know the exact moment she touches herself, because her eyes close and her lips part with pleasure.

Fuck.

This may backfire on me.

I'm feral at the visual, and I can't help but rub the heel of my palm against the growing bulge in my pants.

She flutters her eyelashes, and the hazy glimmer staring back at me has me in a chokehold. Her attention skims down my bare chest to land below my waist.

"Well?" I rasp. "Show me."

She shakes her head. "No."

I raise a brow. Oh, she thinks she's in charge.

"How is that fair?" I look down. "I'm showing you how turned on I am."

Tessa shrugs, like she's unbothered, but the red spreading across her face tells me otherwise.

A fast sigh leaves her when I toy with the string of my sweats. "The difference between you and me is that I'm not afraid to cross the line to show you just how much you turn me on."

She forces out a denial. "I am not afraid."

"Then prove it," I say again, testing her.

"You prove it," she snaps.

Say less, baby.

I shove my hand inside my pants and grab a hold of my dick with a tight grip. My head falls backward from the pleasure, and I give myself a few good pumps, my entire body tensing when I loosen the tight hold. I pin her with a stare, her breaths fast and sharp. A soft swallow wobbles against her throat, her bottom lip glistening from her licking it.

"It feels good to give in," I groan. "You can stand there and watch me if you want. I'm not afraid to show you what you do to me." I squeeze the end of my cock and hiss between my teeth. "Plus, you can deny it all you want, Tess. I know what I do to you without you saying a word."

There's too much hot tension between us not to know.

She leans back onto the wall, her fingers teasing the waistband of her shorts. Our eyes remain locked with my hand moving up and down in my pants. Our breaths are heavy, and the nibbling on her lip grows rougher.

Time to amp this up. I shove my pants farther down so she can see more. "You don't mind, do you?"

Her eyes grow wide.

The buds of her nipples poke through her shirt, and all I want is to lick them.

"Damn it," she hisses.

Then, she gives in.

Fuck yes.

Her eyes roll back, and her hand disappears beneath her shorts.

I give her a few seconds of pleasure, with flames crawling up my back, before I can't take it anymore.

I walk over to her and stand inches away. "Show me," I plead, voice husky.

Her eyes fly open, and her teeth sink into her lip. Without touching her, I grab the thin cotton of her shorts in between my fingers and tug.

She doesn't stop me.

The piece of clothing falls to the floor, and she steps out of them.

No panties?

I can't form the words to tease her, because her fingers go right back to the spot she needs, and I watch in awe as she plays with herself.

"God damn." I squeeze my cock and stare between her legs.

A moan comes from her.

I grind my jaw back and forth and release the hold I have on my cock, because if I'm getting off tonight, it's going to be inside her.

I cage her against the wall again, careful not to brush my leg against hers.

"Get off for me," I whisper, mouth hovering beside her ear. "I want to hear your whimpers."

"Rome," she whines my name like she wants me to save her, and I will.

"You're beautiful like this," I admit, watching every little action.

She sucks in a lungful of air and arches her back against

the wall. Her breasts skim my bare chest, and I wrap my arm around her so she doesn't fall from pleasure. "That's my girl," I whisper in her ear. "You got off without me even touching you."

She doesn't deny it. Instead, she takes me by total fucking surprise by putting her hands on my shoulders and jumping up into my arms. Her bare pussy, wet and dripping, is there for the taking.

My dick throbs.

I stare at her, and she stares back.

A hot swallow works down my throat when she tightens her grip.

I can tell from the look in her eye what she wants, and I'm not righteous enough to stop the game we're playing. A shaky breath cascades out of her, and I position myself in between her legs. My fingers dig into her thighs, and I hold her steady. I slide inside, and her sweaty forehead falls to my shoulder.

Holy fucking hell.

I'm too swept away to get a condom.

The restraints loosen, the pull between us releasing as we both surrender.

"Fucking Christ," I croak.

I carry her over to the bed and lay her down beneath me. Her soft wavy hair splays below her head, and I can't help but go for her mouth.

I kiss her hard, my mouth covering hers possessively.

My balls tighten, and I thrust without reservation.

She breaks the kiss for a split second. "Make it good, cause we both know this is wrong."

In other words, this isn't happening again.

Her legs widen, and I touch her breasts one by one, sending her squirming below me.

"Yes," she whines. "Faster."

Whatever you want.

I move fast and try to chase away my orgasm so this can last longer, but with Tessa's pussy squeezing me mixed with her hot moans, I can't hold back.

"Fuck," I groan.

I try to pull out of her, but she digs her heels into my back, so I stay put and shoot my cum inside of her without a single fuck given.

The orgasm lasts long. Tessa's legs shake, and my entire body stills. It takes too long for me to pull out of her, and when I do, she winces.

Shit. "Did I hurt you?"

With her eyes closed, she shakes her head softly. "It's just been a while," she says, voice low and subtle.

That shouldn't give me a sense of pride, but it does.

I roll over and lie beside her, my breath labored, whereas Tessa's has slowed to the point that I think she may be asleep.

I'm afraid if I make a noise, she'll snap out of her dazed state and leave. So I don't say a word. Instead, I lie unmoving until sleep takes me.

And when I wake up the next morning for Italy, she's gone.

Chapter Thirty-Three

TESSA

THIS IS A HIGH-SPEED TRACK, and it couldn't be more fitting for the past few days. Taking in the historical data and sim runs, it's clear that this circuit is fast and reckless, just like Rome and me.

We're cutting corners and crossing lines, destined to crash and burn.

However, right now isn't the time to linger on what we did and, instead, focus on what's in front of me. Which is twenty sleek cars vibrating to hit the throttle, all with a hunger to succeed.

Including me.

"Radio check," I say into my headset. "Can you hear me?"

"Even when you're not speaking, I can hear you."

Heat creeps up my neck.

"I heard that sigh, Princess."

I shake my head, my lips twitching to smile.

"It was full of irritation."

His dark chuckle sends a chill down my spine. "I don't doubt it."

"You need to focus," I stress.

"I am focused," he argues. "Are you?"

He doesn't wait for me to answer.

"Did you drink your Diet Coke yet?"

How does he know about my favorite drink?

"No...I didn't have time to get one."

"I know." I hear the smile in his voice. "That's why I had one sent over to you."

What?

I glance around in search of this infamous Diet Coke, and the moment I land on a Styrofoam cup with my name on it, I blink back in surprise.

"Find it?" he asks.

I grab it with shaky hands and suck on the straw, taking in three huge mouthfuls. The carbonation tingles the inside of my mouth, and I moan quietly.

He clears his throat. "I'll take that as a yes."

After another sip, I ask, "Is this a bribe?"

He snorts. "A bribe? For what exactly?"

I bite my tongue, refusing to say the words.

"For you not to dip out early next time?" he asks.

Sweat prickles my skin. "There is no next time."

It's going to be green in less than a minute, and this is not the conversation we should be having, especially on a radio where anyone could listen.

"Hey, Tess?"

"What?"

"Don't make that noise again."

My eyebrows furrow. "What noise?"

"The moan you just made when you took a drink of your Diet Coke..."

Oh.

"It sounds an awful lot like–"

"Rome!" I shout.

His chuckle is throaty, and if he could see me, I would flip him off.

Embarrassment stains my cheeks, and I sigh. "Will you please focus on the race? It's minutes from take-off."

"Fine."

Rome's deep breaths filter through my headphones as the race nears, and like a switch, he's ready.

The countdown starts, the beeps matching the rhythm of my heart.

5...4...3...2...1.

I hold my breath when the light turns green.

Take-off is one of the most critical parts of a race. Depending on where you start on line, it decides your position and can limit any overtaking opportunities.

The first few seconds, Rome manages his clutch control, and I stay quiet, trusting that he knows what to do.

I reach for my Diet Coke and take another two mouthfuls, the burn of the soda easing my nerves for a split second.

"Take the outside," I stress.

Rome says nothing.

He does exactly as I say and moves to the outside to come around Vinny. He moves to third, where he started.

"Yes!" I squeeze out between clenched teeth.

"Good call, Princess."

I roll my eyes. "Stop calling me that, anyone could be listening."

He chuckles. "Everyone calls you Vanstone's Princess."

"There's a difference, and you know it."

A few laps pass, and Rome does a phenomenal job holding his position. However, the track is fast, and some of the drivers are driving aggressively, whether on purpose or not, I'm not sure.

"Behind," I say.

Milo King, a driver from the Australia team, is forced off the racing line, causing some unnecessary drama between a few cars. One spins into a curb, the other two nearly sliding against one another.

I wait for the flag to change and stare up ahead.

A blur of yellow catches my eye.

"Yellow..." I announce, blinking a few times.

"Who was it?" Rome asks.

I have an overwhelming urge to sit, so I take a seat.

"Um..." I take a deep breath, but it seems slower than I mean for it to be. "King, I think."

"You think? What?"

I can't focus.

"Sorry, yeah. It's King," I mumble.

"You sound off."

I reach for my drink. "I just...my mouth is dry."

My fingers are outstretched, but I can't seem to reach my cup.

The flag changes colors, and the race resumes, and I can't remember if I said anything.

I finally grab onto the Styrofoam cup and pull it toward me, only it falls from my grasp and spills everywhere.

Dylan curses and grabs me by the arm. "Tessa, are you okay?"

Seconds stretch.

I try to look at him, but there are three of his head, and they're all swaying.

Something is wrong.

My stomach rolls, and a cold sweat breaks out along my forehead.

Rome's voice cuts through the ringing in my ears, the panic catching me off guard.

"Tessa, talk to me."

"Rome?"

"I'm here, Princess. What's wrong? You don't sound right."

I try to talk, but nothing comes out.

"Fuck, I'm pulling into the pits."

"No!" I shriek, except it's delayed.

Suddenly, Beck materializes right in front of me. He grabs onto my arms to steady me and whips off my headset. He puts it on his head, and I know his mouth is moving, but I can't hear him.

I slump forward, my forehead resting on his chest. "I... I...don't feel good."

My body shakes uncontrollably, but everything else is slow.

"Tess." Beck shakes me, and my head wobbles back and forth. "Did you take something?"

I have tunnel vision.

The outer part of my vision narrows, and the last thing I see is Beck's heavy browline and Gia running toward me.

Chapter Thirty-Four

ROME

PANIC TRAVELS to the tips of my fingers as I squeeze the wheel.

I'm going 207 mph on the track and 2,000 mph outside of it.

"Fuck, I'm pulling into the pits," I say.

A noise leaves her, filling every single empty space in my brain. Then comes her refusal, only it's slow. "N–n–no."

I bite down on my tongue to keep myself focused.

My heartrate is all over the place.

There's a shuffle through my headphones, and I blurt, "What the fuck is going on?"

No one answers.

"Tessa!"

One more corner and the pits will be in view.

"Stand by, Rome—medical on the pit wall. Dylan is taking over."

"No, the fuck he isn't."

Static cuts through the radio, mixing with Beck's voice.

"Tess! Did you take something?"

There's a pain in my chest, and worry like I've never felt before gnaws at me.

"I'm pitting."

"Gia, get medical. She just passed out." Beck sounds far away, and I think it's because my heartbeat is too loud inside my ears.

Dylan's voice cuts in. "Rome, stay on course. Finish or you'll be DQ'ed."

Getting disqualified is the least of my worries right now. Does he really think I'll be able to continue on after what I just heard through the radio?

"Call me to the pits now," I snap.

"Rome–"

I growl. "Don't make me regret trusting you, Dylan."

"For fuck's sake. Fine."

A second later, he calls out a feigned strategy check. "Box, box."

I head right for the pits and come to a sudden halt. I'm out of the car within five seconds.

"Goddamnit, Rome." Dylan's hair sticks up in different directions beneath Tessa's headset, his face red and sweaty.

I search around the pit wall. "Where is she?"

If I just get eyes on her, make sure she's okay, I'll be fine.

Dylan tracks my jerky movements as I unzip my race suit. "Are you not finishing the race?"

"That depends," I answer.

I spot an EMT and push past Dylan.

Beck stands above her with his arms crossed and a mirror of the worry I carry on his face.

I'm out of breath when I step in line with him. "What's going on?"

"What the hell are you doing?" Beck looks past me and sees the race still commencing. "Bro, the race!"

Having visual confirmation of her was supposed to make me feel better, but it did the opposite. My stomach tenses, and my heart continues to bang off the inside of my ribs.

It's the exact feeling I had as a young boy when I watched my mom being taken by an ambulance. Only, she never came back.

I shake away the uncomfortable thought and lock onto Tessa.

She's lying there on a stretcher, her rich brown hair a halo around her head. The color is gone from her face, the adorable pink always evident on her cheeks now white. Her head flops to the other side, a line of pain in between her eyebrows.

I step forward when the EMTs head for the ambulance, but Beck puts a hand on my chest and blocks my way toward her.

I bare my teeth, and he lifts an eyebrow.

"I'm going with her," I announce. "Move."

A second of tense silence passes between us. An entire race is happening at our backs, but neither one of us seems to notice.

"Gia," Beck calls out.

She appears out of thin air like a witch.

"Stay and smooth things over with the media. Inform my brothers as soon as you can. Tell them we have it under control and to finish the race."

He looks at me, and we take off into a full-on jog past the rest of the pit walls and their teams.

Pierce Racing is four down from us, my attention snagged by the red and yellow colors that I grew up wearing.

My dad glances at me briefly in between making calls to

Beau on the track.

Time slows.

I recognize the look.

His smirk lacks remorse, and he remains unrepentant, already taking advantage of there being one less driver on the track—and a good one at that.

Anything to win, right, Dad?

Beck calls for a taxi, and I leave my father and Pierce Racing behind.

Once we're settled, I stare after the ambulance in front of us as Beck texts his parents.

I'm certain, by now, the commentators have mentioned that there was a medical emergency on the pit call, and given the fact that I'm no longer racing, they'll know it has something to do with our team.

"What exactly happened?" I ask, my gaze trained on the ambulance.

The lights aren't on, and there is no siren, so that's a good sign. *Right?*

He sighs. "I don't know. Dylan waved me over, and when I got to her, she was disoriented."

My hands begin to sweat.

"Did she say she was going to be sick? Is it food poisoning or something?" My mind is racing, my body filled with more adrenaline than when I was in my car, traveling over two hundred miles per hour.

Beck shakes his head, and for once, he remains quiet.

"Has this happened before?" I ask.

Does she have a medical condition that I'm unaware of? Is this a common thing? Was it nerves?

I clearly don't know everything about her.

Sure, I know the noises she makes when she's turned on, and the way her eyes flutter closed when she's falling over the edge with pleasure. I know the exact shade of her eyes and the way her soft hair feels in between my fingers, but that's all physical.

Now, I find myself wanting to know *everything*.

I want all the in-betweens.

What is she afraid of? Aside from Vanstone, what else does she want in life? Marriage? Kids? Me?

"Rome, come on." Beck is standing outside of the car with the door open.

Thoughts of Tessa's deepest wants and desires scatter when my foot lands on the pavement. I spot her on the stretcher, already hooked up to an IV.

Her eyes open and close, her thick eyelashes drifting up and down. She glances around in confusion, her lips parted and chest moving quicker than it should.

I step into view, and we lock onto one another.

My heart skids to a complete stop.

Tess.

Her tiny shoulders relax, the fear lessening the longer I keep her attention.

I'm here.

Chapter Thirty-Five

TESSA

I CAN'T STAY AWAKE.

Every time I'm able, I peel an eye open, only to close it when I realize how blurry my vision is.

There are voices in and out and a beeping noise.

I shake my head and try my hardest to keep a steady view of what's going on in front of me.

Where am I?

It's so bright in here.

I reach on the top of my head for my sunglasses and pout when I don't find them.

My blinks are slow, and thankfully it helps steady my vision instead of make it worse. There's a TV in the corner, and the race is on.

I sit up quickly. I fling the blankets off my legs and scrunch my nose at the hospital gown I'm wearing.

Vague snippets of what happened fill my fuzzy head, but I push them away to get back to the race.

"The race," I mutter. "I have to get back."

"Tess."

I let go of the bed and buckle at the knees.

Rome reacts quickly and wraps an arm around my lower back, pressing me to the front of his body.

"Lie down, Princess."

Gently, he guides me back to my bed and sits me on the edge of it. He bends at the knee, his race suit bundled around his waist, to scoop my legs up and over before covering them with the blanket.

He sits in the chair beside my bed, his attention on me instead of the race. "How are you feeling?"

"Confused." I fight through the throbbing in my temples. "Why aren't you in the race?"

He blinks slowly. "Because you're in the hospital."

I rest my head against the pillow. "That's why I'm not there. I asked why you weren't."

Rome's blue eyes dart, and I think I see a pinkish hue spread across his face. "You really think I could've kept racing after knowing something was wrong with you?"

"You should've." I close my eyes, too tired to keep them open.

"I couldn't."

The heart monitor starts to beep a little faster than before, which is more than annoying. Whose side is it on? Mine or Rome's?

"I've never known Rome Pierce to stop racing for anything," I whisper.

Rome leans forward, elbows on his knees. "Well, then I guess you're not just anything."

My pulse jumps, Rome's attention moving to the heart monitor.

He leans even closer to the bed. "You like knowing I care about you, Princess?"

I cross my arms and tuck my chin. "No."

His deep chuckle makes my toes curl. "Yes, you do."

The door opens, cutting our conversation short.

Out of the corner of my eye, I watch Rome turn the TV off, the race no longer important.

A tall, tanned-skin man in a white coat comes around the bed. "How are you feeling, Ms. Halston?"

His accent is thick, but I manage to understand him. "I'm tired," I say.

And confused for more reasons than one.

He nods. "Understandable."

Rome interjects himself with his eyebrows knitted. "Did the test results come back? Do you have answers as to what happened?"

The doctor glances at me and then back to him.

What? What isn't he saying?

"Tessa, did you happen to take anything today?" He flips a paper on the clipboard. "Like any medication?"

I shake my head.

"What about drugs?"

I bundle the bedsheets in my fingers. "What? Of course not."

"Are you sure?" he asks, clearly not convinced.

"She said no," Rome repeats. "Don't make her say it again."

The doctor glances at Rome briefly then back to me.

"Then someone drugged you."

My heart sinks, and the room narrows. "What?"

"Excuse me?" Rome's voice is distant.

I channel through the events before the race and can't come up with a logical reason for what the doctor is saying.

"Did anyone give you something? Food? Or a drink that wasn't sealed?"

"No—" I lock onto Rome.

His face pales, and he turns back to the doctor. "Are you saying someone spiked her drink?"

"If she is telling the truth that she didn't ingest the medication on her own, then yes."

"I don't take medication, and I certainly don't do drugs," I stress.

Rome stands and ends up in between the doctor and me. "What medication?" he asks, voice throaty.

"Inderal." The doctor sighs. "It's used for anxiety or sometimes a heart condition. It can lower blood pressure and heart rate, likely why she fainted. It can also make an individual feel slow, or heavy, maybe having slurred words and confusion."

Rome's fists clench.

A cold sweat breaks out on my forehead, and I slowly lower myself back to my pillow. Exhaustion settles in again, my limbs heavy.

"We're going to keep her here for a little longer to make sure her blood pressure stays steady, but then she should be okay to be discharged."

Rome scoffs. "Should?"

The doctor attempts to hide his amusement, turning around with a half-smirk. "I misspoke. She will be fine to be discharged."

Then he walks out, leaving me and Rome alone in a tiny hospital room with too many unanswered questions.

His back remains rigid, the long-sleeve white undershirt stretched across his taut muscles.

I exhale slowly.

Seconds pass, and he doesn't make a sound. I peek an eye open, and he stands in the same spot, spine stiff.

"Rome?" I rasp.

His piercing blue eyes find me over his shoulder, and

flutters fly to my lower stomach. The whites of his eyes are stark against the blue, his eyes wide and breathing shallow. "Tell me you know I wouldn't do that."

I place my hands on the bed and sit up tall. "Of course you wouldn't. Why would I think that?"

He turns around and walks the short distance to me. He peers at me, a line of worry on his forehead. "I was the one who ordered the drink, Tessa." He runs a hand through his unruly, dark hair. "Your first thought wasn't that I drugged you to create some kind of chaos within the team to overtake it in the end?"

I flinch backward and repeat what he says in my head.

A month ago, I probably would've jumped to that conclusion right away and threatened his life. Today, the thought didn't even occur to me.

I don't know what that says about me, or us, but it means something.

"N...no," I stammer. "The thought didn't cross my mind once."

Rome stares at me for so long my heart rate rises again. He glances to the monitor and then back to me before making his way around the bed to sit in the chair. With his legs out wide, he leans back with his arms crossed against his chest, seemingly lost in his head.

My eyelids grow heavy, and I think I fall asleep for a short time before springing awake. Concern is still etched onto Rome's face.

"Don't tell my brothers someone drugged me," I mutter.

His shoulders fall. "Tess."

"No." I shake my head slowly. "They'll tell my parents, and my dad will worry. The stress is too hard on his heart. It was probably a mistake anyway. The medication is for anxiety, someone probably had it mixed in their drink, and it was given to me by accident."

Rome swallows slowly. "And if it wasn't?"

I shrug. "I guess they'll have to try harder next time."

He glares at me, and I sink back onto the bed with a half-smile and drowsiness.

"What do you want me to tell them?" he asks a short while later.

I curl up on my side and face him, my eyelids too heavy to keep open for long. "I trust you to figure it out," I say.

His eyebrow flicks upward. "So you trust me now, Princess?"

It's too hard to hide a smile, so I don't. "Well, you did stop in the middle of a race to make sure I was okay...so yeah, I guess I do."

Seconds stretch into minutes, and I think I fall asleep, until something soft strokes against my cheek. I'm pretty sure it's Rome's thumb.

Chapter Thirty-Six

ROME

BECK HAS CHANGED *the group name.*

Salmonella—or Salmontessa

I glance at him from the other seat in the hospital room and shake my head. He's typing away on his phone with a shit-eating grin on his face.

For the record, I didn't say anything about Tessa having Salmonella poisoning. Just that she had a virus the night prior and was dehydrated, causing her blood pressure to drop.

My phone goes off again, and I glance up to make sure Tessa is still asleep. Every time I lay eyes on her, my heartrate slows, like she's my calm in the raging chaos.

BECK

Don't worry, fellas. Tess is fine.

NOAH

Food poisoning? What did she eat?

GRAHAM

I thought you shit yourself when you had food poisoning? Isn't that what you did, Beck?

VAN

He did. All over Mom and Dad's bathroom.

Noah has changed the group name.

Beck is the Reason We Can't Have Nice Bathroom Rugs.

GRAHAM

I swipe out of the texts and open my search engine. I shield my phone so Beck can't see and type in the name of the medication the doctor mentioned. My fingers clench around my phone as the information pops up.

The room tilts on its side.

The nagging truth buried beneath a layer of denial grows like a fucking weed.

Inderal, also known as propranolol...

Propranolol.

I shut my eyes and travel back in the past. The pill bottle appears, along with tiny, orange pills scattered in father's hand. He took one before every race, like some type of good-luck charm.

I stand abruptly, and Beck jerks in his seat.

"Are you about to throw up?" he asks, panicked.

"I have to head back to the track." The lie effortlessly leaves my mouth. "Gia texted, and she wants me to meet with the media to explain my reasons for not finishing the race."

"Good luck with that," he chuckles.

I glance at Tessa, nestled on her side. A piece of her long brown hair lies over her face, and my fingers twitch to move it out of the way, but I've already shown my cards once today to the public. I can't allude to anything else.

Not with her brother watching.

On the way back to the track, with my gut churning the closer I get, a text comes in from Vince.

VINCE

Most team owners would hang you dry for doing what you did today.

I'm aware. My own father would have beat me.

VINCE

But most fathers would thank you.

ME

Which one are you right now?

The taxi comes to a stop near the back of the track, and I slip out in an attempt to blend in.

VINCE

I'm a father first. Always.

ME

Then you're welcome.

I shove my phone in my pocket and quickly remember why I'm here in the first place.

Gia didn't text me, but I know the media will want me to comment on what happened, and I will.

But first, I have something else to take care of.

Most of the crews are busy taking things down and

loading up their gear. A few nod as I pass, but the rest are too busy to notice me.

The yellow-and-red tent pulls me like a magnet.

My knuckles ache with anger as I stand outside of it. I crack my neck and flex my fingers before curling them into fists at my sides.

I step inside, and Beau has a girl on his lap with his hand in between her legs.

She turns and yelps.

"Get out," I rumble.

Beau leans past the half-undressed fan. "Wrong tent, bud. Remember?"

I shift my glare to his plaything, and she quickly jumps from his lap to scurry away. He stands and pulls his pants up to charge me.

My veins fill with an eagerness.

I wait until he's less than a foot away and plow my closed fist into his jaw.

The shock renders him motionless, but I'm quick on my feet.

I grab him by the collar of his shirt and haul him toward me.

"Did you know?" I seethe.

"What the fuck?" Bloody spit flies from his mouth. "This is a suspension, minimum. Wait until I get the FIA involved and tell them you just came into *my* private tent and fucking hit me."

My lip curls with anger. "You really want to get the FIA involved? Because they won't just investigate me, but you too. And I'm not sure you want them that close to Pierce Racing."

"This again?" He moves to shove me away, and this time, I let him.

He stumbles backward and wipes his bloody mouth on his shirt. "You're just angry because you can't handle losing. Did punching me make you feel better about not finishing the race today?" He rolls his eyes. "Taking after your dad, huh?"

My skin burns from quiet fury.

There is no other insult that would get me this worked up.

"Answer my fucking question," I seethe.

"And what question is that?" a familiar voice asks.

Beau shifts, and a chill works itself down my spine. I turn with my body tense.

It's like looking into a mirror.

The only difference between me and my father is the gray peppered throughout this dark hair. We share the same blue eyes and square jaw. His thirst for winning was passed down to me for years—until I left. I never thought I'd be able to quench it, but it turns out I have a thirst for something else, and it isn't necessarily winning.

My father raises an eyebrow in a challenge, but he should know me better than to think I'll back down.

On steady feet, I walk the short distance over to him and look him straight in the eye. Surprise takes over when I grab onto his Pierce Racing jacket and give it a shake. I hear the sound of pills rattle against a bottle. I shake my head with disappointment.

His eye twitches, a sign that he's irritated, yet he still manages a sick smile. "How's the youngest Halston kid? What's her name again?" he asks, chuckling. "Tes–"

My hand snaps to his throat, and his eyes widen. I bask in his sudden shock and squeeze his windpipe for good measure. "If you *ever* fucking do something like that again,

I'll rip that fucking NDA you forced me to sign to shreds and take you down with me."

Fuck the legal fees.

Fuck the future of my career.

Fuck my reputation.

Fuck Pierce Racing.

I force myself to step away. My hands shake with adrenaline, and I have to look elsewhere before I do something that neither of us will be able to brush under the rug tomorrow.

My father exhales, but it comes out like a growl. "Is that a threat, son?"

"It's a warning, and it's the only fucking one you're getting. Son or not."

He grins, but I see right through it.

I storm past him, and he grabs me by the arm. I turn sharply with flared nostrils, and he immediately releases me. However, his glare remains.

"Mom was right about you," I mutter. "And so was Vince."

His ears turn red.

I look him dead in the eye and shake my head. "It's a shame I didn't see it until you almost killed me."

Chapter Thirty-Seven

TESSA

I GROGGILY SNUGGLE into something soft. A wistful sigh leaves me when my hand touches something warm. I move closer to the heat and get comfortable.

"Will you stop groping me?"

My eyes spring open, and a purplish-blue light glimmers above Rome's sexy smirk in my direction.

I pop up quickly and scramble off his lap to search for Beck.

"Relax, Princess." Rome reaches forward and pushes my hair behind my ear. "Beck's in the cockpit with the pilot, pestering him instead of me."

I skip my attention toward the front of the jet and relax when I see the closed barrier.

His attention flutters over my face. "How are you feeling?"

"Not you too," I say in a raspy voice. "I'm fine."

My brothers playfully poked fun at me for what happened at the race, but given the fact that they drew straws to see which one of them was going to hop a ride on Rome's jet to keep an eye on me shows they're worried.

I shove the thin blanket off my legs and stand to stretch, only I'm not as stable as I think. A dizzy spell hits me, and my body sways.

Rome palms my hips and pulls me toward him. I land on his lap in a straddle, and his eyes light up.

"First you grope me, and now you're straddling me? All while knowing we could be caught at any given second?" He shakes his head. "You're full of trouble, Princess."

My heart flutters.

"I fell," I whisper.

"Funny you should say that." He eyes my mouth. "Me too."

A soft breath slips from my parted lips, repeating what he just said in my head to dissect it, but my thoughts scatter when one of his hands grazes my spine slowly. I shift above him, my stomach somersaulting from the growing pressure in between my legs.

"And you think I'm the troublemaker?" I rub against him with my eyebrow cocked.

A slow swallow moves against his neck. "I think you like it."

It's becoming more and more clear to me that I like a lot about Rome Pierce, despite all the reasons not to.

I gently raise a shoulder, flicking my attention between his eyes. "Maybe," I whisper.

Rome grabs the side of my face, his fingers lost in my hair. He brings me closer, our breath mingling as we stare at each other.

"I don't like the way I felt earlier," he admits.

"What do you mean?" I ask quietly.

His hand squeezes my hip, like a warning. "When I heard Beck call for an ambulance..." his words fade, and he shifts away.

"Tell me," I beg.

I'm desperate to hear the words he shouldn't be saying. My skin heats from the wait, the air around us charged with something so electrifying that I'm afraid if either of us moves, something will snap.

Rome's edgy features soften, the grip on my hip light. "I was terrified." He shakes his head back and forth slowly, his gaze pinned to mine. "Nothing has ever come between me and racing...until you."

My teeth sink into my bottom lip. "That doesn't sound like a good thing," I admit guiltily.

He huffs out a laugh. His fingers dive into my hair farther, and our faces move closer so our mouths are a breath away. "I disagree."

I sink into him as our lips touch. I whimper in desperation, and he shushes me before going in for more.

The kiss is deep.

Rome's mouth swallows mine, like he can't get enough, and I'm right there to match every single stroke. My hips move on their own, my legs spread wider around his thighs, desperate to add fuel to the passion.

I lose my breath from the faint tracing of Rome's fingers skimming the inside of my leg.

A sharp gasp comes between us with the touch of him moving my sleep shorts to the side, and I tremble everywhere.

"Stay quiet," he whispers, breaking the kiss for a second before sealing our mouths again.

My nipples tighten with one swipe of his thumb. I bite down onto his lip, and his chest rumbles.

I arch my back with his finger inside of me, his palm against my clit. I move my body, too driven by lust to care that my brother could walk in at any given second.

"So perfect." His words flutter across my neck, his lips pressing there next.

"Rome." I force his name between my lips, and his shush brushes against my skin.

"You have to stay quiet, Princess. I'll make you feel good, but just stay quiet."

The thought alone sends me spiraling.

He palms my ass, his fingers delving beneath my shorts while he works me into a frenzy at the front. I grind over his hand and chase ecstasy like my life depends on it.

"That's it," he encourages in a low, gruff tone. "You're doing so good being quiet."

His words are like gasoline to a fire. My body burns bright, the orgasm right there, dangling in front of me, until I'm tipped over the edge and melting right into his hands.

He forces his thumb between my lips. "Stay quiet, baby."

In the midst of riding out my orgasm, I open my mouth and suck on his thumb to keep quiet.

He curses under his breath, my body making a complete mess between my legs.

Wow.

That was *hot.*

Once he realizes I'm slowing down, he pulls his thumb from my mouth. He runs the pad of it over my bottom lip. His fingers stay inside of me as he peers up at me with hunger.

"I have never witnessed something so fucking beautiful before in my life," he says in awe.

My cheeks warm, and I send him a tiny smile.

"Come to my house later," he pleads.

I don't have it in me to deny him. I nod, and he exhales, like he was holding his breath until I agreed.

A noise sounds from the cockpit, and I hastily scramble from his lap. Rome grabs the blanket I was using earlier and bundles it on his lap to hide his erection. I shut my eyes and pretend I'm still asleep so Beck can't see the flush on my neck.

Rome shifts, and my foot just so happens to end up on top of his lap. There's a shift in the air, and I know my brother has walked out of the cockpit.

"If she knew she had her legs on you in her sleep, she'd probably kick you in the balls," he says with humor.

Rome huffs out a fake laugh, and I smile to myself. I subtly press down on his hard length, just to mess with him, and his entire body stiffens.

A few seconds pass, and his hand wraps around my ankle. He gives it a good squeeze, and I happily drift back off to sleep, eager for time to pass.

Only this time, it isn't to get away from Rome, but to get *closer*.

Chapter Thirty-Eight

ROME

IT'S hard to keep my attention elsewhere.

Especially with Tessa sitting directly across from me at her parents' dining room table.

No more than three hours ago, I had her in my bed without a single piece of clothing on. That's all I can think about. Each time she wraps her rosy lips around the end of the straw, I have to force myself to look away.

She's doing it again.

I chew my bite of salad slowly, not even noticing the acidic bite of the vinaigrette dressing. The fork slips from my fingers and clatters to my plate.

Everyone glances up from their food, even Vivian.

Tessa has me wrapped around her pretty little finger, and from the looks of her grin behind her napkin, she knows it.

Vince clears his throat, pulling the attention away from me. "Have you taken a look at the weather this week? It's going to be cooler than the previous year for the upcoming race." He pulls out his phone with his wife pursing her lips from him using it at the table.

Tessa's fork hovers in the air in front of her mouth, seemingly frozen. She looks as if she's been caught doing something she shouldn't, and unless her father turns his phone and there's photo proof of us together, then it's fine.

However, I'm not sure how long we can keep this up.

What even is *this*?

"It'll get down to forty-nine the night of the race, according to this model." Vince furrows his brow while gazing at his phone screen.

The color on Tessa's face has drained. She's less lively, and I don't really like it.

"Grip is going to be touchy," Noah adds.

I'm still staring at Tessa.

It isn't until she nudges me with her foot that I snap out of it.

"Yeah, means we can't fully trust the sim this week," I add.

"You're breaking the rules!" Vivian shouts, drawing the attention to her. "No talking about racing at the dinner table! That's all you talk about! It's all you care about."

Van sighs, "Vivian."

Her bottom lip wobbles, and then she slips out from her chair and takes off through the back door.

Tessa stares after her niece with a frown.

Again, I don't like it.

"That's what I'm referring to," Rose says softly to Van. "She's been having these emotional outbursts lately."

I look past my plate at the opened back door. "Can I go after her?"

Noah chuckles. "Since when are you a therapist?"

"You?" Van questions suspiciously.

My shoulders tense, and I shift my gaze to Tessa. She stares at me with those curious doe-like eyes, and it knocks down one of my carefully constructed walls. "I used to do the same thing as a kid."

"I remember that," Vince notes.

Tessa looks from me to her dad, her brows pulled inward.

Unfortunately, he knows a lot more about me than anyone else at this table.

Or at least, what I was like as a kid.

Van drops his shoulders. "If you think you can fix it..."

I scoot my chair out. "I'm not sure I can fix it, but I can relate."

Beck catches my ear on my way to the door. "Okay, fine. Rome isn't as big of an asshole as I thought he'd be."

"No, but his dad sure is," Graham says.

If only they knew half the shit Vince and I know.

Then there's the fact that he spiked Tessa's drink for a better advantage against our team—something I can't seem to admit to anyone, not even her, because the truth of the matter is that I'm partly to blame.

It's no longer a rival between Pierce Racing and Vanstone. It's too dirty and corrupt for that now. It's something much more dangerous, and if the FIA doesn't catch on soon, I may have to follow through with my threat and ruin myself just to ruin him.

Faint sniffles pull on my heartstrings the closer I get to the tree in the center of the Halstons' backyard.

With steady steps, I walk across the soft grass until the tree branches are a canopy above me. Instead of telling Vivian to climb down, I place one foot on the trunk with my hand on the branch above and pull myself up to her.

She wipes her wet cheek and turns away. "Go away."

"You know, I think you're just as stubborn as your Aunt Tessa."

Vivian remains quiet and flips a braid off her shoulder. She does her best not to sniffle again, because she doesn't want me to know she's crying.

"When I was your age, I had my very own hide-out deep in the forest. I made it myself." I turn, and my legs dangle off our branch. "It had a blanket, some water bottles, and snacks."

It had a photo of my mom too because I was so naive that I thought having her photo with the torn edges was going to make everything better.

It takes Vivian a few minutes, but eventually her childish voice cuts through the silence. "Why in the forest? So no one could find you?"

I shake my head. "No one cared to come find me."

And there goes another wall tumbling down for a Halston.

She turns to look at me, her tear-streaked face the first thing I notice. "That's sad," she says.

"It is, and it's not something I share with just anyone." I raise my brow. "So you better keep my secret."

She stares at me before looking at the grassy ground beneath us.

I hear footsteps in the distance, but whoever it is stays hidden. It isn't until a familiar floral scent swirls with the light breeze that I realize it's Tessa.

Reaching forward, I tug on one of Vivian's braids. She glowers at me, and I grin. "Besides me, does anyone else look for you when you run away?"

She nods.

"Who?"

"Everyone."

"Do you know why?" I ask.

She turns away and shrugs. "Because..."

I tug on her braid again, and she looks over at me. "Because they care about more than just racing."

She thinks for a second. "Do you?"

I toss a piece of bark at her. "I'm here, aren't I?"

Her nose scrunches, and she tries to hide a smile, just like Tessa does ninety percent of the time.

"I once heard Aunt Tess say that you were an arrow and cared about nothing except winning."

I repeat the word in my head and chuckle. "An arrow?"

"Arrogant!" Tessa whisper-shouts from below.

Vivian peers at her and smiles wide. "Catch me."

Without warning, she slips from the branch and lands in Tessa's arms with an *"Umph."*

"What are you doing up there with him?" Tessa asks her. "Don't you remember our motto?"

What motto?

Vivian nods excitedly.

Tessa pokes her belly. "Start it..."

"Girls rule..." Vivian gazes at her aunt, who just so happens to be peeking at me with a pretty smile on her face.

"And boys drool," Tess finishes.

They high-five, and Tessa whispers something in her ear. Vivian's eyes light up, and she hops out of Tessa's arms, barreling toward the door, leaving me with my sneaky, glitter-eyed eavesdropper.

"What did you say to her?" I ask.

She glances at the back door. "I told her that Uncle Beck was taking her to get milkshakes for everyone." Her soft laugh settles me in every way. "It was a lie, but he can't say no to her."

"Kind of like how I can't say no to you?" I mutter.

Tessa rolls her eyes and then looks at the trunk of the tree.

"Well, what are you waiting for?" I ask. "Get up here."

She peers behind her and then back to me.

I cock an eyebrow with a silent challenge and watch her walk over to the tree with a grin plastered on my face.

Chapter Thirty-Nine

TESSA

"KEEP YOUR HANDS TO YOURSELF," I warn, taking hold of his hand.

He hauls me toward the branch, and I straddle it before scooting back against the trunk.

"I'm serious," I add. "My parents have cameras."

Rome leans forward to look through the tree branches. "They do? Where?"

"Worried I'll watch it and overhear all the secrets you told Vivian?"

Those soul-crushing blue eyes shift to me. "As if you didn't already hear them?"

My cheeks heat, so I turn away to play it off. "What are you talking about?"

Rome snorts out a laugh. "You're a terrible liar, Princess."

I cross my arms. "I hate when you call me that."

Without looking up at him, I know he's staring at me. Each time his eyes scan me up and down, it's like a trail of flames brush against my skin.

"See?" His voice drops. "Terrible liar."

I nibble on the inside of my cheek and stare at the pieces of bark chipping away from the tree.

"Was that true?" I ask. "Everything you said to her?"

I spread my fingers along the branch, the splintered parts cutting into my palm. My heart anxiously beats, waiting for his answer, like I'm afraid he's going to lie.

"I may be an arrow, but I'm not a liar. Of course it was true."

My lips twitch, a beg for me to laugh, but I don't because my next question blurts out too quickly. "Even the part about you caring about more than just racing?"

This time, I can't help but look at him. His head tilts, the setting sun painting a glare on the side of his face.

"A month ago?" He turns away with a shake of his head. "I would have said no. The only thought in my head aside from tormenting you was winning the cup and beating the shit out of my dad's team."

I huff out a laugh. "Kind of like how the only thought in my head, aside from not being able to stand you, was proving myself as a female engineer in a male-dominated industry."

He grins from the side. "And now look at you, up here all alone in a tree with me."

I swing my legs back and forth. "And I haven't threatened to push you off once."

He turns with a half-smirk waiting for me. "The night isn't over, Princess."

"And neither is the season."

Rome's smile slips, and the space between us grows tight.

I fiddle with the bark again, afraid to look into his eyes for too long. I came out here for a reason, and it's taken less than a minute with him to forget why.

I force a breath through my lips and stare at his hands against the branch. "Sitting at the dinner table, I decided I was going to come out here and tell you we needed to stop whatever it is we're doing."

The cords in Rome's forearms flicker. "Because your dad mentioned the weather conditions for the race."

My spine presses against the trunk. *How did he know?*

"I'm a distraction," he adds.

He is. A *big* one.

"I haven't bothered to think about the next race since touching down from Spain," I admit. "It's so unlike me."

"Would it make you feel better to know that I haven't thought much about it either?" he asks.

We both know why neither of us has paid attention, and being this wrapped up in something—*someone*—is dangerous, especially when there's so much at stake for both of us.

His career.

My career.

Both of our reputations.

If there's even a single slight between us, those things all come crumbling down.

"Whatever I do to you...you do it to me too." He gazes at me from across the branch, the truth written all over his face. "You always have."

A frown pulls at my lips. "What do you mean?"

"There's always been something about you, Tess. Even when we were kids, before your dad left Pierce Racing, I was drawn to you." He glances at me briefly. "Don't you remember me always coming to your rescue when your brothers would torment you? Or what about the time you bumped into the tire trolley, and one of the tires clipped my dad's ankle?"

The memory plays out like a movie in front of my eyes.

"I forgot about that," I whisper.

He stays quiet.

"You took the blame."

"I couldn't bear the thought of him yelling at you," he admits.

I wince, remembering what happened next. "He hit you."

Rome crosses his arms and gazes at the side of my house. "And your dad stepped in to smooth things over, like always."

"I'm beginning to think my dad knows more about you than I do."

"Why do you think he let me join Vanstone?" he asks. "Despite your earlier assumptions, it isn't to take it out from beneath him. That's something Lucas Pierce would do, and honestly..." A swallow works down Rome's throat. "I'd wreck a thousand times over again if it meant knowing the truth."

He snaps his eyes to mine, the shock evident in every little movement he makes. The way his hands curl around the branch, the tense bunching of his shoulders with corded muscles straining along his neck.

I sit up taller against the trunk. "The truth?"

"Fuck." He squeezes the bridge of his nose, his eyes clenching shut. "You're going to have to let that one slide, Princess."

"And if I can't?" I blurt.

His hand drops, and he looks to the ground instead of at me. "You have to."

My mind spins, old memories of Pierce Racing and a younger Rome filling every tiny void.

Rome jumps down from the branch and lands on sturdy

feet. I quickly lean forward and find him staring up at me with his arms out wide.

He wants me to jump? Now?

He calls up to me, "You don't trust me?"

"Should I?" I ask.

His chest expands, his arms remaining open. Without thinking, I swing my legs over and jump. He catches me with ease, one arm under my legs and the other pressed against my back.

I wrap my arms around his neck and look into his eyes. "I guess I do trust you," I say. "But I don't think you trust me."

The grinding of his teeth is loud enough to hear over the breeze in the air. I almost reach up to grab his jaw so he'll loosen it.

"I trust you more than I've ever trusted anyone, Tess."

I wiggle in his grip, and he places me on flat feet. I cross my arms. "Then why won't you tell me?"

"I already told you that I can't." He swallows. "It's not that I won't tell you; it's that I can't tell you." His hands disappear into the pockets of his jeans. "And that has to be good enough for now."

Before I'm able to say anything else, my dad's voice echoes into the yard. "Rome?"

We both look to the porch just as my dad walks through the back door.

"Meet me in the den. I have to talk to you..." My dad glances at me with a soft smile. "Alone."

Rome starts past me but not before whispering, "Just trust me, Tess."

I don't say anything, but I do trust him.

Chapter Forty

ROME

VINCE SLIDES his phone across his desk. "Did you do this?"

I already know what it is before scanning the photo on the screen.

"I didn't peg you for someone who reads GRID," I say.

Vince makes a noise that resembles a chuckle, though there isn't much humor on his face. "I don't. An old colleague sent it to me. Apparently, when asked, Beau answered by telling them that another driver—who shall remain anonymous—came into his quarters and sucker punched him."

"Or my dad slapped him around like he used to do to me."

Vince leans back in his chair.

Instead of meeting him eye to eye, I scan his office and every last accomplishment he has achieved.

It's impressive.

"My dad really couldn't stand that you were better than him," I joke. "He'd probably burn this office to the ground if he saw it."

"He also can't stand that you're better than him," Vince stresses. "You need to be careful out there. Watchful."

I grip the sides of the chair I'm sitting in, my hands wrapping around the arms tightly.

He has no idea just how watchful I have to be—on and off the track.

"And you should keep your hands to yourself too."

My chest tightens, and all I can think about is my hands on his daughter. The curve of her hips, the tight buds of her breasts against my palms, her soft, velvet-like skin.

"The FIA won't tolerate physical violence," he adds.

What about a driver becoming obsessed with his engineer?

Or how he's sleeping with the team owner's daughter?

I shove the thoughts away and say, "But the FIA tolerates illegal modifications to cars and cheating?"

His lips pull into a hard line. "His time will come, Rome. Like I always say, what goes around comes around."

I'm not sure about that.

Things are getting worse, and the secrets I'm continuing to keep because of a flimsy little piece of paper that tells me to have begun weighing on me. It wasn't so much of a problem when I was only worried about myself. But things have changed.

"Grandpa!"

I swing around in my chair. Vivian skips into Vince's office without so much as a knock, carrying a cow-print plastic cup with a purple straw coming out the top.

"A milkshake for me?" His eyebrows rise to his hairline.

She nods. "Yeah, but it's sugar free."

"Of course," he mumbles grumpily. "Whose idea was that?"

She hands over the cup. "Grandma."

"Excuse me..." I throw my hands out. "Where's mine?"

Vivian smiles with smeared ice cream surrounding her mouth. "Tessa took it because she said she was in the mood for chocolate instead of strawberry."

"She took my milkshake?" I narrow my gaze at Vince's opened office door.

Vivian giggles when I stand up and pretend to be angry.

She climbs on Vince's lap to steal some of his milkshake. "I told her she better hide from you."

"Where is she?" I ask.

Vivian scrunches her nose. "I can't tell you where she is! Remember...girls rule and boys drool!"

"Fair enough. I'll find her myself."

"Good luck!" Vivian calls from behind.

I leave Vince's office and stand against the wall next to the door. I pull out my phone and click on the **_Halston Siblings + Rome_** group text.

ME

If Tessa were hiding with my milkshake, where would she be?

VAN

Ask Vivian.

ME

I did, and she hit me with 'girls rule and boys drool'

TESSA

That's my girl.

I grin.

ME

Don't drink my milkshake.

> **TESSA**
>
> Too late.
>
> **BECK**
>
> When we were kids, she used to hide in the dryer.

"I forgot Tessa used to hide in the dryer," Noah laughs from the living room. "She never did it again after I turned it on that one time."

"Noah!" Rose scolds her son. "What?"

"It was for, like, three seconds," Graham adds. "And she was six."

> **BECK**
>
> Check the towel closet upstairs. She's short enough to fit in there.

Suddenly, there's a thump from above and then quick footsteps that follow it.

I chuckle and make my way to the stairs.

I've never been upstairs, and I can't help but wonder what Tessa's room looks like. Is it the same as when she was young? Or have Rose and Vince turned it into something else? A guest room? Another trophy room?

With every step I take, I look at each framed photo of the Halstons.

The first was taken on some sort of ski trip, with a young Tessa on Vince's shoulders, her brothers in the snow below. The next is a camping trip–all the kids with a marshmallow on the end of a stick, except for Beck. From the looks of his puffed cheeks, he has several stuffed in his mouth. There's a beach photo beside that one and then one of Tessa in a cap and gown with her pink cheeks and bright smile, her brothers standing beside her with their arms around each other.

The last one makes me pause.

It's as if the picture comes to life right in front of my eyes, with Tessa reaching out of the photo to squeeze my heart.

She's holding a baby wrapped in a pink blanket, who I assume is Vivian, with tears in her eyes as she smiles into the camera. Van stares at his daughter from behind Tessa's shoulder with the rest of her brothers in the same stance.

Fuck me.

The first wall I ever built around myself is starting to crumble, and Tessa is right at the center of it.

I want a family and a home full of laughter. I want someone as worthy as Tessa to be there at the end of the day with soft eyes and a warm heart. I want our children to be exact replicas of her, and I want them to be able to count on me for encouragement and strength, not disappointment and fear.

A thick swallow works itself down my throat, and I continue on my way up the stairs. I move from room to room, searching high and low for Tessa.

Never mind the milkshake—I want her.

"Where are you, Princess?" I whisper.

My heart beats for something other than myself, and I chase it like I'll never survive without it.

I push open the last door and smile to myself at the light-purple walls. There's a checkered-print blanket on the bed and a bulletin board above a tidy desk that is full of inspirational quotes. There's a certificate hanging crookedly by a single pushpin that says, *Tessa Halston, Voted Most Responsible,* with her high school name and the year she graduated below.

I trace my finger over her dresser and pause to look into the mirror. In the reflection, I spot her crouched beneath her desk, tucked behind the chair.

"Ugh!"

She scoots the chair away to stand and rolls her eyes playfully with the cow-print cup thrusted in my direction. "I guess you can have the rest since you found me."

I reach for the cup, our fingers brushing as I take it from her. "I don't want the milkshake," I say.

A quizzical look takes over her face, but it's gone as soon as I grab onto her wrist and haul her into my chest. Her sweet, chocolate-scented breath hits my face, and I breathe her in.

"I want you, Tessa. Fuck the milkshake."

Chapter Forty-One

"HERE?" I squeak.

I lean my face into the palm of his hand when he winds his fingers through my hair. I run my tongue against my lips, licking away the leftover chocolate.

Rome presses his forehead against mine, and my stomach flutters. "Everywhere."

There's something different lingering as he stares at me —a silent pleading or maybe desperation.

His other hand falls to my chin, keeping my face steady, as he leans in to kiss me.

My childhood bedroom fades in the background as I give in to him. I'm weightless and floating away with each stroke of his tongue against mine. He palms my hips, and my hands land on his strong shoulders. He moves us over to my dresser and plops me down so he can stand between my legs.

Goosebumps rush to my arms from the flitting of his fingers against my skin as he toys with the hem of my shirt. I arch my back as he pulls it from my body. It falls to the floor.

"This is risky." I move to unbutton my jeans.

Rome helps me in between placing hurried kisses against my lips.

"What is?" He's out of breath, both of our jeans on the floor beneath his feet. "Me taking you in your childhood bedroom or..."

I let my head fall backward when his fingers delve beneath my panties to slide them down my legs.

"Or what?" I ask breathlessly.

"Or how fucking in love I am with you."

I snap to attention.

My heavy breasts press against his chest, his heart beating so violently they thump against my skin.

I suck in a mouthful of air when he pushes into me.

His eyes shut, and he rests his forehead against mine.

"What did you just say?" I ask breathlessly.

Rome moves his mouth over my ear, his fingers digging into my skin as he grips my waist. "I said...that I'm in love with you."

Everything stops.

My breathing.

My heart.

"Now, tell me, Princess..." Rome's teeth skim my earlobe, and I'm floating. "Has anyone taken you in your childhood bedroom before? Or will I be the first?"

He pulls back, and our eyes lock. The fall is endless when it comes to him. I just continue to slip right into his arms.

I shake my head slowly.

"So I'll be the first?"

I nod.

"Thank God," he murmurs.

Our lips collide, and we can't seem to get close enough.

I meet him halfway with every slow thrust. His hands are everywhere. *He's* everywhere.

I look up into his eyes, and he pushes in deeper. He keeps a hold of my gaze, sliding out slowly before doing it again.

"Rome." His name quietly falls off my lips.

The build-up is too much.

I'm not sure where I start and he ends. Everything is messy, in the most wholesome way.

I dig my fingers into his shoulders when the knot in my lower stomach begins to untie.

"Let yourself fall over the edge," he murmurs against my mouth. "I'll catch you."

My orgasm starts off slow, unraveling thread by thread before it completely takes over, and I'm lost. I don't know where I am, and I don't care.

Rome puts his hand over my mouth to keep my moans quiet. His head falls to my shoulder, and then he stills inside of me a heartbeat later. Heat mingles in between my legs, and I'm on fire.

There's a light sheen of sweat on his hairline when he slowly leans back, his hands still wrapped around my waist, keeping me still.

"Wow," I whisper.

It's the only thing I can say.

Rome nods.

Seconds stretch, our eyes both bouncing back and forth between each other, with so many quiet thoughts lingering.

"Aunt Tessa?" Vivian calls from the hallway. "Did Rome find you?"

Rome panics. "Fuck."

He's out of me within a second, and we both bend in

search of our pants. Rome zips his jeans up, and I'm still searching for my panties.

"Oh, fuck it," I hiss, quickly shoving one leg in my jeans and then the other before Rome is pulling on the denim and zipping them for me.

I tug my shirt over my head, and the door opens just as Rome swipes my panties up off the floor and into his pocket.

"You found her!" Vivian shifts her attention from Rome to the mostly melted milkshake on the dresser.

He swipes it off the dresser. "Don't even think about it," he warns, raising a brow. "It's mine." His lips wrap around the straw, and he walks past Vivian for the door.

Good idea. We *clearly* need to be separated.

I catch his eye before he steps out into the hallway, and when his lip lifts into a grin, I blush like a fool.

"Aunt Tess?"

I blink and shake myself out of whatever trance I'm in. "Hmm?"

"Why is your shirt backward?"

I look down, and my face heats.

"Oh, you know." I brush her off. "I...spilled my milkshake and had to clean it off. I guess I wasn't paying attention when I put it back on." I'm stuttering over my words like a toddler.

Vivian nods, taking in my quick movements as I fix my shirt. "It's okay, Aunt Tess. I do that all the time."

Funny she should say that.

Because I don't.

Chapter Forty-Two

ROME

A TEXT MESSAGE from Tessa flashes over the screen in my car, and I instantly become engaged. I pull over, two streets away from my house, because waiting until I get home to text her back seems too long.

TESS

So…

That's what her message says?

I sigh and decide to let her sweat a little by acting completely nonchalant over what just happened at her parents' house.

Try admitting you're in love with someone and showing them just how much by taking them on top of a dresser in their childhood bedroom then walking downstairs to hang out with her family as if nothing life-altering had just occurred.

ME

Hey, what's up?

I turn my headlights off and rest my head against the seat, phone in hand.

TESS

What do you mean "what's up"? You know what's up!

That's where she's wrong.

When it comes to her, I'm uncertain of just about every-thing. Besides what she calls through the radio during a race, I'm flying blind where she's concerned.

ME

You tell me.

My chest fills with air, and I exhale slowly. The typing bubble appears, then disappears, and then appears again.

The moment my phone vibrates, my stomach knots.

TESS

You told me you were in love with me.

I sure fucking did.

ME

I know.

The bubbles pop up again, and this time, her message comes swift.

TESS

And?

Does she want me to pretend like I didn't say it? Take it back? Say it again?

ME

And what?

She has me all tangled up. I can't think straight.

TESS

Well…did you mean it?

There is no hesitation.

Of course I meant it. Can't she feel it? It's nearly suffocating.

ME

I don't say things I don't mean, Tess.

TESS

You weren't just caught up in the moment?

I think the moment has lasted long enough, and I'm not going to pretend it's anything less than what it is—wrong or not.

ME

I'm caught up in you, Tessa. Not a moment, not a kiss, not a fleeting glare from across the table in the middle of a meeting.
Just you.

The bubble of her typing pops up again, and this time, it stays. My pulse thrums the longer she makes me wait to the point that I flick my headlights on, ready to drive over to her house.

TESS

Fine. Then we need to set some…
boundaries. At least until the season is over.

Fear claws up my back.

ME

> What kind of boundaries?

"Fuck," I mutter.

I just laid it all out on the line for her, and for what? For her to set boundaries between us? If she expects me to work alongside her, knowing her heart doesn't stop when I walk into a room like mine when she does, then she's going to be upset.

TESS

> We can't fraternize at work or in front of the media. When we're practicing, we stay focused. When we're in a meeting, you can't brush your hand against my thigh beneath the table and expect me to not blush, because I will, and then I'll forget my own name. When you're in the thick of a race, we're nothing more than what everyone believes we are: racer and engineer.

My pulse is off the charts, and my fingers speed across the screen.

ME

> And when we're not doing those things? Then what?

Say it. *Please.*

I've never wanted something more in my entire life.

I thought sitting behind the wheel with a taste of victory on my tongue as I pulled up to the podium was the only thing I'd ever want in this world.

But God, was I wrong.

I want her. My little spitfire of an engineer and her sweet breaths in my ear.

I exhale, and it's like breathing for the first time.

She's mine, and suddenly nothing else matters to me.

I don't have to explain.

She knows what I want.

My phone vibrates in my hand, and I answer her call without thought.

She exhales, and I wish I could feel it against my skin.

"I love you more than I've ever hated you, Rome Alexander Pierce."

Her words stun me.

"Now go to sleep. I expect you to be ready to go tomorrow so we can be prepared for this week."

My lip curves. "So bossy."

"Goodnight, Rome." There's a smile in her voice, and I find myself smiling too.

"Night, Princess...I love you."

I wait with a tight chest.

"I love you too," she says, hanging up a second later.

My cheeks ache by the time I pull into my garage. I drag a feeble hand down my face, in an attempt to wipe my smile away. I'm not sure how I'm going to sleep tonight, especially with my sheets still smelling like her.

I round the front of my car and stop dead in my tracks. A leather shoe is in my peripheral, snapping my spine into place.

"What are you doing here?" There isn't a breeze in the air, yet I'm ice cold.

I knew he'd be arriving in Vegas soon, for the race, but I didn't expect him to show up at my house.

My father's steps are steady, each foot dragging over my driveway until he's right at the edge of my garage. I look him directly in the eye without even a fraction of the fear I once held when it came to him.

"Surely you expected this." He slips his hands into his pockets casually. "Just like I expected you to end up in between Vince's daughter's legs."

He's baiting me.

I shake with anger but bite down on my tongue to keep myself from giving him the reaction he wants.

When he realizes I'm not playing his games, he tilts his head and laughs. "I don't think he's going to be so open to having you on his team when he realizes what you've been doing behind his back." He pulls his hand out of his pocket with something held in between his fingers. "And then there's the FIA. I don't think they're going to be too pleased to know you're fucking your engineer either."

"There aren't any rules prohibiting fraternization in the sense of personal relationships."

I've looked it up, so he can take his fear tactics and get the fuck off my property.

He clicks his tongue, and something snaps inside of me.

"And it's really rich of you to stand on my property and preach what the FIA will or won't be pleased about." I cross over the threshold of my garage and press a finger into his chest. "Because if they knew what you did to my car for a chance to win, you'd be banned for life."

He looks at my finger, and I snatch it away before he can grab onto it.

"Yeah, well, they don't know, and what they don't know won't hurt them."

I scoff. "But fuck me, right?"

He rolls his eyes. "I didn't realize I raised you to be so dramatic. You didn't die, Rome. You hardly even sustained an injury."

I laugh sarcastically. "You didn't raise me to be anything but your fucking puppet behind the wheel."

He looks at my house, and it's obvious he's judging the size of it. Then he scans the cars in my garage before swinging back to me. "Sure looks like you were a puppet…"

"Leave," I say as level-headed as I can.

"Sure." He rocks back on his heels. "But what was it you said about the FIA not having any rules prohibiting fraternization in the sense of personal relationships? Do you think this would go against any ethical codes?"

Whatever was in his hand slips from his fingers, floating to the ground in between us. I follow the flimsy paper until it lands at my feet, and I'm suddenly rocked to the core.

"You can keep it. I have copies."

Fuck.

By the time my ears stop ringing, he's already taking off down the street with nothing but his taillights in sight.

I bend at the knees, and vomit hits the back of my throat.

A grainy picture of us in Spain, me in my race suit and Tessa on her knees with my dick in her mouth, moments before the race, stares back at me.

Chapter Forty-Three

TESSA

WE'D HAVE A BETTER chance not getting caught in a compromising position if we spent time at Rome's house instead of mine, but the last three nights, he's shown up on my doorstep, hours after leaving work for the day, with desperate kisses and rushed hands.

Instead of asking him what's wrong, I give in to the pleading in his eyes and drift off to sleep with him running his fingers up and down my spine, only to meet up with him again the next morning at work.

The media is breathing down our necks. Not only are they curious to see if I'm in good health because of the last race, questioning Rome every other second, but this is also one of the first races of the season that my dad is present for.

Gia grabs onto my arm and pulls my attention to the paddock.

A beefy man has a microphone pointed in Rome's direction, and I'm not sure what he's asked, but if looks could kill, he'd be six feet under right now.

Rome's lips pull back into a snarl, and the reporter

quickly moves on to the next driver, who just so happens to be Beau.

"What is with him?" Gia asks. "Is he testy or is it just me?"

Rome stomps toward the private driver sectors, which thankfully are more than just a tented area like in some of the other races.

"I'm going to go figure it out. I'll be back."

I dart behind a few race trailers and head in the same direction as Rome. Once inside, I hurry past the door with Noah's name on it and slip inside the one next to it with Rome's name.

He spins around angrily, until he sees it's me.

"Hey," I say softly. "Are you okay?"

His light eyes, usually soft for me, are hardened and icy. "I'm fine."

I take a step toward him. "You don't seem fine."

The muscles along his jaw tighten, and he looks away. A heavy sigh leaves his mouth.

I've never seen him like this, and not only am I worried because he's about to race, but I'm worried because there's clearly something wrong.

I move right in front of him, and he peers down at me with the same worry line in between his eyebrows. "Are you nervous?" I ask.

He shakes his head.

I purse my lips. "You're tense." I bounce my eyes back and forth between his and give him a flirty smile. "I can help."

My eager hands move to his race suit bundled around his waist. I start to push it down, but Rome's fingers wrap around my wrists.

"No," he snips. "Not here."

I jerk away. "What?"

His jaw tightens again, and he won't look me in the eye.

"What is wrong with you?" I ask. "You're not acting like yourself."

He drags a hand down his face and scoffs. "I just need to be alone."

Ouch.

The rejection cuts deep, and I instinctively step backward. Confusion fills my head with all sorts of questions, but I bite the inside of my cheek to keep them on the inside.

This isn't the time.

We aren't supposed to do this here, and I should have known better.

"Okay." I do my best to keep my voice steady and turn around.

"Tess...wait," he pleads.

My throat tightens with unshed tears and vulnerability. I clear my throat and open the door. "I'll see you out there."

"Tessa."

"I'm fine," I insist. "Clear your head and find your center. I'll see you out there."

I tell myself to do the same, but the entire walk through the paddock, over to the pit wall, is a blur. I have never had a hard time finding my own center.

But as I slip my headset on and stare across the paddock, I realize something that's terrifying. Somehow, over the last few months, Rome has become my center.

I can't help but feel lost without his icy eyes pointed in my direction during the national anthem. I opt out of searching for him when the drivers climb into their cars so I can save myself from even more rejection and confusion.

It's time to focus.

I smile at Gia when she hands me a Diet Coke in a can,

unopened. I pop the top, take a quick sip, and lower the mic to my lips.

"Radio check." I push away my nerves. "Can you hear me?"

"I'm sorry," he says.

I exhale. "Rome, can you hear me?"

"Yes, and I know you can hear me." His voice is strained. "I'm sorry. I know you—"

"You don't have to explain," I interrupt him.

His scoff echoes inside my ears. "Just give me until after this race, and I will be able to explain. Okay?"

Out of the corner of my eye, I spot my dad stepping up onto the pit wall beside me. "Front-row seat?" I ask him, faking a smile.

"Give your dad the headset," Rome says. "Quick."

I don't argue. I slip the headset off and give it to my dad, who takes it with one eyebrow raised.

"Rome?" He's cautiously on guard.

I nibble on the end of my thumbnail and look down the pit wall. Everyone is in their rightful place with the race starting in less than a minute. Things are shaky, though. Something isn't right, but maybe it's the sudden wedge between Rome and me that has me on edge.

My dad hands the headset back to me, but I don't have time to question what Rome said to him.

The countdown has started, and Rome's evened breathing is in my ear.

"After the race, it'll all make sense, Princess."

"Focus," I say to him.

But really, I'm the one who should focus, because right as Rome takes off, my attention is on my dad and the way his shoulders tense as he glances down the line at Lucas Pierce.

Chapter Forty-Four

ROME

THE MARGIN for error on a street circuit like this is next to nothing. One minuscule mistake and you're in the wall, which is why my focus should be laser sharp. Which has never been an issue. Until now.

My head is in another place.

Driving is second nature to me, so I'm doing okay in position due to my qualifying, but it isn't until Tessa's demands come in that I'm pulled back in at the last second.

"Remember turn six is sharp. Watch the walls."

I cut it close every time but manage to squeak by without damage or losing position.

"Yellow! Box this lap."

"Who hit the wall?" I ask.

"Focus, Rome." Her voice is flat, and I'd rather have her sass than this, but I say nothing because I can't.

Not yet.

Not until after the race.

I've been back and forth since Sunday, replaying everything my dad said and picturing the photo of me and Tessa that I ripped up and threw in the trash. The bomb has been ticking since the second he sped off from my house, and it won't be long until it explodes right in front of my face.

It'll destroy me, but more importantly, it'll destroy her, and that's not something I can ignore.

Not after catching a glimpse of his smug grin today in the paddock after a reporter posed a question that I'm certain my father paid him to ask.

After I pit, Tessa's voice sounds in my ear. "Wait...wait!"

I slow for a second until she shouts, "Go now!"

My car vibrates beneath me as I slip back onto the track and blend in with the rest of the cars.

"Oh my god, yes! You gained two positions!"

I smile at the excitement in her voice, and it gives me more than the position gain.

"Who's up ahead, Princess?" I ask, feeling more like myself than I did at the beginning of the race.

"Beau is in first, and then Noah."

I growl. Beau is in first on a street circuit?

"Did you say Beau?" I ask.

"Yes," she says. "Focus. Turn six is coming up."

My thoughts are spinning quicker than my wheels. I make it past turn six without skimming the wall, and I hear Tessa curse under her breath.

"How is he doing that?" her whisper cuts in and out.

"Who?" I ask, knowing she isn't talking to me.

She doesn't answer me, and I grow suspicious.

"Tess."

"Make sure to use the long straight for your battery," she reminds me. "Keep your position."

It's a strategy we've talked about all week, and I should follow her cue if I want to take us to the podium, but there's a nagging thought in the back of my head that has me going against her advice.

"Rome!" She sighs in annoyance. "What are you doing?"

"What's going on up there?" I try to keep my own car steady while keeping a close eye on Beau and Noah.

"Nothing that concerns you!" she snaps.

"Tess!" I shout. "Tell me."

She sighs loudly in my ear. "Oh my god, you are impossible! Beau is cutting the corners much quicker than I thought possible. That's it. Now focus!"

It's like repeating a fucking nightmare, only I'm not at the center of it anymore. I'm on the outside looking in.

I focus up ahead and move closer without caring about the dirty air affecting my car. I look past the blur of teal from Noah's car and focus on Beau.

My pulse flies, and I wait for the exact moment he should brake.

Only he doesn't. His lights flare too late, and my stomach drops.

Too late. He's braking too late, just like I'd done when driving that exact car.

My fucking father has done it again.

"Where is your dad?" I ask Tessa in a panic.

"What?" she exclaims. "I don't know. I've been focusing on the race!"

I'm out of breath.

This could be my chance.

If the FIA would just take a second look at the way Beau is braking around those corners, and how it's practically impossible to do so, they'd have enough for an investigation. They'd have enough to deliver the consequences my dad deserves for dangerously cheating his way to the top and risking everyone's life on this fucking circuit.

The next corner comes into view, and it's the same damn thing.

He brakes late.

"How is he doing that?" Tessa mutters more to herself than me.

I bite down on my tongue to keep the truth there.

"It's not skill, Princess." *So don't get that twisted.*

A barrier comes into sight, and my gut churns.

"Tell Noah to back off," I stress.

To my surprise, Tessa doesn't question me. There's a subtle shuffle in my ear, and my exact words leave her mouth.

Good girl.

I fly around the barrier and lift off immediately.

No.

"Crash! Crash!" I shout.

I'm instantly hyper-focused. I search for a way to avoid an impact, quickly whipping my car over to the outside line, only to turn quickly to the inside to move around a chunk of debris.

The smoke is too thick to see, but with the scattered debris and Tessa's gasp inside my helmet, I know it's bad.

"I'm coming."

My view stays obstructed until I get closer to the pits, and I can't help but notice how quiet the other end of the radio is. I race into my spot and climb out of my car within five seconds, unlike the rest of the drivers, who remain in their cars, idling. My helmet drops to the ground quickly, and I anxiously search around for Tessa.

I spot my pit crew on the wall and jog over.

They're staring at the monitors with horror. Dylan's fist is pressed against his mouth, and the only Halston I see is Vivian, who has her face buried against Gia's shoulder.

I haul myself up and climb onto the pit wall. I rush over, completely out of breath. "How bad is it?"

Dylan meets my eye but doesn't speak.

When I turn to the monitor, vomit hits the back of my throat.

Fuck.

Chapter Forty-Five

TESSA

EVERYTHING HAPPENS WITHIN A FEW SECONDS, but the winding of Noah's car seems to go on for ages.

A gasp leaves me, and there's a high-pitched ringing in my ears.

I rip the headset from my head and rush off the pit wall. Someone shouts my name, but I keep running.

I don't stop until my dad pulls up beside me on a golf cart with Beck and Van inside. Graham, who stays in the garage most of the race, is already standing near the wreckage when we pull up to the horror.

I glance to the starry sky from the sound of the whirring of the helicopter. My body grows cold, despite the fire yards away. Orange and red flames lick against the spilled gasoline with fury. Beau's car is unrecognizable, not much left of it besides the rubber. Yet, he stands off to the side on his own two legs with a couple of paramedics tending to him.

Noah, however, is not standing.

I grab a hold of Beck and dig my fingers into his arm to steady myself. He moves closer to me but says nothing.

Our dad ignores the fire and everyone who tells him to stay back. He makes it over to my brother on a stretcher, and I watch the color drain from his face before letting myself get a good look at Noah.

Droplets of blood dot his face with a wide-open gash on his forehead. He's unconscious, and I'm stunned into a panic. I can't move. I can't speak. I can't do anything other than stare as my dad climbs into the helicopter with the EMTs and Noah on a gurney.

Then they're off.

"Tess!" Beck's wide eyes appear in front of my face, and everything comes whooshing back in.

Van is on the phone with our mom, who's already on her way to the hospital.

Graham is bent down to the ground with his head hung low, his hand pulling on the strands of his unruly hair.

A thousand worries rush me, and the last few minutes swarm in like tiny shards of glass, cutting me with every little detail.

I shift my attention to Beau. With furrowed brows and reddened cheeks, he stares at his car, as if it's to blame. Then he slowly shifts to Noah's, which is completely torn in half with only one tire remaining.

Pushing past Beck, I walk out onto the track.

The fire is under control now, but nothing about the situation is.

"What did you do?!" I shout.

Beau snaps out of his trance and looks down at me. He blinks several times with his usual arrogance muted. "I...I... my..."

"You what?!" I shout. "I saw the way you were taking those corners!"

"Tessa!" Van calls for me, but I keep my back to him.

Remorse falls to Beau's face, and he shakes his head. "Rome was right."

Anger flies to my fingers. With my palm open, I'm ready to slap him, but someone tugs me backward. Rome's arm is wrapped around my belly, and he hauls me into Beck's arms. "Get her out of here."

"No!" I claw at Beck's arm.

He doesn't let up, and I eventually stop fighting when Rome takes my place in front of his stepbrother. His fists are flexed by his sides, and he shakes his head, but I can't hear what he's saying.

Then comes Lucas.

He walks slowly and takes in the scattered debris and wreckage.

The longer I watch him assess the scene, the less angry I am and the more worried I become.

Noah.

Dad's heart.

Our family.

Vanstone.

"Oh, shit," Beck mutters in my ear.

His arm loosens, and my feet touch the ground.

"Rome," Van warns.

Time stops.

Beau remains beside his stepbrother, and they appear like a team instead of enemies.

Lucas stands feet away with his arms crossed. There isn't a single word muttered. Lucas stares at Rome, shifts to Beau, raises an eyebrow, and then looks back to Rome.

I know a challenge when I see one, and everyone knows that Rome Pierce accepts every challenge thrown his way.

Even when it comes to me.

His steps are calculated, each one heavier than the last.

"What is he doing?" Beck whispers.

"Causing issues," Van snaps.

I slowly gaze around the open area, and everyone is at a standstill with the cameras rolling.

It was pure chaos earlier, and now it's eerily calm. There's no breeze whipping around us or reporters coming to assess the wreckage. It's Rome and his father at the center of everyone's attention.

I read Lucas's lips easily. "Think before you act."

Rome glances over his shoulder at me.

Our eyes lock.

"I love you," he mouths.

Beck's voice comes through like a thought in the back of my head. "Did he just say what I think he did—"

One moment, Lucas is standing in front of his son, and the next, he's stumbling backward away from Rome and his fist.

"The FIA will not tolerate—" Rome swings on him again, ending the threat right then and there. He goes in for more, and suddenly, I can't breathe.

Graham runs over with Dylan. They hold Rome back, who only thrashes a few more times before he towers over his bloody-nosed father.

"I will fucking end you for this," Lucas threatens while being helped up by someone on his team.

Rome shakes his head and points a finger at him. "Just like I'll end you for that." He gestures to the wrecked cars. "I am done with the threats and the dangerous game you're playing."

I step backward as confusion and shock set in.

Rome's name is called to the stewards, and both Dylan

and Graham release him. Lucas's eyes narrow into slits, and Rome smiles sickeningly at him.

Nausea rips through me, and I grab onto my stomach.

His back is to me as he walks over to the golf cart awaiting him, and then they take off in the opposite direction toward the FIA's race control center.

Chapter Forty-Six

ROME

EVERYTHING IS FUCKED.

My throat is tight with worry, my shoulders tense with anger. Each stride I take down the long hallway toward the steward's room is another step I take toward ending my career.

An entire scandal is going to come of this.

There will be legal fees and fines.

But none of that deters me from spewing the truth.

There is much more at stake than my career, validity as a driver, and reputation.

No one will trust me after this comes out—maybe not even Tessa, despite Vince holding onto this secret too, because I have more than just one secret.

Pain comes with the thought of losing her. Sharp, soul-crushing pain. There are consequences, though, and losing her might be mine.

The door opens, and all the stewards, each in their white collared shirts, stare at me from the long table lined with monitors. I glance behind me to the door shutting in my face.

The silence is deafening.

I swallow and take a seat at the one open chair at the end of the table.

The men have the crash pulled up onto the screen but paused right as Noah's car splits into pieces.

He wasn't conscious.

The thought alone pulls me to open my mouth.

"I should've come to you sooner. But legally..." My words trail.

One of them eyes me closely. "Did you sign an NDA?"

I nod. "I did, but after what just happened out there..." I point to the screen. "I refuse to ignore it any longer."

Not to mention the threats, drugging Tessa, and so much more.

I force a breath from my tight lungs and place my hands flat on the table. "My father—"

"Don't."

I flick my eyes to the man at the very end of the table, who's pressing a button on his keyboard. It clicks every few seconds as he replays something over and over again.

"Don't what?" I ask.

"Don't say a word," he mutters.

My spine locks.

"Jerry?" someone questions.

If he expects me to brush this under the rug for the second time, I will destroy the entire fucking sport if I have to.

I vibrate with quiet anger. "I will not let him get away with this again. Noah Halston was just taken by fucking helicopter because of my father—"

The man slaps the table. "Don't!"

I grip the sides of the chair.

"Jerry, what's going on?"

He turns his screen toward us. "Watch."

Instead of the crash replaying in front of us, it's a red-and-yellow car zipping around each corner faster than the one before. Then, he does something and switches the feed over to my last race as a Pierce driver instead of Vanstone.

It's seconds before my brakes give away.

My braking is a replica from what Beau's was today, even though his lasted longer than mine. Both of our cars reacted in the same way—temps grew too high, and the brakes went out.

"Illegal modification," someone notes.

I bite my tongue, and the metallic taste of blood fills my mouth.

Fucking finally.

My head falls forward, and a rush of relief flows into my body.

"Did you willingly drive knowing that you had modifications?"

I raise my chin.

Jerry points at me, and his eye twitches. "Be careful with your words."

Understood.

I shake my head and answer without technically answering. "Why do you think I switched teams?"

At the same time, the door barrels open, and my father stands there with dried blood smeared across his face. "That's a fucking lie."

The steward closest to me speaks up. "This is a closed meeting, Lucas."

His icy glare lands on me. "He's lying!"

He thinks I've told them everything. I lean back in my seat and raise a brow. "About?"

"You're trying to get back at me for threatening to tell

Vince that you're fucking his daughter." The haughtiness in his tone from revealing something much less worrisome than what just occurred on the circuit is pathetic.

My jaw aches when he pulls out his phone.

He tosses it on the table, and I already know it's the photo of Tessa and me, in the act.

The first steward gapes at it, but before anyone else can get a good look, I snatch it out of their possession and chuck it across the room. It hits the wall with force and lands on the floor.

"Did you really think I was going to allow you to disrespect her in my presence?" I shake my head angrily and try to keep my temper in check. "I gave you a warning after what you pulled in Italy where she was concerned." My ears burn from the rise of my blood pressure. "I know it may be hard to hear this, but there are more important things than this fucking sport and winning."

The crack in the door grows wider with Van's hand pushing on it. "Are you saying he had something to do with her passing out?"

I don't have to answer for Van to snap.

The most level-headed man I've ever met leaps across the room and grabs my father by the collar of his shirt. I spring from my seat to jump in between them.

"Van." I grab a hold of his face and make him look at me. "Remember, you're in a room full of stewards."

Whom I can't help but notice aren't doing a single thing to stop this.

Van seethes, spit flying from his mouth. "His actions have not only landed Noah in the hospital, but Tessa too? I will not stand here and let him hurt my family."

"What the hell do you think I'm doing here?" I snap.

"I'm willing to give up my career to fix this. Do not risk yours on top of it."

Van's phone rings, and he scrambles to answer it.

Tessa's name flashes across the screen, and I let go of him. The shaky sound of her voice stabs me in the chest. My stomach knots, and I turn away from him as he steps into the hallway.

My dad angrily brushes his hands down his shirt.

"I want him fined!" he yells, pointing to Van.

"You're fucking unbelievable," I mutter.

Van hangs up the phone, and we make eye contact. His face pales, and I hold my breath.

"He's in the ICU."

A hush works through the room.

I turn back to my father, and if I'm not mistaken, there's the smallest line of worry in between his eyebrows.

I point at him. "If anything happens to him, it's on you."

"Are you coming or not?" Van asks me.

I quickly glance at the stewards. "You know where to find me."

Then I give my dad one last look. "And fuck you."

Chapter Forty-Seven

TESSA

I HAVEN'T UTTERED a single word in the last several hours. Exhaustion sweeps in, the caffeine from my Diet Coke well beyond gone. My dad stares through the glass at my brother hooked up to various machines with a large bandage wrapped around his head while my mom bounces her worry back and forth between the two of them.

She's fussing at my dad to sit and eat, worried that the stress of this evening will set things off for his heart again, but he's refused to do either.

Instead, he just stares blankly.

Lost in his thoughts.

Kind of like me.

I drift in and out of a light sleep, and eventually, my head lands on Quinn's lap, who showed up shortly after we did. I jerk awake from the squeaking of a tennis shoe on the floor or the elevator beeping to see her head resting on Beck's shoulder, only for my eyes to flutter closed again.

There's a muttering of voices that belong to my brothers.

It isn't until I hear Van that my heart skips a beat.

He's here, which means that Rome may be here too.

Assumptions start to pile in my head, rocking the boat of confusion again. I keep my eyes closed, but my ear strains in the direction of Van's low voice.

"Are they both asleep?" he asks in a hushed tone.

"Quinn is drooling on me, so I think so," Beck says.

I keep as still as possible.

"Where's Rome?" Graham asks.

The disappointment is swift, knowing that he isn't with Van.

I'm confused, and I know there are things going on that I'm unaware of, but right now, all I want is everyone I care about to be next to me.

"He's here, but he's keeping his distance."

"What? Why?" Graham asks.

"If I had to guess, it's because he's ashamed," Van answers.

"Ashamed?" Beck questions.

"What aren't you telling us?" Graham asks.

There's silence, and my heart beats faster.

"Can you fucking spit it out?" Beck snaps.

I hear the scruff of Van's hand against his five o'clock shadow, and I imagine him dragging his palm over his face in frustration.

"Lucas added an illegal mod to their car, which is why Beau's brakes gave out and caused tonight's crash. Same with Rome's from last season. Apparently, he had Rome sign an NDA and threatened him with it...amongst other things."

It takes everything in me to keep my eyes shut.

"Fuck, no way. Is that why he came to our team? Because he found out his dad was cheating?"

"Yes," Van says. "But there's more."

There's more?

"Like?" Graham asks.

"Let me remind you that Noah is in the ICU, and Mom and Dad are barely holding it together, so keep yourselves under control after I tell you this."

"I'm intrigued," says Beck.

Me too.

"Lucas drugged Tessa."

I stop breathing.

Quinn shifts, and then I hear her sleepy voice. "Excuse me?"

"What do you mean Lucas drugged Tessa?" Beck asks.

"In Italy. When she fainted and had to go to the hospital. I guess he slipped something into her drink to mess with Rome. He's been holding shit over Rome's head to make sure he doesn't renege on the NDA and tell the FIA about the illegal modifications."

"Does Tessa know this?" Quinn asks.

I open my eyes and slowly lift my head off her lap. They all turn to look at me.

"No," I whisper. "I didn't know."

Van and I lock eyes, and it's obvious he knows more.

In fact, he may know everything.

My nose burns, and my throat tightens. "Where is he?"

He flicks his attention to the curve in the hall.

I stand on shaky legs, but Van does too. He follows me on my way, and I turn around and face him.

"Don't tell them the rest," I whisper. "Please."

"Wait." He tries to keep me from going after Rome, but I shake his grip away and head in the opposite direction on quiet feet.

My heart stutters to a complete stop when I spot him.

In black sweats and a backward hat, he sits on the floor with his back against the wall near the other set of elevators. His knees are bent with his head hanging low.

My shoe makes a noise on the floor, and he quickly glances at me.

"Tess..." he whispers.

A piece of my heart clinks to the floor. There's too much space between us, but I don't move closer. I nibble on the inside of my cheek and pull my eyes from his. The air in the empty hall is at a standstill until he speaks.

"How is Noah?"

I sniff. "Fractured skull. They're keeping him in the ICU for at least twenty-four hours to watch for brain swelling."

He swallows, the noise loud through the silence. "I'm so sorry," he says.

I know he is.

That's why this hurts so much more.

"Me too," my voice cracks.

"Why are you apologizing?"

I erase some of the space separating us but leave enough to where our arms can't brush. I press my back along the wall and slide down to sit like him. I look to the ceiling to keep my watery eyes under control while I let the next words flow from my mouth. "I'm sorry for not putting a stop to us before it turned into this." A choked noise leaves me, and I bite down on my wobbly lip.

"Tess," he rasps.

"Your father used me to control you. He threatened you through me. And now Noah is in the hospital because I'm a weakness to you. To the entire team. I'm a liability."

"That is not true." His jaw tightens. "I could have told the FIA sooner, but I chose not to because of the NDA."

I bite down on my lip again, this time harder. "I was still used as leverage, Rome. Our relationship has complicated everything." I swallow past the lump in my throat. "There is no going back after this. Say this all blows over with the FIA...do you really think we can carry on like we are now? Our team needs trust and clarity, and I don't see how that's possible after all of this."

He clenches his eyes shut and drops his head in between his knees.

It hurts to watch him, because I know him well enough now to know his chest is tight like mine.

Seconds stretch into minutes before he eventually shifts beside me. I peek over at him, and the blue in his eyes is so vibrant I lose my breath.

He nods subtly. "I understand."

My heart falls, and I look away. A tear slips out of the corner of my eye, despite my efforts to keep it intact. Rome's finger sweeps across my cheek, and he flings it away, letting his hand linger there for longer than it should.

Why does this hurt so much?

We sit in the quiet for too long before I can't take it anymore.

I quickly climb to my feet and sniff up the rest of my emotions. Rome is a part of our team right now, even if it's messy between us, and it's time we pull ourselves together.

"Let's go sit with the rest of the team," I say.

Surprise flickers across his face, but he pulls himself to stand.

The FIA is likely looking into each aspect of the race, the modifications, Vanstone, Pierce, and everything in between, and whether or not my heart can take it, he's not going anywhere yet.

I'd told myself Rome came here to burn Vanstone to the ground, but somehow, we were the ones who ended up being the match.

Chapter Forty-Eight

ROME

I SIT beside Vince inside the glass-walled conference room, and surprisingly, I'm calm. The past week took my nerves and unraveled them one by one, now leaving me unperturbed for this FIA hearing.

Jerry, one of the only stewards I know by name, pops up on the screen first, with the rest of the FIA members following shortly after.

"Vince," one of them says, nodding at my boss.

Vince nods back. "Leo."

"How is Noah?"

Vince drums his fingers over the conference table. "He's awake and talking. They discharged him yesterday, and he's at home where Rose is monitoring him closely."

Jerry nods. "That's good to hear. Considering he's a Halston, I assume he's itching to race again."

Vince chuckles. "It was the first thing out of his mouth when discharged. But it'll be at least four to six weeks until he's fully cleared."

Which means Beck will get his chance to drive.

"Well, why don't we get started," Jerry says.

I swallow and sit up taller in my chair.

They start off by listing article numbers and regulations, repeating the incidents that followed after Noah and Beau crashed on the circuit, none of which I need a reminder of.

"Clearly, your actions after the collision had nothing to do with the incident itself, but we assessed the footage, and we cannot disregard the unsportsmanlike conduct between you and Lucas Pierce."

I'd do it a thousand times over again.

"Understood," I say.

"For the physical altercation, we have decided that a two-race suspension within a twelve-month timeframe is punishment enough for your actions. I'm sure you are familiar with it, but that means if you have another altercation with any other driver, you will serve the two-race suspension immediately following."

So, in other words, I'm on probation with the FIA.

Which is shockingly lenient, given the situation.

I clear my throat. "I understand."

"Now..." Leo's gaze is shifty, and it puts me on edge. "As for the conflict of interest brought to our attention by Lucas Pierce."

Fuck.

Vince interrupts them. "What conflict of interest?"

Leo glances at me, and I take it as a warning for what he's about to say.

"Lucas Pierce informed us of a romantic relationship between Rome and his head engineer..."

Also known as your daughter.

Vince remains still; he doesn't utter a word.

I'm a dead man walking if the FIA has possession of the photo.

The only one who saw it before I threw my dad's phone across the room was the steward in the bottom left corner of the screen.

Leo gestures to him. "With the photo that Lucas showed Robert–"

"About that..." Robert interrupts.

Leo pauses, and I swear there's a slight uptick of his mouth.

"It could have been anyone or anything," he says. "I didn't get a good look at the photo."

Out of the corner of my eye, I see Vince look in my direction, but he's pulled back to the screen when Leo clears his throat.

"Well, given recent events and the investigation regarding Pierce Racing, it would be unfair to take Lucas's word for anything without physical proof, given his unethical behaviors as of late."

Thank God.

"However..."

I hold my breath.

"If there were a conflict of interest...we would strongly recommend reassigning positions within Vanstone Racing to avoid such an issue again."

"Understandable." Vince nods.

After saying our goodbyes, each steward's face disappears one by one as they hop off the call. My palms sweat, and my stomach knots, but in the last few months, I've grown humble enough to turn and face him to repent for my wrongdoings.

I don't regret falling in love with Tessa, but if I could go back, I'd do it right.

We could have avoided the mess we found ourselves in, and maybe I'd be able to sleep at night if she were beside me, instead of tossing and turning with thoughts of her keeping me awake.

Vince waits patiently for an explanation. He doesn't glare or press me. He just waits.

I exhale and force myself to look him in the face. "I won't lie to you," I say.

"I know you won't."

"Tessa and I were in a romantic relationship–"

"Were?" he asks.

A slice of pain cuts into my chest, and I nod. "I don't want what happened between us to affect her as one of Vanstone's head engineers. She's phenomenal at her job, even when I didn't make it easy on her. I will gladly step down and remove myself from this team if that's what it takes for her to remain in her position."

I start to list all the different scenarios I've come up with in the last several days with Vince listening intently.

"I know Beck isn't as seasoned as you'd like, but when Noah is back on his feet, Beck could take my place. That way, you'd still have two active drivers representing Vanstone–"

Vince clears his throat. "Are you trying to terminate your contract? Because as far as I know, you haven't breached it, correct?"

"Well..." I take a breath. "I don't think I've breached it."

"You haven't," he says.

I open my mouth, only to close it a moment later. My mind runs in circles.

"Right now, I'm going to speak to you like a father instead of like your boss."

Here it comes.

The reprimand.

I knew it was wrong to get involved with my head engineer. *His* daughter.

"The most important thing in the world is family and having someone to lean on. That's all I've ever wanted for my children."

I nod, but there's a sadness behind the action.

Somehow, over the last few months, Tessa became the most important thing to me, and Vanstone turned into the family I never knew I needed. And now, they're all slipping right though my fingers because of a man who was never really there for me to start with.

I forcefully swallow and drag my attention to Vince. He reaches out and puts his hand on my shoulder and gives it a squeeze.

"And son...you deserve that too."

Son.

My throat grows tight, and suddenly, I'm a young kid again.

He squeezes my shoulder again before letting go and turning to gather the papers in front of him.

"Why do you think I left her out of the contract?" he asks.

What?

He's grinning from the side and continuously flipping through the papers. "I've already discussed this with the others, but Van will be your engineer moving forward. Tess will work with Beck until Noah is back on his feet. Oh, and they're well aware that I knew what your father was up to years ago, so you don't need to worry that they'll hold this against you."

"You're–" I clear my throat, noticing the rasp in my voice. "You're sure? You don't mind Tessa and I working... near each other?"

"No one has been able to tame that girl besides you, Rome." He chuckles to himself. "Even when you two were kids running around the paddock."

Just like no one's ever been able to make me stop dead in my tracks with a single glance in my direction besides her.

Vince stands, but before he's able to leave, I turn around abruptly. "I'll do it right this time. With Tessa," I clarify. "I'll wait as long as I need to, but I'll do it right."

He nods and walks out the door, leaving me in shock.

A few minutes later, the group text goes off.

> **BECK**
>
> Well? What's the verdict, Rocky?

I snort.

Van texts back before I can.

> **VAN**
>
> Two-race suspension within 12-month timeframe.

> **BECK**
>
> That's it?! Probation?

> **ME**
>
> I'm just as surprised.

> **GRAHAM**
>
> Congrats on not getting booted out of Vanstone.

> **BECK**
>
> Or the family.

Tessa's typing bubbles pop up, and my pulse skyrockets.

I walk out of the conference room and over to the

balcony that overlooks the bottom floor of Vanstone, hopeful I can get a glimpse of her.

TESSA

Beck, I swear to God, if you don't get here in the next ten minutes, I'm going to lock you in the sim room all night long.

The thought of racing without her in my ear pulls the knot in my stomach tighter.

NOAH

I can be there in three.

TESSA

YOU ARE NOT SUPPOSED TO BE LOOKING AT A SCREEN!

I'm calling Mom.

I chuckle at their texts and head to the elevator.

NOAH

Are you kidding? You seriously called her?

TESSA

Yep. Now put your phone away.

VAN

Rome, are you coming down anytime soon, or are you going to stay up in the conference room all day?

ME

Stepping into the elevator now.

I hit send, and the doors open to reveal my heart living right outside my chest.

Tessa inhales sharply, her phone in her hand. Our eyes lock, and my world stops.

Will it ever get easier? Seeing her and not being able to touch her?

The only thing I want to do is back her into the small space, press her against the wall, and beg her to let me in again.

I step into the elevator, just as she steps out.

Our arms brush, and I'm rooted in place. I turn slightly toward her floral perfume, but I keep myself from following after her and push myself farther into the elevator.

I'm leaving the cards in her hands, and when she's ready—*if* she's ready—I'll be here.

Chapter Forty-Nine

TESSA

SEVERAL WEEKS LATER

"PUT ME THROUGH TO ROME," Beck says through the radio.

I huff. "That isn't even possible. Now pay attention!"

"I'd just like to know how the hell he dealt with your demands while driving, because I'm having a hard time."

"Just do what I say, and you won't have a hard time!" I snap.

Beck sighs loudly.

I glance at the monitors, and I can't help but secretly root for Rome. This is the fourth race where he's been paired with Van, and Beck with me. Per usual, we each had to work through some kinks, but both Beck and Rome have been placing better with each race.

Rome is in second with only a few corners left until the checkered flag.

"Inside!" I shout to Beck.

He listens and takes the inside lane instead of the outer, and sure enough, he gains a position.

"Thank you!" I exclaim and throw my hands up. "Finally!

Beck whistles. "Hell yeah!"

I want to say, '*See what happens when you listen to me,*' but I'm too swept up in the front of the line where Rome is.

My adrenaline peaks with my heart in my throat.

Come on, come on. Use the DRS.

I hold my breath as he jockeys for first, waiting for the perfect moment to overtake Milo.

As soon as he dashes forward, I jump out of my seat and slap my hand over my mouth.

"He did it," I whisper, talking to myself.

I press my lips together, fighting a smile.

"Who? What?" Beck asks.

The checkered flag waves. Van and the rest of his crew cheer so loud I can't help but look over at them. My oldest brother smiles like a kid in a candy shop, and I shoot him the smile I was trying to hide.

"By the sound of your voice, I bet Rome got first, huh?" Beck chuckles, and I'm tempted to rip my headset off.

"What is that supposed to mean?" I ask.

I know exactly what it means.

"I bet he'd trade getting first if it meant getting you."

I roll my eyes and ignore his teasing.

Rome and I haven't been alone or had a conversation that didn't involve the rest of the team since the hospital. Even in our group text, it's been cordial. Like, when I congratulated him on the last race and he sent a simple *thank you* in response.

I hate it.

Just like I tell myself I hate when I catch him staring at me from across the room, only to love it deep down.

It's the same contradiction everywhere I see him.

I always search for his car when I pull into Vanstone's parking lot, and butterflies fill me when it's there. If his hand brushes mine during Sunday dinner, I crave the rush of heat that follows.

It's hard to remember all the drama that occurred from before. There's still an investigation being conducted against Pierce Racing, and Rome is still on probation. Yet it seems like years ago that he was softly skimming my cheek with his finger as I fell asleep in his bed.

And right now, as he pulls up to the number one spot and climbs out of his car, I can't help but dash over to him with the rest of the Vanstone team. I linger in the back as Van and the others jump on top of him with the crowd roaring in the background.

After the truth surfaced about Pierce Racing, the fans seemed to have fallen even more in love with Rome and our Vanstone team. There's a sea of teal and purple in the crowd, all of whom are on their feet, cheering for him beside us.

Beck walks over and hugs him, both of them sweaty. My brother leans close to his ear and says something over the cheers.

Rome's blue eyes fly over to mine, and the smile on my face disappears.

He caught me.

His eyebrows dip for a split second.

My heart stops.

Beck is mid-conversation with him, but Rome isn't paying attention. He takes a step toward me and stops.

When I stay in place, he takes another one.

And then another.

Until he's inches from me.

A swallow moves against his neck the same time a bead of sweat drips down the side of his cheek.

I exhale, but it comes out shaky.

His eyes bounce back and forth between mine, and everything around me disappears. "I thought winning would make me feel whole again," he admits.

A sadness moves through me. "It doesn't?"

His head moves back and forth slowly. "Not unless I get to share it with you."

There are thousands of eyes on us, yet all I see are his.

"I'll keep winning," he says, "just for a chance to feel your arms around my neck, celebrating with me."

Rome.

Gia shouts his name for an interview, and when I say nothing, he turns away.

I watch him go, but panic propels me forward. I bump into his back, and he spins around to peer down at me. I rise on my tiptoes and hesitantly wrap my arms around his neck.

He pulls me in close, and we both exhale.

Like neither of us could breathe without the other.

"Tess..."

His warm whisper coats the side of my neck, and I pull back to look into his eyes. The blue is glossed over, and he glances at my mouth.

The smallest smile pulls at my lips. "Congratulations, Rome."

He sniffs. "Thanks, Princess."

I grab onto his scruffy jaw. "Now kiss me so we can really celebrate."

He presses me closer and kisses me heatedly, and for the first time, neither of us cares who's watching.

ROME

Where are you?

I PURSE my lips and roll my eyes.

ME

You know where I am.

ROME

Come to my tent.

ME

This sounds familiar...

You know, like that one time his dad spied on us before a race and used it as a way to threaten him.

ROME

If I can't have your voice in my ear while I drive, I at least need it before. The fate of this race is in your hands, Princess.

I slip my phone into my back pocket and grab Van's attention.

"I'm going to get a Diet Coke," I tell him. "Want one?"

He holds up an energy drink.

"Where'd you get that?" I ask. "And it's rude that you didn't get me one, but I digress."

Dylan leans past Van with a smirk, holding *his* own energy drink. "Vivian's nanny."

I glance at my brother, and I *swear* he blushes before turning away to put his headset on.

He recently hired a live-in nanny for Vivian, who now travels with them race to race. She's a former teacher with a kind smile and full of energy, who had zero reservations about traveling from country to country. And although it's only been a couple of weeks, Vivian is so much happier.

I think Van is too.

Though, my parents miss having her at the house.

I quickly dart past a few cameramen and slip in between two trailers.

Rome and I are exclusive, so it wouldn't be surprising to see me with him before a race, but given the dip in my belly from his text alone, I know that the second I step into his tent, things are going to move quickly.

His famous *Do Not Disturb, Does not apply to Tess* sign is taped to the front of his tent. I push past it, and he turns around swiftly to pick me up. My legs wrap around his waist with my arms going to his neck.

"I hear the fate of your race is in my hands," I say in a flirty tone.

Rome shakes his head and stares up into my face. "The fate of my life is in your hands, Princess."

I press my mouth to his, my tongue sweeping in

quickly. Our kiss doesn't break until he sits on a chair with my legs falling to the sides of his.

He pushes my skirt up to my waist. "Have I ever told you how much I love this little get-up you wear?"

I gasp softly with his fingers skimming my panties.

"I do it on purpose," I whisper into his ear.

He teases me, brushing the pad of his thumb over my clit.

"What purpose is that?" he asks gruffly.

I reach in between us and work at shoving his race suit down. He helps me, and when I feel his hard length between my legs, I position him where I need him. "Easy access."

I sink down onto him, and he hisses between his teeth.

"Fuck, baby."

"Shh," I shush, my lips right above his ear. "We've gotta be quiet, remember?"

Rome grips the sides of my face and brings my mouth to his. I meet his rough, needy kisses, one by one, and we move in sync.

The entire race could start, and I don't think we'd stop.

He knows exactly how to get me going, and my orgasm sparks in less than a minute.

"Oh my god," I moan quietly against his mouth. "I love that you know just what I need..."

He presses into me harder. "And I love watching you come for me."

He barely gets the last word out before he's coming too.

His alarm goes off seconds after he finishes. He chuckles with me still on top of him.

"Do you think they'd notice if we were missing?" I ask.

His fingers dig into my hips, and he looks up at me with

a dangerously enticing glint in his eyes. "Don't tempt me, Princess."

But where's the fun in that?

The End

Thank you so much for reading Overtake and jumping into this new world with me!! For more information on the next book in the series, head to sjsylvis.com!

Vanstone Racing

Overtake

Untitled

Bexley U Series

Weak Side

Ice Bet

Puck Block

Chicago Blue Devils

Play the Game

Skate the Line

Rush the Edge

Test the Ice

Shadow Valley Series

Sticks and Stones

Heart of Thorns

The Christmas Playbook

Cross the Line

English Prep Series

All the Little Lies

All the Little Secrets

All the Little Truths

St. Mary's Series

Good Girls Never Rise

Bad Boys Never Fall

Dead Girls Never Talk

Heartless Boys Never Kiss

Pretty Girls Never Lie

Standalones

Three Summers

Yours Truly, Cammie

Chasing Ivy

Falling for Fallon

Truth

S.J. Sylvis is an Amazon top 50 and USA Today bestselling author who is best known for her new adult sport romances. She currently resides in Arizona with her husband, two small children, dog and cat! She is obsessed with coffee, becomes easily attached to fictional characters, and spends most of her evenings buried in a book!

Stay up to date at: sjsylvis.com

Acknowledgments

Readers, thank you *so* much for jumping into this new era with me! I hope you loved this new world, and are ready for the next book in the series! From the very first text message between Tessa and her brothers, I fell in love with the Halston's and I cannot wait to write the rest of the books in the series!!!

Emma, also known as Booktastic Blonde— I will never be able to repay you for all that you do. From your endless encouragement to your one-of-a-kind friendship, *thank you*. Thank you for picking me up when I'm down, and for remembering all the things I forget on a day to day basis. I love you!

To Mary, my PA, and handler of anything I can't seem to handle, thank you for all of your hard work!! I appreciate you so incredibly much!!

To my editor, Jenn, I cannot say thank you enough for your patience with me. You are beyond understanding when I'm down to wire (every single time).

Lastly, thank you to my family for loving me through my stressful deadlines (sorry), and to my closest friends who are always willing to help. I wouldn't be able to do this without any of you!!

Xoxo

SJ